Desperate
Decisions

Desperate
Decisions

Marilyn Mayo Anderson

www.urbanchristianonline.net

Urban Books, LLC
78 East Industry Court
Deer Park, NY 11729

ISBN 13: 978-1-60162-824-4
ISBN 10: 1-60162-824-2

First Mass Market Printing March 2012
First Trade Paperback Printing February 2010
Printed in the United States of America

10 9 8 7 6 5 4 3 2 1

Distributed by Kensington Publishing Corp.
Submit Wholesale Orders to:
Kensington Publishing Corp.
C/O Penguin Group (USA) Inc.
Attention: Order Processing
405 Murray Hill Parkway
East Rutherford, NJ 07073-2316
Phone: 1-800-526-0275
Fax: 1-800-227-9604

This book is dedicated to my Lord and Saviour, Jesus Christ, the one and only wise God.

Acknowledgments

As always, I give all the praise, honor and glory to God. I have to thank Him for blessing me with the gift of writing. Thank you, Jesus, for inspiring me to write this novel as a tool to minister your love through the written word.

To my mother, Mable Parker Mayo, you are a kind and wise mighty woman of God. I am blessed that God chose me to be your daughter.

For my late father, George Rufus Mayo, from whom I inherited the passion of reading.

To my sons, Antonio and Kenneth, I thank God for both of you. I'm blessed to have such caring sons as you.

I have to thank my family for being supportive. I love you all.

Thanks to the many readers who read my previous novels; I sincerely appreciate your support and encouraging words. I pray that this novel will not only entertain, but minister, inspire, and encourage your hearts. My prayer for you is 3rd

John 1:2: *"Beloved, I wish above all things that thou mayest prosper and be in health, even as though soul prospereth."*

Chapter 1

"This pain is unbearable! Hurry up and turn this thing on, *please!*" Diana lay in the hospital bed in excruciating pain. The morphine drip the nurse had given her seemed to have no effect.

The nurse gave Diana a stern look. "It is on, Mrs. Thompson; you have to be patient." After checking and recording her vital signs, the nurse exited the room.

Diana stared up at the ceiling and willed herself to calm down. The memory of the events of what had happened to her just weeks before a tractor trailer plowed into her, played before her like a movie.

"Make up your mind," Diana raised her voice at the man. "Sir, you're wasting my time. I'll be glad when my time is up here. I'm sick of this," she mumbled as she rolled her eyes upward. Diana was about to walk away, but she noticed her supervisor's frowning face. She took a deep breath and turned back to face the homeless

man. "Sir, I'm sorry I spoke to you that way. I'm having a bad day. Please forgive me."

"No kidding?" the man snarled at her. "You should walk a mile in my shoes. Every day is a bad day for me."

Diana lowered her eyes away from the man's intense stare. She shifted her eyes to the next person in line. Her eyes widened a bit when a young lady moved forward and stood before her with three small children in tow.

"Hi, Miss, I don't mean to be intrusive, but what are you doing here? Are these your children?"

"Are you for real?" the young lady asked Diana in the most sarcastic tone she could muster up. "What does it look like I'm doing here? I'm trying to feed my three children and me. Don't be turning your nose up at my children either. What planet did you beam down from?"

"I—I'm sorry, Miss, I'm just surprised to see a young girl down here, that's all. And with three small children too." Diana's supervisor, Kendra, walked up to her and clasped her hands together tightly. "Is it my break time, Kendra?" Diana asked her.

"No, I need to talk to you, Diana," Kendra told her grimly. "Ms. Mable is here to take your place." Diana stepped back and handed the *plastic gloves to Mable. "Diana, just discard those. Ms. Mable can retrieve a new pair from the box under the table."*

Kendra glanced at Diana from head to toe. Diana was dressed in black slacks, a frilly white blouse and black four-inch stilettos, which made her five-feet-four-inch stature appear tall. Her oval shaped, banana colored face was masked with heavy pecan tan makeup, and her big, brown, doe eyes were heavily lined with black mascara. Her dark coarse hair was carried up in a French roll.

Kendra sighed. "Come into my office, Diana." Diana sauntered into the office behind Kendra. Kendra motioned for her to sit in the burgundy high back Queen Anne chair.

Diana sat down and kicked off her heels. "Thank you for replacing me, Kendra. I don't know how much more of these people I can take."

Kendra gave Diana a solemn look. "Diana, you do understand why you are here, don't you?"

Placing a perfectly manicured, pale hand on Kendra's desk, Diana laughed fictitiously. "Yes, of course. Kendra, thank you for pulling strings with Judge Winthrop and convincing her to order me to perform community service instead of doing jail time," she smirked.

"I'm glad I could be of assistance." Kendra returned the smirk that Diana was wearing. *"I couldn't imagine you doing thirty days in jail."*

Diana crossed her legs as her eyes scanned the scarce pine furniture that was scattered around the small office. "The thought of it scared me silly. It's good to have friends in high places. I really appreciate you taking my case."

Kendra relaxed her back in the office chair. "When you walked in the door all chipper this morning, I thought maybe since someone had shown mercy to you, God had inspired you to do something to make someone else's life brighter. Maybe even say something kind to someone."

Diana waved her hand in the air dramatically. "That's funny, Kendra. You know I don't waste my time in dumps like these. Considering the circumstances, I'm doing the best I can. Frankly, I'm surprised to know you're here and in charge of this place too. After we graduated high school and went to college, we swore we wouldn't take a second thought to run down places like these."

"Well, we both were young and dumb back then. Thank God I met a wonderful man in college, who led me to the Lord."

Diana sat upright and scowled at Kendra. "Humph, who needs God when you have money,

honey? I have money; my husband is a success-
ful oncologist about to start his own practice,
and we own a five thousand square foot home
sitting on a hill in Camden Estates. And being
able to vacation twice a year in places that I
could only dream of when I was a child is awe-
some," she said emphatically.

Kendra's eyes pierced Diana's. *"That's a bless-*
ing, Diana, but do you have Jesus?"

Diana's face became distorted. *"Is that why*
you called me away from my duties; to talk
about religion? My time is precious. All I want
to do is my time here and go back home so I can
supervise my maid on how to clean my house."

Kendra's eyebrows furrowed. *"Diana, what's*
happened to you?" She sat up straight in her
chair. *"Having money shouldn't make you a*
cruel snob. I know some wealthy people, and
I've yet to have encountered one of them to be-
have as terribly as you."

Diana snickered. *"Don't be so melodramatic,*
Kendra. We both know that I was destined for
success when I was in high school. And you,
being a successful criminal defense lawyer, are
wasting your time with these people."

Frown lines creased Kendra's forehead. *"Di-*
ana, I'm disappointed in you. It really hurts
me to see how you've changed. Your heart has

turned to stone," she said sadly. Kendra thought for a moment. "Please come to church with us Sunday. Maybe attending one of our services will do you some good."

"I don't think so, Kendra." Turning up her nose, Diana said, "I haven't attended church since my mother's funeral twenty-two years ago. I lost my faith in God when He let her die from sickle cell anemia. If anybody deserved to live and be happy, it was my mother. She was an angel."

"Diana, I'm sorry about your mother's death too," Kendra told Diana in a soothing tone. "I loved Ms. Anna dearly because she took up a lot of time with me while my mother ran the streets with one man or another; but that was then and this is now. I learned to forgive my mother, and now she is a faithful member of our church."

"Good for you and your mother." Diana clicked her tongue. "As for the Lord and me, I haven't found it in my heart to forgive Him or forget what my mother went through."

Kendra suppressed the tears that welled up inside of her. "Well, I'll pray for you, Diana."

Diana's countenance hardened. "Don't waste your breath," she said indignantly. "I'm doing just fine like I am."

Kendra shook her head. "I'll still keep you in my prayers, regardless of what you say."

Diana laughed. "That's comical, Kendra. It's hard to believe you are 'saved' anyway. It's funny how we've switched roles, isn't it?"

"What do you mean?" Kendra had a puzzled look on her face.

Diana smirked. "When we were in high school, before my mother passed, my sister and I were the ones who were saved and going to church every Sunday and trying to get you to come, but you were a heathen if ever I saw one."

Kendra's facial muscles relaxed as she slumped in her chair. "You're right, Diana, but thank God for His grace and mercy. I probably would have ended up turning tricks or getting strung out on drugs if you hadn't convinced me to go to college with you."

Diana nodded her head in agreement. "Yes, I'm glad you agreed to go with me because after Momma died, I didn't have a soul in the world to depend on anymore. My sister had left town with that so-called pastor of our church, and after God betrayed me and took my momma, there wasn't a reason to believe in Him anymore."

Kendra pulled her posture upright and took a deep breath. "I didn't know any better then, but now I know that that statement couldn't be further from the truth. Whenever we're in the valley of despair, that's when we need to put our trust in God so He can bring us through our trials."

Diana waved Kendra off. "Like I said before, I don't need a God who refused to heal my mother when I needed her the most." Kendra stared at Diana mournfully. "Don't feel sorry for me, Kendra. I can't stand pity. Anyway, as you said, that was then and this is now, and believe me, now is a lot better than then." She sighed loudly. "Is the sermon over for the day? I need to get back to my duties. The sooner I get this over with, the better. Six hours down, one hundred and fifty-four to go," Diana exclaimed sarcastically.

Kendra tapped her fingers lightly on her desk. "You've done enough for today, Diana. My schedule is for you to come in on Wednesdays and Fridays, from eight to two." Kendra scrutinized Diana's face. "So check your attitude at the door before you come in." Diana smirked, but Kendra kept a serious expression on her face. 'These people' as you call them, are homeless, not inhuman. Please make sure that you remember that when you come in Wednesday, so whatever my assistant, Ms. Mable, assigns you to do, do it."

Diana looked at her nails and sighed. "Sure, Kendra, whatever you say."

Kendra stood up. "By the way, Diana, you should wear more comfortable clothes next time. I'm sure you were in pain, standing in those stilettos for six hours." Diana grimaced and rubbed her feet. Kendra laughed. "A simple T-shirt and a pair of jeans or a summer sweat suit and sneakers will be ideal."

Diana stood and scanned Kendra's conservative navy, pinstriped pantsuit. "I dressed this way because I was under the impression that I would be working in the church's office for you. I didn't know my home girl would have me doing hard labor, like I was a common criminal."

Kendra raised her eyebrows at Diana. "Diana, but for the grace of God, you would have been. Driving while under the influence of alcohol is a serious offense."

Diana nodded her head in agreement. "You might have a point." Diana bent over in the chair and put her heels back on. She stood up and headed for the door. "I'll see you Wednesday morning at eight, but don't expect me to come in here with a big smile pasted on my face."

A sharp pain shot through Diana's back, jolting her back to her present state in the hospital. She just wanted the pain to go away. For a moment she thought maybe she should pray. She laughed inwardly and said to herself, "Yeah, right. I'm sure if I prayed, God would just look down at me and laugh." Diana drifted off into a deep sleep without so much as parting her lips to say a prayer.

Chapter 2

Twelve weeks prior.

Aquila and her three children, Daniel, Darius, and Abigail, sauntered back to her friend, Pricilla's, tattered two-bedroom house. It was only four blocks from the church, but in the searing North Carolina August heat, it seemed more like four miles. Still, she was grateful to have a safe place to stay.

Lord, she prayed silently as she rounded the corner and walked the few yards to reach the dilapidated front porch, *I thank you for making a way for me to escape the torturous life I was trying to survive in while back in Nashville, Tennessee.*

"Auntie Cilla!" Daniel, Darius, and Abigail screamed excitedly as they ran ahead to meet their adopted aunt.

Pricilla stretched out her arms to greet them.

"Are you done with school, Auntie Cilla?" Abigail questioned.

"I'm finished with my classes for today, sweetie. I bought you guys some chocolate covered ice cream bars. Go look in the freezer and help yourselves to one."

The children, ages six, five, and three, raced into the house.

Aquila sat on the porch, with its warped planks, beside her childhood friend. She wiped the sweat that ran down her face on her long-sleeved blouse. "Pricilla, you don't have to buy things for them. You've already spent a lot of money on bus tickets for us. I know how tight money must be, with you going to nursing school full time and only working part time."

Pricilla shrugged. "I don't mind at all, Aquila. When you called me the last time talking about that husband of yours and how he had slapped you around again, I knew God wanted me to do something to get you and those kids out of that hell hole. Sending money for you guys to come to Raleigh was the sensible thing to do."

"Yeah, but Pricilla, you barely have enough money to take care of yourself. Although I appreciate you for helping us, I feel really bad living off of you," Aquila told her apologetically.

Pricilla used the napkin that she held to dab at the sweat on the back of her neck. "I imagine you thought I had a huge house to live in when I sent for you all, but unfortunately, it only has two bedrooms. I'm sorry that all I could offer you was the couch to sleep on. You're probably disappointed, but this is the house I bought."

Pricilla had moved to Raleigh from Nashville, Tennessee to go to school. She rented the house for a year, and then the owners asked her if she wanted to buy it. The couple was retired from the military and had made their home in Phoenix, Arizona. They didn't plan on coming back to Raleigh to live, so they concluded that paying taxes on the dilapidated property wasn't feasible. The owner told Pricilla that remodeling his mother's house was too costly and collecting rents through a real estate agent had been unprofitable. They quoted a price well below the market value, so Pricilla knew that she couldn't refuse the offer.

Aquila looked at Pricilla and shook her head slowly. "I'm not disappointed. I'm grateful to sleep peacefully on that sofa bed, girl. Although Brandon provided a beautiful four-bedroom three and a half-bath house for us to live in, it wasn't worth the beatings I had to endure whenever he got in the mood to use my body as his punching bag. Believe me; peace is more valuable than material things."

"I know that's true." Pricilla looked back at her home. "This doesn't look like much, but it's mine. I figured that I could remodel it when I graduated and became a registered nurse."

"That's a great idea," Aquila encouraged her. "You've accomplished a lot since you left Nashville."

"I know you didn't understand at the time, but I was tired of living in Nashville with nothing but sad memories. I needed a change, so in 2006, when I read in a magazine article that Raleigh was voted as the second best place to live in, I decided to move here to see if I could start a new life. I hopped on the first bus out of Dodge, moved to Raleigh, and found me a place to live because I had a plan."

Aquila glanced at Pricilla and giggled. "You always did have a plan. Ever since we grew up in the orphanage together, you've had a plan."

Pricilla and Aquila grew up in an orphanage in Nashville Tennessee. Pricilla had been adopted by an older couple who were in their late fifties. Her memories of them were vague, but she remembered feeling loved. Her adopted father was an innocent by-stander that was killed during a convenience store robbery. Five months later, her adopted mother died from a massive heart attack.

Pricilla was only six years old at the times of their death. Being that her adopted parents didn't have any living relatives, Pricilla was placed in one foster home after another. At age eight, she was sent to the orphanage. She couldn't fully comprehend why her life had been changed so drastically.

She had a hard time adjusting to the orphanage, with so many other little girls of all ages. Ms. Berry, the director of the orphanage, was very strict. She made sure that the girls were fed, had their individual beds, and proper places to keep their scant clothing.

But there were twenty or more girls per employee, so the girls didn't get much individual attention. Pricilla learned quickly how to obey the rules, go to school every day as required, and do what she was expected to do.

Aquila had been sent to the orphanage after her parents died. She didn't have any memory of them. All she could recall was being sent to different places to live. She learned later that she had been placed in four different foster homes. To her recollection, most of the families seemed nice.

She remembered the day a kind, soft spoken woman came to visit the woman she thought was her mother. The two women sat and talked with her and told her that she would be going to live in a special house. She remembered crying and reaching back for her 'mother,' but her mother only looked away as Aquila was driven away by the visiting woman.

Sometime during the car ride, Aquila had cried herself to sleep. The lady woke her up and walked her into the huge house with a lot of other girls. She was taken to a bed by Ms. Berry, the director, who told her with a somber face, "This is where you'll sleep." She instructed one of the older girls in the room to guide her until she was familiar with her surroundings. After Ms. Berry left the room, Aquila fixed her innocent eyes on the girl for support, but the girl gave Aquila a mean look, turned on her heels, and walked away. Aquila shyly looked around at the other unfriendly looking girls in the room and fell on the bed and cried pitifully.

One girl came over, sat on her bed, and tried to comfort her. She told her not to be afraid because she would take care of her. That girl was Pricilla. Since then, Pricilla Battle, age eight, had called Aquila Forest, age six, her little sister.

Pricilla propped her right foot up on the bottom cement step. "Yep," she said confidently. "My first plan was to go to college. I'm fulfilling my dream of going to nursing school. I hope to start my career as a registered nurse shortly after graduation. It was my dream to own a house, and now, I own a house. It may look like a shack to some people, but it's mine. So far, my plans are working. The only thing that's missing is my biological mother," Pricilla said sadly. "But I'm going to find her too, if it takes me the rest of my life."

Aquila smiled. "Don't worry, Pricilla," she encouraged her. "I believe you're going to find her too. That's been important to you for a long time."

Pricilla dropped her eyes toward the ground. "I hope so. When I find her, I hope that she will be proud of me too."

"Why wouldn't she be?" Aquila asked her defiantly. She then sighed softly and told her in a soothing tone, "I'm very proud of you."

Pricilla raised her head back up. "Thanks, Aquila. I might have always had a plan, but you've always had something kind to say to anyone that you've encountered."

Aquila's countenance saddened. "I should have had a plan for my life. Unfortunately, my only plan was to meet a nice man and marry him; you know, my knight in shining armor."

Pricilla stood up, stretched, and watched the heavy afternoon traffic whiz by only a few feet from her tiny fenced in front yard. "I understand what you're saying, but that was *some* knight you chose."

"Well, when all your life consists of is an orphanage, a girl couldn't help but dream of someone to love her." Aquila lowered her eyes toward the ground. "Only my knight was twelve years older than me and as mean as a snake."

"I had a funny feeling about him when you introduced me to him in the park, but I dismissed those feelings after you dated him for months and he treated you so well. I was shocked when you told me that you were going to run away from the orphanage and move in with him."

Aquila gazed toward the traffic. "That was one of the dumbest things that I've ever done."

Pricilla sat back on the porch and clasped her hands together behind her head. "You didn't know what the future held, Aquila. Like the saying goes, hindsight is better than twenty-twenty," Pricilla told her with conviction.

Aquila nodded her head in agreement.

Aquila had been gone a week before Ms. Berry, the director of the orphanage, had noticed that she was unaccounted for. She questioned all the girls and staff members, but they had no idea where she was. Aquila had disappeared without a trace. Pricilla had graduated high school a year earlier, moved out of the orphanage and into a nearby boarding house. She worked full-time at Wendy's fast food restaurant. She had visited Aquila at least once a week at the orphanage, so Ms. Berry's first contact person was Pricilla. Ms. Berry had hoped that Aquila was with her, but she wasn't. Ms. Berry reported Aquila's absence to the police, but they didn't put much effort into trying to find her.

Pricilla knew where she was, but Aquila begged her not to divulge her location, so she didn't. A few weeks later, Aquila turned eighteen. She flew to Las Vegas with Brandon Savino, where they got married in the beautiful Tropicana Wedding Chapel at the Tropicana Hotel Resort & Casino in Las Vegas, Nevada. She became pregnant two months after the wedding with Daniel, and Darius was conceived ten months later. During the first two years of their marriage, Aquila was happy.

Brandon provided a good life for her and the babies. He had a great career as an air traffic controller at Nashville International Airport. Within that two-year period, he had purchased a beautiful home in a prestigious neighborhood for them to live in.

However, Aquila noticed a sudden change in his behavior once they moved into their new home. Brandon became increasingly verbally abusive and forbade her to leave the house without his permission. He was unusually jealous and accused her of being attracted to any man that she looked at for more seconds than he thought she should. He insisted that she stop using public transportation, citing that it was too dangerous for a young woman with two small children. Brandon demanded that she stay at home until he got there, and he would drive her everywhere she needed to go.

Aquila was a strong-willed individual. She thought he was being ridiculous and told him as much. She continued to travel throughout the city, riding on the public bus system the way she was accustomed to while in the orphanage. To keep the peace, she made it a point to be home before Brandon returned home from work.

One Friday afternoon, she'd taken the bus to the community college to enroll in the adult high school diploma program. She got home later than usual, at four fifteen and had anticipated having dinner ready by five thirty. Brandon usually walked in the house at five forty every day. But to her surprise, on that particular day, he was already sitting at the kitchen table waiting for her when she walked in the house. Aquila perceived that his whole body language emitted anger. Despite this, she walked into the kitchen and greeted him warmly. He stood up abruptly and began to yell expletives at her. Aquila usually tried not to aggravate his temper by staying quiet while he vented. But that day she was fed up with him. She used a few expletives of her own, but she was utterly shocked when he slapped her so hard that she landed on the kitchen tile floor. That slap was the beginning of Brandon's cruel, physical abusive behavior toward her.

"I thought Brandon was the best thing that could have ever happened to me," Aquila lamented.

"He had me fooled too," Pricilla admitted. "If I had been able to foresee the future, I would have given Ms. Berry his address. He could have been arrested for child molestation because you were still a minor."

Aquila sighed loudly. "He definitely fooled me into thinking that he was my dream come true."

Pricilla rubbed her hands together. "He *was* a charming man."

"He was a charmer; a *snake* charmer. In the end, all I did was jump out of the frying pan of the orphanage and into the fire with a maniac." Aquila picked up a small twig from the ground and broke it in half. "I should have stayed where I was until I graduated high school like you did, and then gone to college." She threw the two pieces of the twig back on the ground. "Now, here I am; a high school dropout with three young children, no education, and not a dime to my name."

"There's no need to beat yourself up over the past, Aquila. God is still in control, and He is a loving and merciful God. You just keep the faith, and He will give you the desires of your heart."

A single tear rolled down Aquila's face. She quickly brushed it away with her sleeve before Pricilla saw it. "Thanks, Pricilla. I need to be around someone who has faith in God because it will help me to become stronger. You know, I'd never really opened the Bible and studied it until you started quoting scriptures to me when I called you after Brandon decided it was time to teach me another lesson. I tell you, he is the meanest, most jealous man on the face of this earth."

"Don't even give him a second thought, Aquila. He'll reap what he sowed."

Aquila exhaled loudly. "I suppose you're right. All I know is that I'm glad that I finally got away from him."

Pricilla raised her right hand up toward the sky. "Thank God," she said emphatically. She noticed the painful expression on Aquila's face, so she changed the subject. "So do you want to go to my church Sunday?"

Aquila hunched her shoulders. "What church do you go to?"

Pricilla looked at Aquila in amazement. She had assumed that Aquila knew where she attended church. "I'm a member of the church that you and the kids eat lunch at every day, Quila."

"Oh, you attend church there?" Aquila asked in a surprised tone.

"Yeah, girl; the pastor and his wife are really kind people. When I told them about your situation, they advised me to tell you about the lunch meals they prepare for the homeless. They are both lawyers, and he is the pastor of the church too. First Lady Kendra spends her lunch hours in the soup kitchen every day, making sure everything runs smoothly while the homeless are being fed."

Aquila was thoughtful for a moment. "You know, I think I saw her today. I was standing in line waiting to be served and some snooty woman looked at me and asked what I was doing there. I looked at her like she was crazy. And she wanted to know if Darius, Daniel, and Abigail were my children. I usually try not to be rude to people, but that lady pissed me off when she looked down on my children like they were stank or something. Then she had the nerve to say she was surprised to see a young girl down there and with children too. It must have been First Lady Kendra that called her away."

Pricilla shook her head. "It's a sad fact, but some people live in their own little wealthy cocoons and either don't know, or don't care that there are homeless people living in this wealthy country just like there are in other poverty stricken countries."

Aquila rubbed her left arm gently. "I guess you're right. Today was the first time I've seen her. Of course, I've only been in town a few days. But I'm surprised the pastor's wife allowed that lady to work in there. Most of the people sitting at the tables around us were talking about her; how she had a terrible attitude. She must have been born with a silver spoon in her mouth or something."

"I doubt it. If she's working there, I'd be willing to bet she was ordered to do so by the court system. First Lady Kendra allows people to do community services there because she works with the juvenile judicial system. She believes it's the perfect alternative to keeping young people who are first time offenders from going to jail."

Aquila scrunched up her nose. "Well, this lady wasn't young. She looked at least forty or forty-five. It was hard to tell with that pile of makeup she had on. And believe me, Pricilla, she needs more than community service work to get rid of that stinking attitude she has."

Pricilla was thoughtful for a moment. "You know, I think I know exactly who you're talking about. I believe her name is Diana. She's First Lady Kendra's friend. How that came to be, I have no idea, because they're as different as day and night." Pricilla didn't feel comfortable enough with Aquila to tell her exactly how she knew of Diana. When the time was right, she'd explain it to her.

"She sure was a piece of work," Aquila emphasized.

"If she's anything like the way you described her, she's not going to last long in the soup kitchen."

"The lady that replaced her, I think her name is Ms. Mable, looked at her like she dislikes her." Pricilla nodded her head. "And *she* looks just like someone I've seen before."

"It's funny how we see strangers that look like people we know, isn't it? Who does she look like?"

Aquila frowned slightly, trying to remember who Mable looked like. "I don't know; maybe one of the social workers who used to come to the orphanage." Aquila moaned when she stood up.

Pricilla laughed. "What's wrong with you? You sound like an old lady."

Aquila forced a phony smile. "Oh, nothing; I'm just tired, I guess."

The truth of the matter was that Aquila had black and blue bruises over most of her body. She was ashamed to let Pricilla know just how badly Brandon had physically abused her. She hated to admit it, but a part of her felt that she was partly to blame. She didn't have an answer why her husband did the things he did to her. Aquila remembered Pricilla once telling her that God is an all knowing God. If that were the case, then perhaps He knew, and perhaps, in time, He'd reveal it to her.

Chapter 3

Diana dabbed the sweat on her face with a tissue as she scurried to her car. The scorching afternoon sun beat down on her head. Her cell phone rang. "Hello." She pressed the keyless entry to her car, opened the door, and sank into the soft tan leather seat of her pearl white 745 LI BMW.

"Diana, where are you?" Jeffrey, her husband of nine years inquired.

Diana started the car and turned the air condition on full blast.

"Hi, Jeffery," she answered breathing heavily. "I'm leaving the soup kitchen at church. Honey, it was awful. I had to serve homeless people lunch, and some of them smelled awful."

"Diana, don't be so dramatic; they're homeless, what did you expect?"

"I'm shocked, that's all. I expected my community service time to be easier, I guess."

"I think you got off easy. The judge could have sentenced you to jail time. DWI is a serious offense. Thanks to your friend, Kendra, at least, you won't have a record now."

Diana sat back and enjoyed the cool air that blew in her face. "You're right, I should be grateful."

"All of this drama could have been avoided if you had kept your promise to me that you weren't going to drink anymore," Jeffrey complained.

Diana sighed. "I'm really sorry, honey. I only drink when I feel depressed. I should have known better than to drink and drive. I've learned my lesson though."

Jeffrey grunted. "So you say."

Diana carelessly changed lanes without checking her rearview mirror. "I *promise* you that I won't take another drink, Jeffrey," she said apologetically.

Jeffrey approached his next statement carefully because whenever he'd previously mentioned the subject, Diana had gotten angry. "Honey, you should really consider going to a psychologist for counseling about your drinking problem."

Diana bolted up in the car seat. "I don't need a psychologist to tell me what I already know," she said acridly. "I drink to forget the nightmares

I've had since Momma died and since I gave my baby away for adoption. Drinking helps me forget, Jeffery."

"Drinking only numbs the pain. It's been over twenty years since you gave your baby up. We've hired private investigators to find her, but they haven't been successful. Frankly, I'm beginning to think that I'm wasting my money. I'm sure we'll have better luck searching on the Internet sites because it's a high probability that the child's been searching for you too."

Diana sighed. She maneuvered her car into traffic, leaving downtown Raleigh from McDowell Street, and merged onto Capital Boulevard. "You're probably right, Jeffery, but I didn't want to leave any stones unturned, so that's why I hired Terry's Investigative Service. If he doesn't produce any evidence soon, I'll relieve him of his services."

"I think that would be best, honey. As soon as I can clear my calendar for a week at the hospital, and my practice is running smoothly, we can fly out to Nashville and investigate the information we find on the Internet together."

"How long will that take?" Diana demanded to know. "You promised to take some time off over a month ago. It seems that your hours have increased since then, and you come home later and later every day."

"Starting a medical practice takes time, Diana," Jeffrey replied in an irritated tone. "I have to oversee the office set up, make sure the equipment and instruments are of the latest technology, and interview nurses and clerical personnel. By the way, that master's degree you have in health care management would be a great asset to me. Why don't you reconsider working for me and managing the practice?"

"I'll consider it, Jeffery," Diana said reluctantly. "I'm not sure if working together would be a good idea. Besides, my first priority is finding the child that I gave away."

Diana's life had changed drastically after her mother, Ms. Anna Wooten, died a month after her high school graduation. She had suffered from sickle cell anemia all of her life. She didn't survive the last sickle cell crisis that she went through. A few weeks after her mother's death, Diana's sister, Sydney, eloped with the pastor of her mother's church. Sydney had taken the few meager items that their mother owned. The only thing she left Diana was a contact phone number, in the event that she wanted to live with her. But Diana Janine Wooten had big dreams and ambitions; living with Sydney and her husband was not a part of the future that she had envisioned for herself.

The only thing left for Diana was sad memories and the rented house that they'd lived in for years. Diana packed the few items that she owned and moved in with Kendra and her mother for six weeks.

Diana had gotten accepted to the college of her desire. She moved from Raleigh, North Carolina to Nashville, Tennessee to attend college at Fisk University. She was seventeen when she enrolled for classes for her first semester.

Being a naïve young girl who was raised by a single mother and devout Christian, Diana was unprepared to deal with the pressures that were synonymous with college life. She met and fell in love with a young man who happened to be a sophomore in college. Bobby Tarnell was a sophisticated, handsome gentleman from Chicago, Illinois.

Upon being introduced to him, Diana was immediately mesmerized. Bobby was very cunning, and in a matter of weeks, had successfully convinced Diana to sleep with him. What Diana gullibly mistook for his love for her, was merely a player's game for Bobby. Weeks later, Diana realized that she had become pregnant. Unfortunately, Bobby told her that he wanted nothing more to do with her or the child she was carrying.

He coldly offered to give her money for an abortion. To add insult to injury, he informed her that he had married his high school sweetheart, a young lady from his hometown in Chicago. He had put in for a transfer to the college in Chicago where his wife attended and would be leaving Fisk University after the fall semester ended.

Diana asked him to at least go with her to the abortion clinic. He refused, callously stating that she was on her own, and he never wanted to see her again. To say that Diana was hurt and devastated was an understatement. She took the money from him and searched for an abortion clinic via The Yellow Pages.

Although she had every intention of going through with the procedure, she spent weeks agonizing over the decision to kill her unborn child. Her mother's moral teaching against abortion burned in her conscious.

But after considering the fact that she had denounced her mother's religious beliefs after her death, she decided that it wouldn't benefit her to be a single, financially depleted mom. By the time she gathered enough courage to go through with it, she was informed by the doctor that she was beyond the legal abortion stage.

Bobby had left school without giving Diana a second thought. Now her only alternative was to have the baby and raise it alone. But reality raised its ugly head, and she realized that raising a baby alone with no money, education, and no one to rely on would be a monumental task. Dropping out of school was not an option; neither was moving in with Sydney and her husband. In Diana's mind, reliving the poverty-stricken life that her mother had immolated for Sydney and her was repugnant.

She endured the shame of pregnancy throughout the school year and managed to complete her freshman year at college. During the summer, in July, she gave birth to a baby girl and gave her up for adoption. Her problems had been solved; or so she thought. She became more determined than ever to reach her goals of obtaining a bachelor's degree, her master's degree, and working toward gaining financial success.

After receiving her master's in health care management, Diana applied for and was hired in a hospital administrator position at Vanderbilt Medical Center in Nashville. She worked there for three years. She had become homesick for her hometown of Raleigh, so she applied for the position of health care business manager, at WakeMed in Raleigh, North Carolina.

She flew to Raleigh a month later and interviewed for the position. Human Resources offered her the position. After negotiating her desired salary, she accepted it and moved back to her hometown. By this time, she was twenty-seven years old. During the five years that she worked at WakeMed, she met Dr. Jeffrey Thompson. Jeffrey was older than Diana.

He was forty-four and had been a widower for three years. Diana and Jeffrey dated for a year and got married when she was thirty-two, and he was forty-nine.

Having married an established, successful, oncologist, Diana felt assured that she had accomplished her goals of moving toward financial wealth. She moved into Jeffrey's beautiful, immaculate, spacious home that he had shared with his first wife, Denise, who had passed away from breast cancer. Diana wasn't thrilled that Jeffrey's adult son, Michael, still lived with him. After a messy divorce that had left Michael financially depleted, he had moved back into the house with Jeffrey until he finished medical school at UNC Chapel Hill.

Considering the shabby, matchbox home that she had grown up in, she believed that she had hit the jackpot. Diana was assured that she had finally been awarded the life she deserved.

She had looked forward to having a child with Jeffrey. She felt that another baby would relieve her of the guilt she'd been burdened with since she gave her first child away. Unfortunately, her health failed, forcing her to have a hysterectomy. To her dismay, the one thing that she wanted, the chance to redeem herself by having another baby, was now destroyed.

Diana became depressed and started drinking excessively. Jeffrey and she decided that she should take an extended leave of absence from her job. Her leave turned into a resignation. Shortly thereafter, she started having nightmares about the child she'd given away for adoption. She was now on a mission to locate the child that she had given up.

After a two-year futile attempt to locate her daughter, Diana was determined not to let anything or anyone, not even Jeffrey, distract her from finding the child that she ached for.

"I think we'd work well together," Jeffrey assured her. "And truth be told, I'd rather have you work with me every day than have to worry about whether you're home idle or out shopping for unnecessary items, spending money faster than I can make it," he complained.

Diana eased her car onto the 440 beltline, headed for Cary. "You make me sound like I'm a desperate housewife."

"You need to get out of that desperate house-wife role and make a life for yourself."

Diana exhaled loudly into the phone. "I enjoy my life the way it is."

"I just think you would enjoy your life better if you spend your time more wisely. Perhaps if you concentrated on something besides finding your child for a while, you might not have those awful nightmares as often—"

"Why can't you understand that I'm having these nightmares because of guilt from giving my child away?" Diana frowned as she yelled into the phone. "I don't think I'll ever get a moment's peace until I find her."

Jeffrey held his hand up, as though Diana could see him. "I didn't mean to upset you. I can't say that I understand your pain. I can only imagine what it would be like to have a child and not know where he or she is." Diana was silent. "Honey?" Jeffrey waited for Diana to respond.

"I'll be okay." Diana wiped the tears away that had trickled down her face.

Jeffrey continued, choosing his words cautiously. "Honey . . . I think you should at least consider talking to your sister about your child."

"Why? So Sydney can sit on her sanctified horse and judge me?"

"I doubt if Sydney would judge you. She has a daughter, so I think that she'll be compassionate and be there to help you deal with the situation."

Diana exhaled loudly into the phone. "No. Sydney and I have never been close. I wouldn't feel comfortable talking to her. "

Diana and Sydney had been bickering since they were little girls. Their personas were as different as day and night. Diana had a vivacious personality; she was boisterous, but often felt insecure because her self-esteem was predicated on her attire. She was very unappreciative and dissatisfied with the simple life that she was forced to live as a teenager.

Sydney's personality was reserved and soft spoken, but she had a lot of confidence in herself. She was unpretentious and was grateful to receive whatever meager items that her mother could afford to buy for her. She also had a great sense of humor.

As teenagers, their looks were as distinct as their personalities. Sydney was five feet seven inches, slim, with an hourglass figure. She had smooth, chocolate skin, short, coarse hair, and big, bright, dark eyes.

Diana was five feet four inches, plump, with banana colored skin. Her hair was long, hanging four inches past her shoulders. She had big, brown, doe eyes.

Both girls were beautiful, but because of their mother's religious beliefs, neither was allowed to wear makeup or jewelry.

Diana's selfish, greedy attitude prompted her mother to be sterner with her than she was with Sydney. Diana instigated arguments and fights with Sydney, because she was jealous of her. Diana thought that her mother favored Sydney more. Her animosity toward Sydney still existed throughout adulthood. Because of that, the visits and phone calls between them were sparse.

"It's time for you guys to put the past behind you and make amends. Life is short. She's the only family you have," Jeffrey reminded her.

"You're right," Diana agreed. "Maybe one day we'll get it together."

"There's no time like the present," Jeffrey replied.

The person in the car beside Diana blew their car horn loudly at her and gave her a nasty look. Diana swerved back into her own lane. "That was close," she exclaimed.

"What happened?" Jeffrey inquired anxiously. Diana told him what happened.

"Hang up and concentrate on your driving, honey," he said sternly.

Diana's phone beeped. She checked the screen. "Jeffrey, this call is from Terry. Maybe he has some news. I'll talk to you later." Before Jeffrey could respond, Diana hung up.

Chapter 4

Kendra settled at her desk in Matthew's and her law firm. She was admiring an 8 x 10 picture the two of them had taken together days ago. Many people told them that they resembled each other. They both had milk chocolate skin, stood five feet eight inches tall, and both had dimples. Kendra's dark eyes were small and bright, while Matthew's light brown eyes were small and squinty. They both were slim and had well-defined bodies. Kendra's thick, coarse hair hung three inches past her shoulders, while Matthew always wore his wavy black hair cut close to his round head.

Kendra and Matthew met while attending Fisk University in Nashville, Tennessee. Kendra was born and raised in Raleigh, North Carolina. Matthew was born and raised in Louisville, Kentucky.

Their backgrounds were completely different. Kendra's father divorced her mother, Hannah, because of her lack of self discipline, when Kendra was seven years old. Kendra grew up with a single mother who had few moral standards. Hannah was a beautiful, petite woman. She stood five feet one inch tall, and had velvety cocoa brown skin, small dark brown eyes, and long thick coarse hair. Her personality, however, did not accentuate her looks. She used profanity like it was going out of style. Her form of discipline for Kendra was using a string of expletives. She was a heavy drinker, smoker, and ever since Kendra could remember, Hannah changed boyfriends every six months to a year.

After Kendra turned fourteen, Hannah made her do most of the cleaning and cooking, while she spent time with her boyfriends. Kendra yearned for her mother's attention, but she knew that as long as Hannah had a man around, their needs would come before hers. Hannah didn't show Kendra a lot of love, but she made sure that she had the bare necessities: food, shelter, and clothes.

Hannah was determined to work and pay her own way without the assistance of the county. Despite the fact that she partied just about every weekend, when Monday morning came, she reported to her domestic housekeeping jobs on time. She used the meager child support money that she received from her ex-husband on Kendra and always deposited twenty-five dollars a month in an account for Kendra.

Her mother was neither educated nor did she believe in going to church. It was not a priority for her to seek any type of religion. Until Kendra met Diana's family, she had no desire to go to church either. She only went with Diana's family because it was a requirement. She spent many weekends with them, using their residence as a place to relax, while her mother entertained her boyfriends.

Her goal in life was to get her high school diploma; that was the one thing that her mother commanded that she achieve. The second commandment was that she'd better not get pregnant. Kendra managed to adhere to each rule.

Diana convinced her to apply for college at Fisk University, where she met Matthew Woodbridge during her sophomore year.

Matthew came from a middle class two-parent family that urged him from childhood to get a good education so that he could reach his highest potential. He had been showered with love as a child and cherished the memories of being raised in a close-knit family. His father was a lawyer and the pastor of a small church in Louisville. His mother was a professor in the School of Medicine at the University of Louisville. His three siblings and he had grown up in church all of their lives. Needless to say, because of her upbringing, his parents did not approve of Kendra.

Kendra was a challenge for Matthew, but in spite of her street wise, hard core, no nonsense personality, he loved her, so he witnessed to her about the love of God. Many of their dates consisted of going to church, reading the Bible, and studying for their classes.

Despite Matthew's encouragement, Kendra didn't yield her life over to God. She continued to party and go to clubs with Diana. A year before they graduated, Kendra and Matthew both applied to law school at North Carolina Central University, in Durham, North Carolina. They continued dating during their first year at law school until Matthew broke up with Kendra. His reason was that they were unequally yoked and that he couldn't, in good conscious, marry a woman that wouldn't submit her life to Christ.

Kendra was heartbroken. It was during that time that she'd discovered that she was pregnant. She made a decision to abort her child. Weeks later, she was devastated and broken from the heartache of what she'd done. After a few weeks, Kendra surrendered her life over to God. She and Matthew reunited and were married during their second year in law school. After gaining valuable experience with law firms in Raleigh, they started their own business as partners in The Woodbridge Law Firm.

The only regret that she had was that she wasn't able to give Matthew another baby. If she had known she wouldn't be able to have any more children, she would not have had the abortion while she was in college. She felt guilty for not telling Matthew the truth about what she'd done before they were married. To make matters worse, she had been informed by her doctor a year ago that she had ovarian cysts. She often wondered if her infertility was a result of reaping the sin of having that abortion so many years ago.

She was scheduled for her annual exam to have a biopsy performed on the cysts in a few weeks. But she was optimistic that the results would be favorable. Matthew constantly reassured her that no matter what the results, God was still in control and able to heal her. She felt blessed to be married to a good man.

Kendra smiled as she placed the picture back on the mahogany desk and swirled around in her brown, cowhide leather chair, to open her laptop computer.

Matthew walked into the office. "What are you smiling about?"

Kendra placed her left hand over her chest. "Matthew, you startled me. I didn't hear you come in."

Matthew stopped in front of her desk. "I didn't mean to startle you. What where you thinking about that had you smiling so widely?"

Kendra looked into her husband's solemn face. "I was silently praising the Lord for giving me a good husband." Kendra noticed that Matthew's countenance had become distorted. The smile left her face. "What's wrong, Matthew?"

"We have more problems at church," Matthew answered. Kendra raised her eyebrows. Matthew put his right hand over his forehead and rubbed it down to his chin. "Ms. Brown phoned and told me she's resigning, effective two weeks from today."

Kendra opened her hands, palms up, toward Matthew. "Why? I thought she was happy with the three dollars an hour raise we gave her? Did she give you a specific reason why she was resigning?"

"Yes. It seems that one of the mega churches in town has offered her five dollars an hour above the amount we pay her per hour, so she's leaving."

Kendra slowly shook her head from side to side. "I hope that she's considered that the workload will probably be twice as much as the workload at our small church."

"Who knows, Kendra? Sometimes the almighty dollar cancels out people's common sense. I told her that I hate to see her leave, but there's no way we can match the salary that that church is offering her." Matthew stuffed his hands into his pants pockets. "Being that we allot so much money to feed the hungry and the majority of the church's money is allocated to the benevolent fund, the accounts payable is stretched to the limit."

Kendra stood up and walked around the desk to comfort Matthew. "Honey, the Lord knows you are doing the best you can." She pulled his hand out of his pocket, put her hand into his, and squeezed it lightly. "He'll send us someone who's as faithful as you are, and they'll feel blessed to make thirteen dollars an hour. I'll post the position on the church's Web site tonight. I'm sure we'll have more applicants than we can handle within a week's time."

Matthew reached up and pecked Kendra on her forehead. Being that Kendra had on three-inch heels, she stood taller than him. The height difference was not a factor to either of them. Matthew closed his large hand over Kendra's small hand and walked toward the leather sofa that was placed against the wall.

Matthew flopped down in the seat and patted the spot next to him. Kendra sat. "How was your morning?" he asked. Kendra updated him on the situation with Diana. Matthew studied Kendra's sad face and tried to cheer her up. "She'll change, honey. Just give her time. She'll eventually see the error of her ways."

Kendra exhaled wearily. "Let's hope so. I'd love for her to change willingly, because you and I both know that if she doesn't, God will find a way to humble her." Kendra put her head on Matthew's shoulder. "I have a feeling that Diana is about to be yanked off of that high horse that she's been riding."

Chapter 5

Diana listened intently as Terry updated her on her adopted child's situation. "We did find someone born in the hospital with the same date and time of birth as your child, Mrs. Thompson. However, the Office of Vital Statistics wouldn't release any information that wasn't public knowledge. The child was given away for adoption by the birth mother, age: eighteen, race: African American, father: unknown—"

Diana exited 440 to the Cary Parkway, drove the four miles to the subdivision they lived in, and pulled into her driveway. She pressed the button on the car's sun visor to open one of the four car garages that was situated on the side of the huge brick house.

"Terry, is that all the information you have? I could have looked that information up on the Internet," Diana said harshly. "And I know who the father is. I didn't name him on the birth certificate because he didn't own up to her."

Terry closed the drapes in his hotel room in Nashville and sat on the chair that was positioned beside the bed. "Yes, ma'am," he said apologetically. He could hear the frustration in Diana's voice.

Diana expelled a deep breath. "I'm sorry, Terry. I shouldn't be taking my frustration out on you."

"I understand, ma'am. Anyway, I did some digging around; it's funny what people will give up for the right amount of money." Terry bent over to untie his shoe laces. "I got this information from a retired nurse that worked at the hospital twenty-three years ago. I looked up all the nurses that were employed at the hospital that year and her name turned up. Once I found her, I guess she was in a financial bind, because when I bribed her with money to talk, she started singing like a bird. When I showed her your picture, she remembered you. She said she couldn't understand why such a beautiful, intelligent, college girl like you would give up her beautiful baby girl."

Diana frowned. "There were several nurses that waited on me after I had the baby."

Terry kicked his shoes off and propped his feet up on the bed. "This nurse said that you may remember her, because she gave you her daughter's pendant. She said that you were so depressed that she wanted to comfort you."

Diana tapped lightly on the steering wheel and smiled. "Yes," she said excitedly. "I do remember her." Diana recalled that the nurse was a tall, heavy set, multi-racial woman in her fifties. "I can't recall her name, though."

"Her name is Ms. Kemp." Terry picked up his burger and bit into it, then twisted the top off of his beer.

"That's right," Diana exclaimed. "Nurse Kemp was so nice to me. I think that she must have felt sorry for me. I don't know what happened to that pendant, but I kept it close for a long time. It was a gold cat with green eyes."

"Yes, ma'am." Terry finished chugging down the beer that he'd been drinking. "Anyway, it turns out that a middle class couple adopted your daughter; both teachers in the Nashville school system."

Diana exhaled loudly into the phone. "At least some decent people adopted her. That has worried me to no end all these years."

"Don't get too excited, Mrs. Thompson; there's more." Diana stayed silent and listened. "They both passed away three years after they adopted her. My source told me that the woman's mother was the only living relative of the two, but she was too old and frail to take the child in. A few foster families kept her for a few years, but that didn't work out, so the State assigned her to the orphanage. So the child stayed there until she was grown, I guess."

"You guess?" Diana asked Terry in a disappointed tone.

Terry covered his mouth and coughed. "Yes, ma'am. The orphanage burned down four years ago, and all of its records were lost in the fire."

"What did I do to my precious baby?" Diana lamented. "Is there anything else, Terry?"

"No, ma'am. I came to a dead end once I found out the orphanage no longer exists. I'm sorry, Mrs. Thompson." Diana didn't respond. "Ma'am?"

"Oh, I'm sorry, Terry. This is so disappointing. I guess you can fly home tonight or tomorrow, whenever you can get a flight out of Nashville. How are your funds?"

"They're kinda low, but I have enough to get me through the night and back home." Terry cleared his throat. "But I will need the rest of my retainer when I return, plus expenses."

"Just let me know when you return to Raleigh, and I'll write you a check."

"Yes, ma'am. I'm sorry I couldn't do more."

"Me too; but I know more now than I did before. Thank you, Terry. Take care." Diana snapped her cell phone closed, opened the car door, and stood in the garage staring blankly at the floor for a moment. She closed the car door and slowly walked into the mudroom and kicked off her heels. She walked in her stocking feet into the enormous kitchen. June, her housekeeper, emerged out of the adjacent family room.

"Hi, Mrs. Thompson." Diana nodded at June, but didn't make eye contact with her. She was on the verge of tears. June continued. "I finished cleaning the bathrooms, vacuumed the carpet upstairs, and washed and folded a load of towels. I'll be back tomorrow to damp mop the hardwood floors and dust."

Diana blinked back the tears before she gazed at June. "I'm sure you've done a great job. Thank you." Stunned by Diana's warmth and sincerity, June's mouth dropped open as she gave Diana a curious look.

Diana thought she saw concern in the older woman's eyes. Normally, Diana treated June like the invisible woman. But after the disappointing news that she'd just received, she needed some compassion. She realized that no matter how cold she was toward June, June always seemed to respond in a kind manner. Kendra's words echoed in her mind. *"Having money shouldn't make you a cruel snob."* She thought maybe she should consider her atrocious behavior.

June gave her a pleasant smile. Diana cleared her throat. "June, take the rest of the week off."

"Mrs. Thompson," June asked nervously, "you don't need my services this week?"

"You've worked hard, June; take some time off. Here, let me pay you." Diana walked to the kitchen's center island and sat on the stool in front of it. She pulled her checkbook out of her purse and wrote a check for the usual weekly amount, plus a bonus.

June stared at the check. "Mrs. Thompson," she said, handing the check back to her, "you've paid too much."

Diana shook her head. "It's okay, June. You deserve some extra time and money for putting up with me all these years."

June touched Diana on the shoulder. "Are you okay, Mrs. Thompson?"

Diana looked at her and smiled sadly. "I'm fine, June. I'll see you next Monday. Okay?" Diana folded June's hand over the check.

"Yes, ma'am." June walked to the mudroom and retrieved her shoes, looked back at Diana, and walked to the garage.

After Diana opened the Plantation blind in the dining room to make sure June was gone, she walked back to the pantry that was adjacent to the kitchen and retrieved a hidden bottle of vodka. She reached on the second shelf for a paper cup and filled it to the brim. "I promised Jeffrey I wouldn't drink anymore, but just one will calm my nerves."

Chapter 6

It's hot in here," Pricilla exclaimed. She looked at Aquila's attire. "Aren't you hot in those long sleeves and jeans, girl?" She looked at the thermometer that was placed on the wall. "Whoa . . . It is 93 degrees in here. I need to invest in a small air conditioner."

Pricilla and Aquila sat in front of the box fan that was placed in the living room window. They watched the children through the screened door as they played outside under the small oak tree.

"It's a little warm in here, but I'll be all right. In my rush to pack, I forgot to pack my shorts and summer blouses."

"We're about the same size, aren't we?" Pricilla asked her. Aquila nodded. "I may pick up a few pairs of shorts and some blouses from K-Mart for you on my way home from work tonight."

Aquila gazed at Pricilla. "You don't have to do that. I'll be fine."

Pricilla laughed. "I know I don't, but I'm about to burn up just looking at you. You can wear some of my things today if you want to."

"I'm okay." Aquila looked away from Pricilla.

Pricilla wondered why Aquila seemed offended by her offer. She glanced at the clock. "I have to be at work by three o'clock today. Being a nurse's aide is okay, but I'm looking forward to becoming a registered nurse." Pricilla smiled. "If God continues to be with me, I'll accomplish my goal in December." Aquila nodded. "Do you want to drive me to the nursing home, so you can take the kids to Pullen Park? As hot as it is, I'm sure they'll enjoy the Aquatic center."

Aquila looked down at the green and white linoleum floor. "I don't have a driver's license."

"Oh." Pricilla smoothed her short hair down with the back of her cocoa brown hand. "Girl, I thought you had your driver's license, all this time."

"I had a driver's permit, but Brandon didn't have enough patience with me to teach me how to drive." Aquila stood up and walked to the front door to check on her children. "The few times that he took me out, he screamed and yelled at me so much that I lost my nerve for driving."

"That man had you boxed in like a new pair of shoes, didn't he?"

"Basically. He claimed he didn't want me to work, because he wanted me to stay home and take care of his children. His excuse for not allowing me to go to school to get my adult high school diploma was that I should wait until Abigail started pre-school next year." Aquila's eyes were tearful. "I was such a fool, Pricilla. I let Brandon ruin my life. He provided well for us, but I paid my due, that's for sure. Over the years, the kindness he'd shown me earlier in our marriage turned into physical and verbal abuse. I wanted to leave him a long time ago, but with no money or education, I couldn't go anywhere."

Pricilla folded her arms across her stomach. "Aquila, why didn't you report him to the police? Why would you protect his sorry behind?"

Aquila walked back to the couch and sat down, facing Pricilla. She unbuttoned the long sleeves of her blouse and folded them up to her elbows. "I wasn't protecting him. I threatened to call the police several times, but he promised me that if I did, when he made bail, he would kill me. And believe me, Pricilla, he is mean enough to do it."

"It's still not too late to press charges against him." Pricilla stared at Aquila's bruised arms. "Look at your skin. You look like you've been hit by a Mack truck."

"I'll be fine. These bruises will go away; they always do." Aquila stooped over to pick up the newspaper from off of the floor. In doing so, her blouse rose up in the back. Pricilla's light brown eyes widened when she saw the blue and black bruises on Aquila's caramel-colored back.

"Aquila," Pricilla squealed. "What happened to your back?" Aquila stood up abruptly at her friend's query. "Pull your top up and let me see the rest," she said, horrified. Aquila glanced at Pricilla and slowly pulled her top up. "Oh my God," Pricilla gasped. She couldn't believe her eyes. She jumped up and walked closer to Aquila to get a better view of the bruises. "I can't believe this." Pricilla's eyes filled with tears.

"I'm sure that the bruises look worse than they feel," Aquila lied. "I'll be fine."

"What the heck do you mean? I think that you need medical attention. You may have some blood clots." Tears flowed down Pricilla's face. She felt faint, so she sat back down in the recliner. She picked up a magazine and fanned her face. "Lord, my God, what kind of monster would do something like this?"

Aquila pulled her top back down. "Pricilla, I know it must look terrible, but I'll heal. I've finally gotten away from him, so this won't ever happen again." Aquila lowered her voice to almost a whisper. "Please don't make a big deal out of this."

Pricilla gawked at Aquila incredulously. She hunched up her shoulders and threw her hands up and purposely raised her voice. "It is a big deal. That maniac abused you; from the looks of these bruises, he tried to kill you."

Aquila walked back to the door again to see if the children had heard them. They hadn't. Tears streamed down her face. "Pricilla, I was scared that he *was* gonna kill me this time. That's why I called you the next day while he was at work."

Aquila described the episode to Pricilla that led up to her escape from Brandon. Despite Brandon's ridiculous commandment, Aquila was more determined than ever to get her diploma. She refused to be treated like a child any longer because she had developed ambitions too. She planned to get her diploma, and once Abigail started kindergarten, she wanted to enroll in college.

Aquila and the boys had taken the bus to the community college so that she could enroll in the adult high school diploma program. She had taken Abigail to her neighbor's house. The process had taken longer than she expected. She and the boys caught the four forty-five bus back to the bus stop near their home.

They exited the bus and Aquila walked swiftly down the street to their house. Daniel and Darius complained that they couldn't keep up with her. She grabbed each by the hand and pulled them along. She hurried to Ms. Carter's house and picked Abigail up. She thanked her and explained why she couldn't stay for a visit. She told her that Brandon would be home soon and she wanted to be there before he arrived.

Aquila was hopeful that he'd be proud enough of her endeavors to support her. She underestimated Brandon's will to control her life. She was surprised when she unlocked and opened the front door and saw Brandon pacing around in the living room. She nervously explained to him where she had been. To her surprise, he seemed cool about it.

She made dinner, they ate, and an hour later, Brandon supervised the children's bath while Aquila washed the dishes and watched *Ugly Betty* on the small TV in the kitchen. Brandon eventually joined her, and they sat on the couch in the family room and watched *Grey's Anatomy* together.

Aquila finally began to feel relaxed. Brandon didn't mention her activities again, so Aquila assumed that he was okay with it. She couldn't have been more wrong. They prepared to go to bed at the usual time, which was ten o'clock. Once they closed the bedroom door, Brandon painstakingly dictated his rules to her again. Aquila tried to reason with him, but her pleading words seemed to agitate him. The more she talked, the angrier he got. Aquila saw the wild look in his eyes, and she knew what was coming next. She balled up in the fetal position while he tortured her with his fists. She silently prayed and asked God to spare her life. As though hearing her prayer, Brandon stopped suddenly and walked out of the room. She crawled into the bed and tried to go to sleep.

The next morning, Brandon came into the bedroom and apologized profusely. Confident that Aquila had forgiven him, he proceeded to get ready for work.

She pretended to accept his apology as usual, but she felt an underlying hatred for him. Aquila knew that it was time for her to get away from him. She waited an hour, until she thought he was settled at work, before she called Pricilla. Pricilla told her that she would wire her some money immediately to buy bus tickets.

Aquila showered, protecting her bruised skin as much as possible. She packed a few clothes for herself and the children, got the children's birth certificates and immunization records, and fled for her life.

Pricilla held her hand over her mouth in horror while listening to Aquila tell the story. "Thank God you got away. Oh, Aquila, I had no idea that you had such a horrible life with him. When you told me he beat you, I assumed he smacked you around some, which is still a crime, but believe me, if I had known he was abusing you like this, I would have reported him myself."

Pricilla left Aquila standing in the living room. She returned with a camera in her hand. "Turn around. I'm taking pictures of your bruises. They'll come in handy when you take his butt to court. I wish you had reported him, girl, because you would have it on record, as well as these pictures. He needs to serve time in prison for this," Pricilla said indignantly. She snapped pictures of Aquila's back and arms. "I see he thought he was smart enough to beat you where it wouldn't be obvious to the public."

"Yeah; he never touched my face because he knew I couldn't cover it up."

Pricilla's eyebrows furrowed. "And I'm mad at you for covering up these bruises for him. You enabled him to get away with his crime. Now I see why you wear long sleeves and pants in the middle of summer." She picked her purse up off of the couch and put the camera in it. "I'm gonna have these developed, and then I'm gonna talk to First Lady Kendra and ask her to refer you to a prosecutor in order to bring charges up on his butt."

Aquila's lips trembled slightly. "Pricilla, I appreciate your concern, but please don't do that."

"Why not?" Pricilla demanded to know. "Aquila, you're pissing me off with this protective attitude over Brandon, after he's almost beat you to death."

"I'm not protecting him. I'm protecting my children. Once he finds out where I am, he'll come looking for me, and I don't want to be found." Aquila wiped the tears from her face with the backs of her hands. "I just want a chance to heal and start a new life for my children and me. Please don't talk to anyone. I just need peace in my life right now."

Pricilla calmed down. "Against my better judgment, I'll consider what you're saying, but I'm still getting these pictures developed for future reference."

Aquila slumped down on the brown, checkered couch. "Thanks, Pricilla. Thanks for being a good friend."

"I still think you should report him, but I'll respect your wishes for now." Pricilla exhaled wearily. "It's time for me to leave for work. I'll bring you some ointment and bandages for those bruises when I come home tonight." Pricilla rushed into her bedroom and changed into her scrubs.

Ten minutes later, she came back into the living room and picked up her purse. The children had come back into the house and were looking at a show on the Disney Channel. She walked over to where they were lined up on the couch beside Aquila and kissed each of them on the tops of their heads. "I have to go to work, guys. I'll see you when I get back home tonight, okay?" They looked at her and nodded. Each said goodbye to her; Abigail stood up and hugged her.

"Have a good night at work, Pricilla," Aquila said, looking sheepishly at her.

Pricilla nodded. "Thanks."

Once Pricilla was outside, Abigail crawled into Aquila's lap and hugged her tightly. Aquila winced from her touch. "My goodness, you're strong, Abigail," Aquila told her, frowning from the burning sensation. "You hug Mommy so tightly." She lifted Abigail's arms away and kissed her. Aquila gently lay back on the couch and tried to recover from the burning sensation of Abigail's hug.

Chapter 7

Disturbed by the bruises she'd seen on Aquila's body, Pricilla pulled into the driveway of the nursing home where she worked part-time as a certified nurse's assistant. She entered the building and swiped her employee card through the card reader. The registered nurse on duty, Summer, handed Pricilla her duty assignment with the patients she'd assigned her to for the evening. Pricilla glanced at her workload and met the nurse's stare. "You don't actually expect me to handle this many patients in four hours, do you?"

"It's not that hard, Pricilla. You just have to work efficiently." Summer smirked and tossed her blond hair behind her shoulder. "The other *aides* don't have a problem working this floor."

Angered by Summer's snide remark, Pricilla glared at her, but decided it would be in her best interest not to voice what she thought because it would probably cost her her job. Besides, she only planned to work there until she graduated nursing school in December. Pricilla counted to ten under her breath, exhaled deeply, and returned the smirk. "Summer, you sound as though nurse's aides are peons."

Shifting in her seat, Summer appeared to be uncomfortable. "Pricilla, don't be so sensitive. You should know that I didn't mean anything by that," she drawled.

Yeah, right, Pricilla mused. Pricilla gawked at Summer and walked away to start her evening shift. The evening hours passed by quickly as Pricilla attended to the needs of the elderly, making them as comfortable as she possibly could. At ten after seven, she slid her card through the slot and headed outside. Her cell phone rang. It was her boyfriend. "Hi, Jeffrey," she greeted him excitedly.

"Hey, baby. What's going on?"

Pricilla had met Jeffrey at WakeMed during her second year of nursing school. They bumped into each other getting on the elevator. The collision caused Pricilla to drop her chemistry book along with a pile of papers. Jeffrey apologized and bent over to help her recover her items. He introduced himself to Pricilla, and she greeted him coolly. Her first impression of him was that he was arrogant. Pricilla had preconceived notions about him because she had heard the nurses gossiping about Dr. Jeffrey Thompson.

According to them, he was a difficult doctor to work with. On the other hand, some nurses were not shy about expressing their desire to have a relationship with him. It was rumored that he was financially secure and that he was a generous giver. Despite Pricilla's cool attitude toward him, Jeffrey continued to talk to her on the elevator.

By the time they had reached the lobby, Pricilla had changed her mind about him. She thought that he was a sweet, charming individual. Whenever she did her clinical assignments at the hospital, she anticipated seeing him again. However, she had no plans to approach him. She had no intentions of being a part of the drama and gossip that occurred between the other aggressive nurses that wanted him. A month later, they ran into each other again at the same elevator.

Again, Jeffrey dived into a conversation with her. Pricilla felt more relaxed with him, so she opened up and talked freely to him. Jeffrey gave her his business card and told her to call him if she needed a reference for a job. Pricilla thanked him. She told him that she was going to apply for a nurses' aide position at the Sunrise Retirement Home and that she would use him as a reference.

Two weeks later, she called him and thanked him for the great reference that he'd given her. She told him that because of his reference, she got the job. From then on, they talked on the phone at least twice a week. Pricilla shared information with him about why she had moved to Raleigh. Jeffrey shared information with her about the difficult time he'd had after the loss of his loved one. Their relationship started out as friends, but it developed into a mutual love. The chemistry between them was undeniable. Needless to say, their relationship became intimate.

Pricilla picked up her pace. "I'm walking to my car. I worked four hours today at the retirement home, in addition to going to school."

"Oh. You had a long day today," Jeffrey coaxed.

"Yes, today was very hectic. So what's going on with you?" Pricilla asked him sweetly.

"Not much; I'm leaving the hospital now. My day went well, but I'm sorry to hear that you had a trying day."

"My classes went fine, but work was challenging. Some of the patients were very irritable, and two of them were just antagonistic."

"One of my patients was annoyed with me today too, but that's to be expected sometimes in our profession, baby." Jeffrey pulled up to the stoplight and waited for it to turn green.

"You're right. When people are sick, we can't expect them to be on their best behavior. But some people are just mean. I feel sad for two of the patients I waited on tonight. I don't think anyone ever visits them. One man buzzed the desk three times, and all he basically wanted was to talk."

"I'm sure a lot of patients in the nursing homes are lonely and feel unloved."

"Yes, I'm sure." Pricilla sighed loudly.

Jeffrey put his right signal on and moved his foot from the brake to the accelerator when the light turned green. "Are you too tired to meet me at our regular place?"

Pricilla patted her hair down. "I'd love to see you, baby, but—"

"Or, I could stop by your house," he crooned.

Pricilla giggled. "No, I can't tonight, Jeffrey. Remember, I told you my friend from Nashville is staying with me."

Jeffrey frowned. "How is that preventing you from seeing me? I'd like to meet her."

"Because she has been seriously injured, and I promised her that I would stop by the store and get some ointment and bandages for her wounds."

"Shouldn't she see a doctor?" Jeffrey inquired.

Pricilla scanned the dimly lit area while she walked toward her car. "I think she should," she agreed, "but she insists that she's all right."

Jeffrey grunted, then asked, "Was she in a car accident?"

Pricilla opened her car door, got in, and then locked the door. "No, more like a husband accident," she said sarcastically.

"Are you saying her husband abused her?"

"Yes, he did. She's got black and blue bruises all over her arms and back."

Jeffrey whistled. "Did she report him to the police?"

"No; she's too afraid to report him to the police. She's fearful that he'll find out where she is and come looking for her. I wanted to report him, but she doesn't want me to." Pricilla started her car and turned the air condition on full blast.

"So she's hiding out at your place?"

"In a sense, yes, she is." Pricilla expelled a short loud breath. She felt as though Jeffrey was interrogating her. "My place is a refuge for her and the children. She had *nowhere* else to go." Pricilla's voice hardened. "I *told* you she was my best friend, but more like a sister to me in the orphanage. We've always looked out for each other."

"Don't get so defensive, baby. You're doing a good thing by taking care of your friend. Unless she presses charges, there's nothing else you can do."

Pricilla relaxed her shoulders. "I guess you're right. Thanks for understanding. I have early classes the rest of this week and clinical assignments on Thursday and Friday, but I'll make it up to you Saturday after I get home from work," Pricilla told him in a seductive voice.

"I can't wait that long to see you. Maybe we can have lunch together tomorrow in the hospital cafeteria."

"Are you kidding me? Aren't you concerned that the nurses will gossip, Dr. Thompson?"

"No," Jeffrey retorted. "If anyone asks, which I doubt they will, I'll just tell them that you're one of the students from the college. My personal time is none of their business anyway."

Pricilla laughed at Jeffrey's sarcastic remark. "Okay, Jeffrey. You're getting too bold for your own good."

"Everyone is going to know about us eventually, anyway. I plan to marry you some day."

"I wish I was as positive about this as you are." Pricilla sighed. "Jeffrey, can you do me a favor?"

Jeffrey drove into his driveway. "Sure, what do you need?"

"I need money to buy extra food for Aquila and the kids. The refrigerator is almost empty."

"No problem, baby. I'll put the money in your account first thing in the morning."

"Thanks, honey. I'll see you tomorrow in the cafeteria at twelve thirty, right?" Pricilla asked him sweetly.

"Right," Jeffrey confirmed.

Pricilla closed her cell phone, put her gray '94 Nissan Sentra in gear, and drove to Walgreens. Her eyes stung with angry tears as she thought about the ugly bruises that Brandon had left on Aquila's back. Aquila refused to press charges, but Pricilla wanted him to pay for what he'd done.

Chapter 8

Jeffrey entered the side door of his and Diana's house. The house was completely dark. Usually, Diana would have the house lit up, and Jeffrey would complain about her wasting electricity. Jeffrey turned the kitchen light on; there was no sign of dinner. Out of habit, he yelled toward the upstairs bedroom.

"Diana, I'm home, baby!" He strolled into the den, where he saw Diana lying on the couch asleep. He nudged her. "Diana, wake up, baby. I'm sorry it's so late. I stopped by the office to see how things were progressing . . ." Diana's arm fell limply to the floor. "Oh no, Diana, I know you haven't been drinking again." Jeffrey shook her vigorously. "Diana," he called her gruffly. "Wake up." He tapped her on the arm.

Diana's eyes flittered open slowly. She looked at Jeffrey as though he was a stranger, and then she looked around the room. She tried to sit up, but fell back clumsily on the burgundy leather sofa. "Oh, hi, honey," she slurred. "You're home early. I had planned to cook us steaks and potatoes for dinner."

"It's not early," Jeffrey said, irritated. "It's nine thirty. Diana, you promised me that you wouldn't drink anymore."

"I know I promised, Jeffrey, but after the news Terry gave me today, I needed something to calm my nerves."

"What about me? Why didn't you call me back after Terry called you, so I could help you deal with it? I'm your husband. That's why I'm here."

Diana sobbed. "I'm sorry, Jeffrey. I'm never going to find my daughter." She slumped back on the couch.

Jeffrey patted her on her shoulders gently, and then he stood up and walked swiftly to the kitchen. "You need to drink some coffee. I'll put the coffee pot on while we go upstairs and get you a nice hot bath." After he put the coffee on, Jeffrey walked back to the couch and sat beside Diana. "Come on, baby: let's go upstairs." Diana held her hands out, and Jeffrey led her upstairs and into their humongous Mediterranean styled bathroom. He turned the water on in the tub and sprinkled lavender bath beads and bubble bath into the water. She undressed while the tub filled up with water.

Jeffrey helped her into the bathtub. "Do you want to tell me what happened that was so bad it drove you to the bottle?"

Diana relaxed in the warm, soapy lavender and rose hip bath water. She repeated the news that Terry had given her earlier that afternoon.

Jeffrey's eyes were full of compassion for his wife. "It's not good news, but maybe something will turn up sooner or later, honey. You're not going to give up, are you?"

"What else can I do, Jeffrey? Terry came to a dead end. The orphanage burned down, and all of its records with it."

"I know that, but your daughter is twenty-three years old now. She would have left the orphanage at least five or six years ago, so it's a possibility she may be still living in or around Nashville. I still think we should search the Internet and take a trip to Nashville to see what we can find."

"When, Jeffrey?" Diana inquired with doubt in her voice.

Jeffrey washed Diana's back. "I'll try to clear my schedule for two weeks, if I can get Dr. Patel to cover my patients while I'm gone. I can't make any promises now, baby. When I go to work tomorrow, I'll review my schedule, and then confer with him to see if he can work my patients into his schedule."

Diana relaxed her shoulders. "Okay, honey, that sounds reasonable."

Jeffrey sighed loudly. "Diana, it's only reasonable that you see a psychologist—" Diana jerked her body around to protest. "Diana, hear me out. You need to talk to someone that can listen to your problems objectively. When you find your daughter, you need to have a clear head to be able to deal with her. Have you considered the consequences of meeting her with you having all of these hang ups? And baby, you need to deal with this drinking problem too."

"I don't have a drinking problem, Jeffrey. I only drink when I feel pressured," Diana declared.

"That's a classic case of denial," Jeffrey rebutted. "There are other ways to handle pressure. Baby, why don't you pray or at least attend church sometimes?"

Diana hit the water with her fist. "Jeffrey, please don't start up again with praying and religious talk. Kendra's sermon today was enough to drive me up the wall. I don't need to hear this crap from you too," she shouted.

"Well, you're going to hear it more often," Jeffrey said sternly. "Since Kendra invited *us* to attend her and Matthew's church, I thought we could at least show our appreciation for her services."

Diana cut her eyes up at Jeffrey. "We paid her well. We're not obligated to attend their church."

Jeffrey glared at Diana. "No, we're not obligated, but I enjoyed listening to Matthew teach on the Word of God last Sunday. I don't go to church as often as I should, but I'm going to at least start praying more."

Diana shook her head. "That's up to you. God stopped listening to my prayers a long time ago."

Jeffrey exhaled loudly. "That's just the vodka in you talking now."

"No, it's not. It's a fact. God turned His back on me a long time ago."

"That's not true, and you know it's not." Jeffrey had become frustrated with Diana's pessimistic attitude. "You can't keep living like a heathen; your mother didn't raise you to be an atheist."

"I'm not an atheist; I know that God exists, but I just don't believe in Him anymore." Diana stood in the tub and dried off. "Jeffrey, do you know the last time I stepped in a church was at my mother's funeral?"

"I'm well aware of that. It's time you stopped holding a grudge against God and turn your life back over to Him. Maybe then you'll be able to find your daughter."

Diana stopped drying her body and glared at Jeffrey. "God is not the answer to my problems. I just need to find my daughter so that I'll feel whole again. There's been a gaping hole in my heart ever since I gave her up."

Jeffrey stared at Diana incredulously. "Put your pajamas on, Diana," Jeffrey said wearily. "I'll go down and make your coffee."

Chapter 9

Pricilla unlocked the door to her home. The aroma of a home cooked meal met her nostrils. "Hi, Aquila," she yelled. "Girl, what smells so good?"

The children ran to Pricilla and hugged her. She picked each one up and kissed them on their cheeks. They ran back into the living room and continued to play UNO.

Aquila appeared from the kitchen. "Hey, Pricilla," she greeted her cheerfully. "I hope you don't mind, but I baked the chicken drumsticks that were in the freezer. I also made rice, yams, and sweet green peas."

"Of course, I don't mind. That's why the food is here; for you and the children. It's rare that I cook with my hectic schedule, so I'm happy to get a home cooked meal. I usually eat a salad or fast food." Pricilla walked past Aquila and stood in the kitchen looking toward the stove.

"Dinner should be ready in five minutes. I tried to time it to be ready by the time you got home from work." Aquila walked back into the kitchen, opened the oven door, and pulled out the pan of baked chicken.

"Aren't you thoughtful? You didn't have to do that."

Aquila laughed. "I guess I'm trained. Girl, I had to have Brandon's dinner ready when he got home from work. It's a habit, I guess." Aquila set the table for five people.

Pricilla pulled a chair out from under the kitchen table and sat down. "Well, Brandon isn't an issue anymore. You do things the way you see fit from now on."

Aquila's eye's twinkled. "Thanks, Pricilla. I'm gonna look for work here soon. I can't let you struggle and take care of me and the kids. We've eaten your cupboard empty."

Pricilla shook her head. "That won't be necessary, Aquila. Your first priority is to heal and relax your nerves, and then we will discuss what you need to do, okay?"

"I don't want us to be a burden to you. I already feel guilty about interrupting your life. Once I get a job, I can contribute to buying food and at least pay the electric bill while I save money to get my own place."

"Aquila, don't stress, okay? I've got everything under control." Aquila looked down and nodded. Pricilla laughed. "I'm going to wash my hands so I can eat. Everything looks and smells good." She stood up and walked out of the kitchen toward the bathroom.

Aquila relaxed her shoulders and called the children. "Come on, guys. Wash your hands so we can eat."

After everyone was seated, Pricilla blessed the food. She looked around the kitchen as they sat at the table and ate the meal. "Aquila, everything looks so clean and in order. Please don't feel obligated to clean up. I usually try to straighten the house out on Saturdays when I have time."

"I don't mind cleaning. As a matter of fact," she laughed, "that's one thing I can do well. I didn't work outside my home, but I stayed busy cleaning and cooking and taking care of my babies. Brandon used to brag to his friends about what a good housewife I was." Aquila laughed nervously. "His friends had no idea that I had no choice but to be a good housewife."

"Hopefully, that's all behind you now. It's time to make a life for *you*."

The children finished eating and returned to the living room to watch television. Pricilla retired to her bedroom to study for the next day's exam. Aquila washed the dishes and joined her children in front of the television.

Two hours later, Pricilla walked into the kitchen, grabbed a bottle of water out of the refrigerator, and sat in the faded brown cloth recliner in the living room. After giving the children baths, Aquila rejoined her. She settled on the brown plaid sofa. Pricilla was engrossed in watching *The Burning Bed* on the Lifetime Channel until she noticed, with her peripheral vision, Aquila fidgeting in her seat. She changed the channel.

"I'm sorry, Aquila, I didn't mean to be insensitive by watching that movie," Pricilla apologized.

"It's okay. I know you weren't being insensitive. I just hate to watch movies about men battering women. It reminds me of my own life."

"Lord willing, your former life." Aquila nodded and Pricilla continued. "That bag on the coffee table is for you. The items inside should help heal your bruises. You'll need to take a bath in the Epsom salt to help alleviate the soreness." Pricilla picked up the brochure that she had placed on the arm of the recliner that she sat in. "Oh, I brought this brochure from school for you." She handed it to Aquila. "It has the schedule of the spring semester's curriculum in it. I had forgotten about it until I opened my book to study."

Aquila glanced at Pricilla shamefacedly. "I don't even have a high school diploma yet, Pricilla. I need that before I can enroll in any college courses."

"I know that, Quila," Pricilla remarked with a smile on her face. "I talked to the head of the adult high school diploma program, and she said that you can study at your own pace to work toward obtaining your diploma."

"Thanks. I've wanted to get my high school diploma for a while now. I'm going to start as soon as possible." She looked over the brochure.

"You're gonna need that, so you can attend college by the spring semester."

A wrinkle creased Aquila's forehead. "I don't know about college, Pricilla. I thought I should get my diploma so I can apply for work. Besides, I don't have money for college."

"You can apply for a grant. I think you need to get at least an associate degree in something at the community college." Pricilla crossed her legs and clamped her hands together across her knee. "What are your interests?"

Aquila mused. She sat upright and folded her legs under her body. "You know, I've always loved typing. In school, I could type sixty-five words a minute, but that was seven years ago. I'm sure I'm rusty now."

"Typing is like riding a bike; once you learn how, you never forget it."

Aquila looked over the brochure again. "This business office technology program looks interesting. You think I can do that?"

"Of course. You can do all things through Christ, which strengthens you."

Aquila jumped when her cell phone rang. She retrieved it from the oak end table beside the couch and looked at the number.

Pricilla had no idea that Aquila owned a cell phone. She stared at Aquila. "Is that *your* phone?"

Aquila looked up at Pricilla. "Yes." She glanced away from Pricilla's piercing eyes.

She'd packed it in her personal items bag the day that she left Brandon. She decided to pack it for emergency use only, in case she needed to call Pricilla. However, she turned it off as soon as she got on the bus because she knew Brandon would be blowing it up when he couldn't get a hold of her at home. She hadn't unpacked the bag until this afternoon when she discovered that she needed her feminine care products.

Aquila stared at the number again. "It's Brandon," she told Pricilla. Her eyes were full of fear. "What should I do?"

"Give it to me," Pricilla ordered. She took the phone in the kitchen, pulled the kitchen cabinet door open beneath the sink, pulled out a hammer, laid the phone on the floor, and smashed it to pieces.

Pricilla gawked at Aquila. "Now you don't have to worry about him calling you anymore," she stated sarcastically.

No, Aquila didn't have to worry about Brandon bothering her anymore; at least, not by the phone. Now he was left with only one option. And Aquila knew her husband; it would only be a matter time before he followed through with it.

Chapter 10

After Diana drank her coffee and ate the sandwich Jeffrey had made for her, she went upstairs to go to bed. Jeffrey broiled a steak and potatoes for himself and ate in silence. An hour later, he walked quietly up to their bedroom and stood beside the mahogany four-poster bed to see if Diana was asleep. He watched her body as it moved up and down with each inhalation and exhalation. She snored lightly.

He crossed the huge room, his feet sinking into the thick, plush, off-white carpet. Closing the door, he walked into the upstairs foyer and sat on the beige damask chaise, put his elbows on his thighs and lowered his head in both hands.

Jeffrey was raised to be a man of honor and a provider for his family. He was brought up on Eason Farm, in a small community outside of Tarboro, North Carolina. His parents reared him in church and used their meager funds to help him work his way through college, and then medical school. His father taught him to make sure that he not only supplied his family's needs, but do everything in his power to ensure that their future was secure.

Once he became a doctor, he lived simply and saved his money. The largest purchase he'd made in life was the home that he bought for his first wife, Denise. He didn't purchase luxury vehicles and learned how to invest his earnings wisely. After twenty years, he'd become quite wealthy.

Until he met Diana, Jeffrey grieved over the death of his first wife. After her death, he focused solely on his work and rarely dated until he met Diana. Jeffrey was not a strong communicator, but he was attracted to Diana's vivacious personality. He initially watched her for a couple of months before he asked her out on a date.

Diana confided in him about her daughter from the beginning of their relationship. She was honest with him about her lack of religious beliefs. He didn't consider himself to be a particularly religious man, so he tolerated her theory on God at the time, but hoped that she would change.

Their first date went well, and they continued dating for a year until Jeffrey asked Diana to marry him. He was happy with Diana for the first seven years of their marriage. However, Diana's blatant disrespect for God forced him to see her in a different light. Recently he had to keep a constant check on his bank account to make sure that Diana wasn't squandering his money in order to fill the void in her life. To his dismay, his feelings for her had begun to change. He believed he still loved her, but he had no idea how to help her anymore with her drinking problem. He was at his wit's end.

"Is everything all right, Dad?"

Jeffrey jerked his head back up to see his son, Michael, standing there. "Oh, hi, son. I didn't know you were home." Jeffrey leaned back against the chaise.

"I just got here." Michael stared into his father's eyes. What's wrong?"

Jeffrey shook his head. "Your stepmother has been drinking again. I don't know what to do for her anymore. She refuses to get help."

"There's not much you *can* do, Dad, unless you commit her to an alcohol and drug abuse center." Michael sighed.

"And we both know that she'll probably never forgive you for that."

"You're right, son." Jeffrey pulled his six foot two–inch lean body up and ran his hand through his thinning mixed gray hair. His mocha face was distorted with frown lines. "I'm afraid if she doesn't find her daughter soon, she is going to go on another drinking binge, or have a nervous breakdown."

"Has she considered talking to anyone, professionally?"

Jeffrey shook his head. "She won't hear of it. Whenever I mention that, she gets upset. Frankly, son, I'm at my wit's end. I can't take too much more of this kind of pressure."

"Maybe you should reconsider starting your practice for now, Dad. I hate to see you so stressed out."

Jeffrey patted his son on the shoulder. "Thanks, son. I'll find a way. I *can* pray for Diana. As much as she hates the thought of prayer, she needs it, regardless." Jeffrey looked down at the floor. "I need to amend some things in my life too."

"You're a good man, Dad," Michael reassured him. "Mom would have been proud."

Jeffrey half smiled. "I don't know about that, but your mother was a good woman. Although she's been gone for fifteen years, I still miss her."

Michael shifted his body weight to his left leg. "Me too."

Jeffrey looked up and stared at Michael for a moment. "You know, you look more like your mother the older you get." Michael was tall like his father, but he had his mother's complexion; he was light brown with big brown eyes and long eyelashes. His hair was dark brown and coarse. He had full lips and perfect white teeth. "I used to think you looked just like me, but I see more of your mother's features in you now."

Michael smiled. "I think I look like both of you guys." He took a seat on the chaise.

Jeffrey glanced past Michael's head as though he was in a trance. He had a sad smile on his face as he reminisced. "Yep, Denise was a special woman." He looked at his son. "She would have been really proud of you too. She fought her illness trying to see you graduate from high school. That was her dream, to see her baby boy finish high school."

Michael had a sad look on his face while reminiscing about his mother. Both men were silent for a moment.

Jeffrey cleared his throat. "How was work today?"

"Being an intern at the hospital is stressful, but I made it through another day."

"Well, although you had a late start in your profession, you're on your way. You'll be a doctor before you know it. Hang in there, son." Jeffrey patted him on the back.

Michael smiled at his father reassuringly. "You too, Dad."

"I guess I'll turn in for the night," Jeffrey said wearily. "I have an early day tomorrow."

Michael nodded his head in agreement. He stood back up. "Goodnight. Get some rest, now. Try not to worry about Diana, okay?"

Jeffrey exhaled wearily. He was doing the best he could for Diana, but he was beginning to wonder if she was worth the stress she'd caused him for the better part of their marriage.

Chapter 11

Aquila's blue-gray eyes stretched open. Pricilla!" she yelled. "Why'd you destroy my phone?"
"You said you don't want Brandon to find you, right?" Pricilla retorted.

"Yeah, but I'm going to need a contact phone number to give to the employers when I apply for work."

"I'll give you money to buy a prepaid phone. You shouldn't have brought that phone with you anyway." Pricilla put her right hand on her hip. "Have you answered it since you left him?"

Aquila turned on her heels, went back into the living room, and sat on the couch. She folded her arms across her stomach. "No. Why?"

Pricilla followed Aquila, watching her facial expression closely, trying to determine if she were telling the truth. "Because cell phones have a tracking device in them. All Brandon has to do is report you missing to the police, and they can track your whereabouts by your last phone usage."

"Brandon is not going to the police. He would have to give up too much information about himself. If the police interrogated him, he would be a suspect in our disappearance, and he'd have to admit that he's the reason I'm missing."

Pricilla stared at Aquila doubtfully. "Are you sure you haven't felt guilty for leaving Brandon and called him or answered his calls since you left, Aquila?"

"Of course, I'm sure," Aquila answered indignantly. "I listened to the messages and deleted them. He left messages until the inbox was full. Believe me, after listening to those threatening messages, I have no desire to talk to him. When I was there, he called four or five times a day while he was at work."

"How did he get anything done at work, if he spent that much time calling you?"

"He found a way somehow." Aquila exhaled loudly. "Girl, it was so irritating, having to stop my housework just to talk to him."

Pricilla walked back toward the kitchen. Aquila followed her and opened the refrigerator door to get a bottle of water. Pricilla stopped at the table and asked her, "Did he actually have anything worthwhile to talk about?"

Aquila raised her hands up in the air dramatically. "*Please,*" she exclaimed. "He just wanted to keep tabs on me. I'd gotten to the place where I dreaded hearing his voice over the phone."

Pricilla pulled an oak kitchen chair from under the table and sat down. Aquila followed suit. "Brandon had *issues*, didn't he, girl?"

"He's a nut job. The day I left, he'd called me during his half hour lunch break to see what I was doing. I'd just finished packing our clothes; the suitcases were sitting by the door. I told him I was making PB&J sandwiches for the kids' lunch." Aquila smirked. "Actually, I was making sandwiches and packing juices for us to eat on the bus trip here." She opened her bottle of water and took a few sips of it.

Pricilla laughed. "I know he went berserk when he came home and couldn't find you or the kids anywhere."

"I'm sure the first thing he did was go next door to our neighbor's house and ask Ms. Carter if I were there."

"Was she a good friend to you?"

"She was. She's in her sixties. Brandon was okay with me hanging out with her. I guess he thought as long as I hung out with an older woman, I wouldn't get tempted to cheat on him."

Pricilla stared at Aquila momentarily.

Aquila frowned. "Why are you looking at me like that?" Aquila asked.

"Oh, I was just thinking that you are a beautiful young lady. Despite the fact you don't wear makeup and you dress like an old lady, I'm sure you still get a lot of attention from guys. Maybe he was so insecure about you because he's twelve years older than you, and he knows that if you wore makeup and entered the workforce, he'd have some competition. That's why he kept you locked away from the world."

Aquila slumped back in her chair. "Ms. Carter said the same thing."

"Did she know that Brandon beat on you?" Pricilla put both elbows on the table and cupped her face in her hands.

Aquila hunched up her shoulders. "No, not for a fact, but I think she suspected he did. She always extended the offer to help me with anything if I were in need, and said that I could knock on her door day or night, no matter what time it was."

"If she said that, she knew. She was just waiting for you to ask for help." Pricilla sighed. "People don't know you need help if you don't ask for it, Aquila."

"I know. I just felt so ashamed. I wanted to tell her, but I couldn't."

"I understand, but sometimes what we consider to be shame is really pride." Pricilla sat back in her chair and crossed her legs.

Aquila shook her head in agreement. "You're right. In spite of my shame, I wanted to pretend that I had a good life with Brandon." She drank several more sips of water.

"Well, it's time to live in the real world. You can have a good life, but not with someone using you for a punching bag. I'm not trying to be a witch, but you can't afford to slip up and leave clues behind for Brandon to find you."

"You're right. I didn't need to leave the phone lying around so one of the children could answer it, and blurt out that we're living with you, either."

"Did you tell Ms. Carter that you were leaving Brandon?"

"No. She had called me early that morning, as she always does. She wanted to let me know she was going on a shopping trip with some of her friends. I called her before our cab arrived and left a message on her answering machine that I'd gone to visit a friend in North Carolina for a few days. If Brandon questions her about my whereabouts, she can honestly say she doesn't know exactly where I am."

Pricilla sat straight up in the chair; her countenance was serious. "It would have been great if you hadn't mentioned coming to North Carolina, because Brandon knows that I moved here, doesn't he?"

Aquila drank the rest of the water and stood up to put the empty water bottle into the recycling bin. "Yes, he knows that you moved to Raleigh, but he doesn't have an address because the few greeting cards you sent me had a post office box number, remember?" She walked back to her chair and sat down.

"Oh, yeah; I thought using a post office box would be sensible until I established a permanent home address. I had no idea when I moved here that I would actually buy this house. But now I like the security of my mail being delivered to the post office instead of here." Pricilla smiled. "That's fortunate for you, because if Brandon had my address, I'm sure he'd show up on my doorstep looking for you and the kids." The ringing of Pricilla's cell phone interrupted their conversation. She looked at the caller ID. It was Jeffrey. A broad smile crept across her face. She stood up. "Hi, Jeffrey; hold on, honey." She covered the phone. "We'll talk later, Aquila. Okay?"

Aquila nodded and gave Pricilla the 'okay' sign with her fingers. Pricilla waved goodnight and headed for her bedroom, leaving Aquila sitting alone at the dining room table.

Looking around the room, Aquila mused. *This house is in need of repair.* Her eyes scanned the old seventies cabinets. One of its doors was warped. The counter tops were yellow Formica, and one area of it had a burn mark on it where a hot pot had once been placed. The faucet in the single sink needed to be replaced. The linoleum was so faded that it was hard to tell what color it actually was.

Aquila's eyes roamed back to the living room. The walls were a dingy green with small cracks in them, and the faded green and white linoleum needed to be replaced. She concluded that the entire house needed to be renovated. She stood up and pushed the chair under the table. Aquila picked the broom up and swept the shattered phone into the dustpan and emptied the remains in the trashcan. Pricilla's words echoed in her mind about Brandon. She hoped that he wasn't so obsessed with her that he'd track her down. Her body trembled as she thought about Brandon's angry face the night before she left.

He had told her that she was going to learn how to submit or else he would beat her into submission. He warned her not to even think about leaving him because he would track her down like an animal tracks its prey and kill her. Pricilla was right. Telling Ms. Carter that she was going to North Carolina might have been too much information.

Chapter 12

Rays from the morning sun streaked through the Plantation blinds. Diana rolled over; her eyes half opened, and patted the pillow on the other side of bed, feeling for Jeffrey. She opened her eyes.

"Jeffrey?" She looked at the digital clock. Its huge red numbers read: 6:05. She figured he must have gone to work already. She stretched and glanced at the covers where Jeffrey would have lain. The sheets were straight as though they'd been untouched. *He didn't come to bed last night; he must have slept in one of the guest rooms,* she thought.

Lately, Jeffrey had slept in the guestroom more nights than he'd slept in their bedroom. Diana figured that it was because he hated the smell of alcohol. She slid out of bed, put her bedroom shoes on, and walked to the bathroom. After one glance in the mirror, she gasped. "Oh my goodness, I look like crap. I've got to stop drinking, or I'm going to start looking like an old dried up hag. Makeup can only cover so much."

Diana stepped into the spacious Mediterranean styled tiled shower and took a long hot shower, and then toweled herself dry. After lathering lotion all over her body, she ambled to her walk in closet, looking for a casual outfit to put on. "Hmmm, I need to go shopping for some summer sweat suits and jeans for my community service work."

She chose a pink T-shirt that she'd bought from their Tahiti vacation six months ago. She pulled a pair of Levi shorts from the hanger and tried them on. She bent over to get her only pair of sneakers. Losing her balance, she stumbled and fell on the closet floor. She sat there for a moment. Her head throbbed from the pain of a terrible hangover. She pulled herself up, went back into the bathroom, rummaged through the cabinet, and found some Extra Strength Tylenol for her splitting headache.

After taking the meds, she walked slowly to her bed, climbed back into it, and within a matter of minutes, fell asleep again. Several hours later, the bright afternoon sun shone in her face. Diana looked at the clock. It was 1:17 in the afternoon. "Oh my goodness, I've slept half the day away." Feeling better, she eased off of the high sitting bed and proceeded to make it up. She undressed out of the wrinkled clothes she had on, freshened up, and applied makeup, lightly.

After searching through her closet again, she found a thin white cotton blouse and a denim skirt to put on. She searched through the slew of shoeboxes on her shelf and found a pair of white sandals and put them on.

After walking downstairs, Diana stepped into the kitchen and put some coffee in the coffee pot, toasted a bagel, and spread cream cheese on it. The telephone began ringing. "June, are you going to get that?" she called out after the phone went unanswered. The phone rang once more, and then went to the answering machine. She placed her food and coffee on the table. Diana tapped her forehead lightly upon remembering that she had given June the rest of the week off. She walked over to the phone and listened to the voice mail. Jeffrey had called to check up on her. She dialed his office. After the phone rang four times, the voice message took over. She figured he was with a patient. She glanced at the clock on the wall and waited for the beep so she could leave a message.

"Jeffrey, I'm fine, honey. I'm sorry I missed you this morning. I am going to drive to Burlington Outlet on Buck Jones Road and buy a few casual clothes to work in. I hope you're having a good day. Love you."

Diana hung up the phone, sat at the kitchen table, and ate her breakfast. When she finished eating, she washed her cup and saucer. Then she climbed the stairs to get her purse and came back down with the intention of driving to the outlet. Once she started the car, opened the garage, backed out and the brilliant afternoon sun blinded her temporarily, she felt a wave of nausea come over her. Realizing that she couldn't drive in her condition, Diana put the gear in drive and pulled back into the garage. She decided she'd just have to wear some old jeans and a T-shirt tomorrow.

She got out of the car and walked back into the house. After almost losing her balance twice, she stumbled to the end of the stairs and sat on the bottom step.

I have to get myself together, she thought. Diana was aware that Jeffrey's patience had become razor thin. He had tolerated her drinking binges for years. He didn't drink any type of alcoholic beverage, and he detested the smell of the after effects of its odor that seeped through her skin and lingered on her breath. The passion between them had dissipated long ago. She didn't have any proof, but she believed that her drinking had driven him to the arms of another woman. *I lost my daughter, but I can't lose my husband too.* She hung her head down and sobbed uncontrollably.

Chapter 13

Jeffrey and Pricilla sat in the solarium and ate their lunch. As Pricilla predicted, several nurses that worked with Jeffrey inquisitively glanced their way, more than once. "Jeffrey, don't you feel uncomfortable with these women staring at us?"

"No, I don't. We're having lunch, nothing more, nothing less. Believe me, if some of them had the opportunity to sit where you are, they would jump at the chance."

Pricilla sat back in her seat. "Well, aren't you the arrogant one?"

"I don't mean to sound arrogant, honey, but I work with these nurses every day. Some of them are very aggressive."

Pricilla glanced at two of the nurses. "They don't seem too pleased that I'm sitting with you."

Jeffrey looked sternly at one of the nurses. She shifted her eyes in another direction. "That's their problem, Pricilla. We're not doing anything wrong." Jeffrey bit into his burger and swallowed. "How're things going with your friend?"

"Okay, I guess." Pricilla stirred the ranch dressing throughout her salad. "Her husband called her last night."

Jeffrey put his burger down and wiped his mouth with the paper napkin. "What happened?"

"Nothing," Pricilla sneered, "because I took the phone from her and smashed it to pieces."

Jeffrey raised his eyebrows at Pricilla. "I'm sure your friend wasn't happy about that, was she?"

"No, she was upset at first, then I explained why I did it, and she understood."

"What did you say to her?" Jeffrey took another bite out of his burger.

"I reminded her that cell phones have a tracking device, and he might try to find her by that method. She said that she hadn't been communicating with him, but I have doubts. I've heard of women going back to their abusive spouses because they feel guilty, or because they don't think there's a better life for them, especially if they're totally dependent on the guy.

Pricilla swallowed a forkful of her salad, and then continued. "At times, Aquila seems so helpless; we can hardly have a conversation about anything without her bringing Brandon's name up. I didn't want her to break down and call him or answer his calls, so I smashed the phone. You should have seen the fear in her eyes last night when the phone rang. But her reaction to my breaking her phone made me wonder if she's missing him."

"She could be lonely for him in a twisted way. It's sad, but I guess some women feel devastated when they don't know any other way to live and mistake abuse for love."

"I'm trying to convince her that she can have a better life without him, but it's just going to take time, and she needs a plan." Jeffrey nodded and Pricilla continued. "Now I need to buy her a pre-paid phone so she can have a way of communicating. Since I don't have a home phone, she needs a phone in case there's an emergency with the children."

"Do you need money?" Jeffrey reached for his wallet. "I'll do whatever I can to help."

Pricilla held Jeffrey's hand. "Jeffrey, I wasn't asking you for money. You've put money in my account already."

"I want to make sure you're doing okay. Having four more mouths to feed is an additional burden on you." Jeffrey pushed his wallet securely back down into his pants pockets.

"You're so sweet. It's only been a little over a week, but I *can* tell a big difference in my grocery bill. Since she and the kids go to church to eat lunch on Mondays, Wednesdays, and Fridays, that saves me three meals a week."

Jeffrey looked at his watch. "That's great. It's a blessing that Pastor Woodbridge and his wife, Kendra, open the doors of the church to feed the homeless."

Pricilla sighed. "Yes, it is. When I told them about Aquila's situation, First Lady Kendra was so concerned that she urged me to tell her about the soup kitchen so that would be one less meal I'd have to supply them with. I don't mind helping my friend, but when I sent for her and the kids, I wondered how I could afford to help them."

"The Lord made a way, as usual." Jeffrey stared into Pricilla's eyes. "So when am I going to meet your friend?"

Pricilla bit her bottom lip lightly. "I don't think now's a good time, Jeffrey. Aquila needs time to heal. I'm sure she's still uncomfortable living in my small tattered house. Last year, she sent me pictures of her house; it's beautiful and big. Brandon was an abusive jerk, but he provided well for her and the children."

"What type of work does he do?" Jeffrey thoughtfully massaged his chin with his right hand.

"He's an air traffic controller at Nashville International Airport."

"He has a great career. I heard those jobs could be stressful, though." Jeffrey's forehead wrinkled. "You think maybe he took that stress out on Aquila?"

"I don't know; that's possible. He spent twelve years in the Marines, and I believe Aquila said that he told her he was deployed for a year in Afghanistan, and he did a tour in Iraq."

Jeffrey sat back in his chair. "He could be suffering from PTSD."

Pricilla frowned. "What's that?"

"Post traumatic stress disorder. If that's his problem, he should have gotten counseling. I assume those tests are thorough, and any manifestations from his condition should have shown up on his psychological test when he applied for the position with the airline."

"Maybe." Pricilla finished her salad. "Brandon is a very intelligent person. Who knows, he could have skillfully passed those tests with no problem."

"It's possible, but something's going on in that skull that's not quite right." Jeffrey shook his head in disgust. "There's no excuse for a man beating a woman. We're all under pressure, but taking it out on your wife is not the answer."

Pricilla smirked. "Maybe Brandon missed class the day that lesson was being taught."

Jeffrey's beeper went off. He checked the number. "Sorry, baby, I've been called for an emergency." He stood up, pushed his chair under the table, and picked up his trash from the burger and bottled water. "I'll talk to you later. Take care."

Pricilla watched Jeffrey scurry down the corridor, headed for the emergency department. Her phone rang. "Hello?"

"Pricilla?" a baritone voice inquired.

Pricilla frowned and hesitated before she said, "Yes?"

"This is Brandon Savino, Aquila's husband." Pricilla didn't respond. "I know that you are my wife's best friend, so I was wondering if she happens to be with you at your place."

"You don't know where your wife is, Brandon?" Pricilla scoffed.

"It's not like her to leave without asking me, I mean, telling me her plans—"

Pricilla interrupted him. "Brandon, how did you get my cell phone number?"

"I requested her phone statement from last month's phone bill, and I see where she'd called this number several times. To my knowledge, you're the only person she knows in North Carolina."

"So you assumed she'd come to see me because we've had a few phone conversations? What's going on that you're not telling me?"

Brandon hesitated before he spoke. "Pricilla, last Thursday we had a disagreement; a bad one. When I got home from work Friday evening, she and my children were gone. They've been missing for over a week; I'm worried sick. I've exhausted all other avenues to where she could be."

"Brandon, if you were so concerned about your wife, why didn't you report her missing to the police?"

"Because she left a message with our neighbor that she'd gone to North Carolina to visit a friend. So is Aquila there with you?" Brandon asked impatiently.

Pricilla exhaled loudly. "No, I haven't seen her." *Lord, forgive me for lying.*

"Are you *sure*, Pricilla? You don't sound too concerned that your best friend is missing."

"Oh, I'm very concerned. But from what she's told me about you, I'm glad to know she finally left your abusive butt," Pricilla said harshly. "Wherever she is, she's better off without you."

Brandon's voice deepened. "Are you implying that you haven't heard from her lately?"

"I didn't stutter, Brandon. I said that wherever she is, she's better off without you," Pricilla retorted.

"Pricilla, I don't know what Aquila's told you, but she's lying—"

"Brandon, I've known Aquila most of my life. She's like my sister, and I know she's not lying. You're the liar and wife beater," Pricilla scolded. "You're gonna pay for what you did to her."

"I didn't mean to hurt her, Pricilla, I love her, I just; I don't know what came over me . . ." Pricilla heard Brandon sniffle. "So she's there with you?" Brandon persisted.

Pricilla had become highly annoyed at Brandon's amateur imitation of police interrogation. "I said I *talked* to her, Brandon. She wouldn't tell me where she was. But even if I did know, I wouldn't tell you. So do me a favor, Brandon, and lose my phone number."

"You have no right to keep me from seeing my wife, Pricilla," Brandon yelled through the phone. "Let me speak to her *now* . . ." he demanded. Pricilla snapped her cell phone closed.

Brandon was furious with Pricilla for hanging up on him. In his twisted chauvinistic mind, she was just as disrespectful to him as Aquila was. He was certain that Aquila was there with her. Now, it was just a matter of locating Pricilla's address so that he could handle his wife in the flesh.

Chapter 14

The next morning Diana eased out of bed, being careful not to wake up Jeffrey. She took a long hot shower, dressed in Jeffrey's oversized red, North Carolina State T-shirt, a pair of black khaki pants, and the new Nike sneakers she'd bought a week before. She gently rubbed Oil of Olay moisturizing lotion on her face. She jumped when an image appeared behind her in her mirror. Diana held her hand over her chest; her knees felt weak.

"Jeffrey, you startled me," she said loudly.

Jeffrey chuckled. "I'm sorry, honey." Jeffrey put his arms around Diana's waist. "It's only six thirty, and you're fully dressed. You must be anxious to get to your job."

Diana rested her head on Jeffrey's chest. "I'm anxious to get it over with. The sooner I get there, the sooner I can leave."

"I don't have rounds at the hospital this morning, and my first appointment isn't before eleven." Jeffrey gently massaged Diana's shoulders. "Why don't you call Kendra and tell her you'll be in at nine instead of eight. It's not as though your hours are mandatory, as long as you're there for six hours, right?"

Diana's shoulders relaxed and she succumbed to the tingling sensation she felt from Jeffrey's fingertips moving across her body. "Kendra set my hours for eight until two. She said Ms. Mable will be expecting me at that time," she said in a husky voice.

"Can't you call her and tell her something unexpected came up and you'll be in later?" Jeffrey pulled Diana toward the bed. "It's been awhile. I need you."

"I need you too, Jeffrey," Diana said passionately. Jeffrey unzipped her pants and pulled her closer to him. Diana moaned softly. "I was beginning to think that you weren't interested in me anymore. It's crossed my mind several times that you're having an affair."

"Don't be ridiculous, Diana, I don't have time for such foolishness." Jeffrey covered Diana's petite body with his large frame. He couldn't admit that he was partially responsible for Diana's drinking problem. If he hadn't neglected her when she needed him most, she probably could have dealt with her issues in a more constructive way. Although he felt guilty for contributing to her problems, he had not ruled out the pending thoughts of ending their marriage if things didn't change.

Kendra dialed Diana's cell phone number. It immediately went to voice mail. Frustrated, Kendra asked Ms. Mable, "Where in the world is she? Have you heard from her?" Mable shook her head. Kendra flipped through the list of numbers in her day planner. She dialed Diana's home phone. It rang three times before Diana answered groggily. "Diana, why are you still at home? Did you forget you were supposed to be here at eight?"

Diana bolted up in bed and looked at the clock. It was five after nine. "Kendra, didn't you get my message?"

"No," Kendra answered curtly.

"I left a message for you on your home phone. When you didn't call me back, I assumed you were okay with me coming in later."

"I leave home on Mondays, Wednesdays, and Fridays at seven o'clock and come to the church's office to make sure Ms. Mable has everything she needs before I go to work. What time did you call?"

"I called at 6:40." Diana covered the phone with her hand while she yawned.

"I was probably in my dressing room at that time and didn't hear the phone ring. What was your message?"

"I wanted to let you know that something came up, and I'd be there at nine."

Kendra exhaled loudly into the phone. "It's after nine now, Diana," she said flatly.

"I'm sorry, Kendra. I'll be in as soon as I get dressed. It won't happen again." Diana slid out of bed and walked swiftly to the bathroom.

"I hope not. You need to take responsibility for your actions. I can't record your time with the court system, if you don't bother to show up. This isn't a game. If you don't do your community service, your sentence can be revoked, and you'll have to do your time in jail."

"I hear you, Kendra. I'm on my way. Give me an hour and I'll be there, okay?"

"All right, one hour, Diana. Ms. Mable needs your help, so don't procrastinate any longer." Kendra clicked the phone off in Diana's ear.

Diana scurried back into the bedroom and threw the cordless phone on the bed. "I hate the way Kendra talks down to me," she complained. "I can't wait until my time in that dreadful place is over." She bustled back to the bathroom.

Jeffrey followed Diana into the bathroom. "Look on the bright side, honey, it could have been worse. You could be sitting in jail now, doing time for DWI. Kendra is looking out for you as her friend. I don't think she talked down to you; you're overreacting again. She stuck her neck out for you, and you need to be grateful."

"I am grateful, Jeffrey, I just don't want to work with those awful, smelly, people." She turned her nose up, and then shook her head in disgust.

"Your punishment could have been a lot worse. God showed you mercy and favor. You should try praising Him and stop complaining so much."

Diana stepped into the shower. "Jeffrey, I don't want to hear any preaching from you this morning. I have enough problems as it is."

"Without God, your problems are only going to get worse."

Diana scowled at Jeffery and turned the water on. "How much worse could things get?"

Chapter 15

"Aquila, I need to talk to you," Pricilla said with a serious look on her face.

"What's wrong, Pricilla?" Aquila sat on the edge of the couch. "You look worried."

Pricilla waited until Daniel, Darius, and Abigail walked out on the front porch to play to say what she had to say. "I wasn't going to mention this to you, but Brandon called me looking for you."

Aquila gasped. "When?"

"Yesterday. During my lunch break."

Aquila's eyes widened. "How did he get your number?"

"He said he checked your phone bill and he saw where my number appeared several times, and he knew I was the only person you knew in North Carolina. Aquila, that husband of yours is crazy." Pricilla sat on the couch beside her.

"I know he is, girl." Aquila's lip trembled. "Pricilla, did you tell him I was here?"

"Of course not," Pricilla scoffed. "I told him that I'd spoken to you, but I didn't know where you were. I told him that you told me about how he'd abused you, and that he was going to pay for what he did to you."

Aquila twisted a lock of her hair around her finger. "Do you think he believed that you don't know where I am?"

Pricilla sighed loudly. "No, he didn't believe me, but I reiterated that I didn't know where you were, but that I was sure wherever you were, you were better off without him. And then I told him to lose my phone number."

Aquila raised her eyebrows at Pricilla. "What did he say to that?"

"He demanded that I put you on the phone, so I hung up on him."

A single tear rolled down Aquila's cheek. "Oh Lord, I hope he's not gonna track me down here. Maybe I should leave, Pricilla. I don't want to get you any more involved than you already are."

Pricilla's forehead wrinkled. "And go where, Aquila?"

"I don't know," she said anxiously. "I'm afraid for my life." Aquila's breathing accelerated. She had a panicky look in her eyes.

"Calm down." Pricilla told Aquila to inhale deeply and exhale slowly for at least three times.

Aquila practiced the breathing techniques. Pricilla waited until her breathing returned to normal before she continued. "He doesn't know for sure that you're here. He was just bluffing to see if I'd crack and tell him you were. Even if he is stupid enough to come to North Carolina, he wouldn't begin to know where to look for you because he doesn't know where I live."

"I hope not, but don't underestimate Brandon. I wouldn't put it past him to use any means he can to find me." Aquila wiped her tears away with the back of her hand.

"Well, we'll have to be careful and make sure he doesn't find you. I think we should alert the Raleigh police, and maybe you should take a restraining order out on him too."

Aquila laughed nervously. "What good is a restraining order going to do? I've seen too many shows on TV and in the news, where husbands or boyfriends killed women although they reported the abuse to the police. They wouldn't do anything until it was too late."

"That's true, but it doesn't have to be you." Pricilla's phone rang. Without checking the caller ID, she answered it. "Hello?" She paused for a moment, listening to the caller. "Brandon, I told you that I don't know where she is. Don't call me again, or I will report you to the police for harassing me." Pricilla pressed the end button.

Aquila lay back on the couch, her hands visibly shaking. "I should leave. I don't want him to find me; neither should you be in the midst of my situation. I should have never gotten you involved and endangered your life too."

"My life isn't in any danger," Pricilla said with a brazen expression on her face. "I'm going to have those pictures developed and talk to First Lady Kendra too. You have to take steps to protect yourself, Aquila. You can't just crawl into a hole and let Brandon bully you out of a life of peace and freedom. There's a place for guys like him; it's called prison, and by all means, if it comes down to it, I'm going to make sure that's exactly where he ends up."

Chapter 16

Kendra sat at her desk and carefully looked over the resumes that had been e-mailed to her for the secretary position at church. Three months had gone by since Ms. Brown had resigned. The person she'd hired from the temporary service didn't work out. She had already interviewed four people for the position, but despite being highly skilled in the field, none possessed what she was looking for.

Two of the applicants had brassy personalities, and one came dressed in attire fit only for a professional dancer, to put it nicely. The woman that had just left her office, she felt, was overqualified. Although Kendra believed that the word 'overqualified' was a new form of discrimination, she decided it was true in this case.

Samantha had a master's degree in finance and accounting. Being that she had recently moved to the area, Kendra knew that Samantha would only be buying time until a more suitable position came through for her.

There was a soft knock on the door. Kendra laid the resumes down on the desk. "Come in." It was Ms. Mable. Kendra smiled at the older lady. Mable was a short woman, about five foot three inches tall, with bronze color skin, and big bright eyes. Kendra could tell that she had been a very pretty lady in her younger days. "How're you, Ms. Mable?"

"I'm doing okay for an old lady," Mable replied. "I just wanted to keep you posted on how things were working out with your friend."

Kendra motioned for Mable to sit down. "Is Diana still being difficult, Ms. Mable?"

"No, she's doing fine now. After I straightened her out, she calmed down and took her butt off of her shoulders." Kendra laughed loudly. "She comes in and works like a little worker bee now. Thanks for giving me permission to take charge of the situation."

"You're welcome. I knew she would try to take advantage of you. That's why I nipped it in the bud when she came to me complaining about you."

"Well, she's doing great now. I actually like her. She's really a very funny person, when she's not brooding over whatever's bothering her." Mable squinted her eyes at Kendra, hoping she'd give her a little insight on Diana.

Kendra didn't accommodate Mable's indirect inquiry. "She's a good person. We just need to pray for her, Ms. Mable."

Mable nodded her head. "Now, *that* I can do. 'Cause I need all the prayers I can get myself." She stood up to leave. "I'd better get back out there and finish up. I'll see you tomorrow."

"Okay. Thanks for everything you're doing. Let me know if you need anything." Kendra pulled her chair closer to the desk.

"I will." Mable lingered at the door. "Are you done interviewing for the day?"

"No," Kendra said wearily. "I have to interview one more applicant today. She doesn't have any experience, but I promised her friend I'd interview her, since she campaigned so faithfully for her."

"Just remember, Kendra, experience ain't the only thing that qualifies a person for the job. You and your husband gave me a chance, and I sure didn't know anything about running no soup kitchen."

Kendra looked at Mable thoughtfully, smiled, and nodded. Mable walked out of the office and closed the door.

Kendra looked over the resume once more. She stood up and walked down the hall to the bathroom. When she came back, she noticed a well-dressed young lady sitting in the corridor. She had on a navy blue skirt suit with a white blouse, and navy sling back pumps. Her hair was cut in a bang and the rest hung evenly just past her shoulders. She reminded Kendra of Cleopatra, the Queen of Egypt. Kendra smiled and greeted her. "You must be Aquila?"

"Yes, ma'am, I am." Aquila stood and extended her hand to Kendra.

Kendra shook her hand. "Please, call me Kendra."

Aquila nodded and smiled nervously.

Kendra gave Aquila a reassuring smile. "I've seen you a few times in the soup kitchen, but I must say that you've changed your appearance quite drastically. I wasn't sure if you were the same young lady."

"Yes, ma'am," Aquila said, forgetting to address Kendra by her name. "I needed a change," she said coyly.

"I'm impressed. You look very professional," Kendra complimented her. She noticed how nervous Aquila appeared to be. "Would you like some water or maybe juice before we get started?"

"Some water would be nice, thank you." Aquila lightly flipped her hair back behind her shoulders.

"I'll get it for you." She pointed toward her office. "You can go on in my office." Kendra walked to the water cooler and pulled a paper cup out of the machine and filled it with water. She then walked back into her office. She handed the water to Aquila, who was still standing. "Please, have a seat, Aquila." The phone rang. Kendra excused herself to answer it, and Aquila took the opportunity to drink the water.

Once Kendra hung up the phone, she began to interview Aquila. She started with the normal, 'so tell me about yourself' routine. She questioned Aquila about her skills, or lack thereof, and asked her why she believed that she was qualified for the position of secretary for Macedonia Baptist Church.

Aquila was articulate. She described her abilities as a housewife and mother of three small children. She told Kendra that she was organized, and the complexity of multitasking had become a normal part of her everyday life.

Surprisingly, Kendra was pleased with the answers and with Aquila's pleasant personality. She inquired if she would be available to report to work from nine A.M. until five P.M., Monday through Friday.

Aquila replied, "Yes, I live only four blocks from here, so I can walk to work. Two of my children are in school, kindergarten and first grade. Pricilla pays for my daughter to attend daycare, here at the church."

Legally, Kendra couldn't ask her the two questions that concerned her most, about transportation and childcare. It worked out well, because Aquila volunteered that information.

Kendra stood up to indicate that the interview was over. "Aquila, it was a pleasure to talk to you. Pricilla spoke highly of you. She is so proud of your accomplishment of getting your adult high school diploma. And because she cares about you, she gave me insight on your unfortunate situation at home." Aquila lowered her eyes. "Aquila, you have nothing to be ashamed of. I am very proud of you for leaving and even prouder of you for being brave enough to make a new life for yourself and your children."

Aquila breathed a sigh of relief, feeling that she'd gotten through her first interview remarkably well. "Thank you, Kendra. Pricilla spoke highly of you too. I am very grateful that you took time out of your busy schedule to interview me, knowing that I don't have any experience."

"You're welcome." Kendra lightly drummed her fingers on the desk. "I don't normally do this, but being that you don't have any experience, I would like for you to type these letters for me.

There are three of them; I don't expect you to finish them all, but I just need to see what you can do." Aquila nodded. "Here, you can sit at my desk, and I'll give you twenty minutes."

Aquila took a deep breath and said, "Sure, I'll do my best." She sat in Kendra's office chair.

Kendra patted her gently on her right arm. "Don't stress; I'm sure you'll do fine." Kendra set the letters on the stand and left Aquila in the office.

Kendra returned exactly twenty minutes later. Aquila had reclaimed her seat in front of the desk. With a slight frown, Kendra asked, "Is everything okay, Aquila?"

"Yes, ma'am. I've finished the letters. I put them in the order that you gave them to me on your desk."

Kendra walked around the desk and picked up the letters. "You finished all of them?" Aquila responded with a nod. "Well, that's impressive." She looked directly at Aquila and said, "I'll check these over for accuracy, and you should expect to hear from me in a week or so. I still have to interview a few more people. I'll contact you either by a letter or a phone call." Kendra extended her hand toward the door and escorted Aquila outside. "Take care, Aquila."

Aquila walked back to Pricilla's house, which was now her new home, with a sense of optimism. She tied the belt to her leather coat around her. Since she'd been in Raleigh, she was able to get gently used clothes for herself and the children from First Baptist Church in downtown Raleigh.

For the first time in her life, she began to feel like she was really welcomed and appreciated. She had been in North Carolina now for three months. In that short time, she'd managed to get her adult high school diploma, and applied to Wake Technical College's Office Technology Program. With Pricilla's generosity and coaching, she learned how to apply makeup and dress better.

Aquila crossed the street at the corner and walked down the sidewalk toward Pricilla's house. It didn't compare to the spacious brick home that Brandon had provided for them. But on the other hand, she concluded that the price of having to endure Brandon's angry outburst was too much to pay to live in luxury.

The freedom, peace, and tranquility that flowed through the small house made her always state, "It's good to be home."

She unlocked and opened the door. Before she closed the door, she looked back and saw a suspicious looking man, slowly walking by and gazing at her. The man nodded. Out of a new-formed habit, Aquila scanned his features, and stored them in her memory in the event she needed to describe him for future reference. She nodded back and quickly closed the door. A tingle of fear ran down her spine.

Chapter 17

Diana cruised down 440 East, exceeding the posted speed limit. She didn't want to be late for her community service duties. She had worked in the soup kitchen twelve hours a week, for twelve weeks. She had performed one hundred and forty-four hours of community service. With only sixteen more hours to go, she could finally see the light at the end of a seemingly long tunnel.

After three months of enduring Mable's sarcastic remarks, she finally realized that the older lady was a loving person. Ironically, she'd become fond of Mable and realized she would miss talking to her. Diana actually felt comfortable enough to confide in her about having given her child away for adoption.

Mable confided some highly personal information to Diana also. She told Diana that her husband abandoned her, and that Social Services had taken her three-year-old daughter from her because she was a drug addict. She told Diana that after years of using drugs, she was grateful that God had enabled her to overcome the destructive habit.

She admitted that despite God's mercy, at age forty-five, she still continued to make unwise decisions that resulted in her having two more sons by another irresponsible man.

She inferred that at her age, sixty-three, she was raising two sons, ages seventeen and eighteen. She reassured Diana that she was truly blessed, because at least she had a husband that provided well for her. After listening to her, Diana realized that her own problems were minuscule. Diana admitted to Kendra that, except for the fact that Mable was a holy roller, she was a pretty decent lady.

Diana took the Capital Boulevard exit and headed for downtown. Her cell phone rang. "Hello," she answered unenthusiastically.

"Hi, Mrs. Thompson. This is Terry. I know you weren't too thrilled with me coming back to Nashville, but your husband wanted me to give it one more shot."

"Terry, I was trying to make peace with the fact that I might not ever find my child, so please spare me anymore heartaches."

"Actually, this time, I have a lead," Terry said excitedly. "I went back to that nurse's house, and she gave me an old newspaper clipping. In it were the names of all the children that had been in the orphanage at and before the time of the fire."

"What was the purpose of posting the children's name in the paper? Wasn't that confidential information?"

"Yes, ma'am, it would have been, but since the records burned with the place, they had to account for the children that didn't lose their lives in the fire. The only other records were held at the courthouse or the Office of Vital Statistics."

"So how would that matter where my child is concerned? By the time the orphanage caught on fire, the child was gone for at least three years."

"That's true, but in searching through the records of children that had lived there, I ran across a birth certificate that had your name on it." Terry unfolded the old document that he held in his hand. He spread it out on the bed in his hotel room.

Diana was sitting at a stoplight. When she heard this, she became excited and ceased to pay attention to the traffic. "Oh my goodness, Terry," she said nervously. "Who, I mean, what, where is the child?"

"You're not going to believe this, but she lives in Raleigh."

Diana gasped. "Are you kidding me, Terry?" she exclaimed.

Terry chuckled at Diana's excitement. "No, ma'am. According to my source, she has been living in your city for a while now."

"Who is she? Do you know her name?" Diana asked impatiently. "Tell me, please. I just want to know her name," Diana said nervously.

"Okay, Mrs. Thompson. It's—" Terry heard a loud crash through the phone line. "Mrs. Thompson," he said into the phone. "Mrs. Thompson, are you okay?" The phone went silent.

Diana's light was still on red, but in her excitement, she had let up off of the brakes, stepped on the accelerator, and pulled into the path of an oncoming tractor trailer.

Chapter 18

Over a month had passed since Aquila had interviewed for the secretary position at church. Kendra called her two days after the interview and hired her for the position. She now sat in the tiny office adjacent to Kendra's and typed the church program for Sunday's services.

She quietly sang along with Dave Hollister as he sang the song "Grateful" that played on the gospel radio station, *103.9, The Light.* "Grateful, Grateful, Grateful, Grateful, from my heart I love you, for setting me free . . ."

Kendra stuck her head in the office door. She carried a bouquet of beautiful vibrant red roses in her hand. "Aquila, I'll be leaving in five minutes. Do you need anything before I go?"

Aquila muted the volume on the radio. "We're a little low on computer paper; other than that, we're fine."

"Go online and order it from Office Depot, and I'll stop by to pick it up on my way to the office

in the morning, okay?" Aquila smiled and nodded. "Whatever you need for the office, Aquila,
just order it. And by the way, you're doing an
excellent job."

Aquila's countenance beamed with happiness.
"Thank you, First Lady Kendra." Aquila had started calling Kendra, 'First Lady' Kendra; shortly
after she'd started working for her. "I really appreciate you giving me this golden opportunity.
I've never earned my own money before, and it
feels so good not to have to ask for money like a
little child."

"God is good, Aquila. Life is going to get better and better for you. Keep trusting in Him, and
God will bless you exceeding abundantly above
all you can ask or think; Ephesians 3:20. Read it
for yourself."

Aquila jotted the scripture down. "Yes, ma'am."

Kendra wagged her finger at Aquila. "Aquila,
please don't call me ma'am. I know that I'm old
enough to be your mother, but I really don't
like that. Just be professional, okay?" Kendra
switched the roses from her right hand to her
left hand.

Aquila couldn't help but wish she'd had a
mother like Kendra. "I'm sorry, First Lady Kendra. I'll be more aware from now on." She looked
at the roses in Kendra's hand. "Those roses are
beautiful."

Kendra looked down and sniffed the roses. "They are, aren't they? I love roses. Matthew had them sent to me."

"I think that is so sweet. My husband used to send me my favorite flowers, which are tulips." Aquila shifted her eyes away from Kendra. She regretted bringing Brandon into the conversation. Kendra smiled and sniffed the roses again. She noticed the sad expression on Aquila's face.

The telephone rang. Aquila picked it up on the first ring. "Macedonia Baptist Church, how may I direct your call?" she asked cheerfully.

Kendra waved good-bye. Aquila smiled and returned the wave. Aquila heard Kendra speak warmly to the cleaning guy before she closed the door.

"Hey, girl," Pricilla replied cheerfully. "You sound so *professional*."

Aquila relaxed her posture. "Oh, hi, Pricilla. I'm doing my best."

"I'm so proud of you."

"Thanks. I love this job." Aquila twirled her left index finger around the phone cord while she talked. First Lady Kendra just told me that I was doing an excellent job." Aquila smiled broadly. "That comment makes me feel really good."

"I'm sure it does. You are a very intelligent person, Quila. You just needed a chance to prove it. Your self-esteem has really improved too."

"I know," Aquila agreed. "I can't thank God and you enough for getting me out of that miserable life I was living."

"Hallelujah, girl. Amen and amen," Pricilla said excitedly. "I can only talk for a minute; I'm sitting in the solarium having lunch. I just wanted to check on you."

"I'm doing great." Aquila opened a drawer and retrieved an envelope to mail the letter that she'd typed earlier that morning. "But the question is how are you doing on your first day as an R.N.?"

Three weeks after Aquila had interviewed for her position at the church, Pricilla sat for the nurse's exam. She was thrilled to have landed a full-time job at WakeMed only two weeks after she passed the exam.

"I'm doing okay. I was blessed enough to work on the pediatric ward today. Hopefully, this is where I'll be for the next three months, or until an opening comes up in the E.R."

"If it were me, I think I'd rather stay in Pediatrics."

Pricilla scrunched up her face. "Not me; I like the excitement of being in the emergency room. You never know what kind of situation you're going to deal with from day to day."

"My point exactly. I hate any type of trauma," Aquila said sadly. "It's the life I've had to live, you know what I mean?"

"I do understand." Pricilla waved at one of her former classmates. He walked over to the table where she was. "Hold on a sec, okay?" she asked Aquila. Pricilla covered the phone's mouthpiece while she talked to him for a moment. After they exchanged greetings, he left. "Okay, thanks for holding." She looked at her watch; she had five more minutes until her break was over.

"Has Jeffrey mentioned how Diana is doing? I feel so bad, having talked to her that way the first time I saw her. I haven't really seen her since Ms. Mable assigned her to the kitchen. I've only waved at her from a distance. I'll pray that she comes out of that coma soon and recover fully."

"She's not in a coma, but she's so heavily medicated, one would think she was in a coma. Jeffrey's really worried about her."

Aquila put the letter into the envelope and sealed it. "I'm sure he is."

Pricilla sighed loudly into the phone. "I hate that Jeffrey never got a chance to tell her about us."

Aquila held her breath momentarily before she spoke. "Pricilla," she said softly, "things happen sometimes that we can't control. Maybe Diana's accident happened for a reason."

Pricilla meditated for a moment. The only thing she could think of to say was, "I suppose you're right."

Aquila sighed. "Just be patient. When the time is right, Jeffrey will tell her about the two of you."

Pricilla didn't say anything. Aquila knew that was her hint to be quiet. The second line on her phone rang. "Pricilla, I need to take this call; I'll see you tonight, okay?"

"Sure," Pricilla said flatly. "My break is over anyway. Talk to you later."

Aquila answered the phone. "Macedonia Baptist Church, how may I direct your call?"

An unfamiliar voice on the other end said, "May I speak to Aquila Savino please?"

Aquila froze for a second, wondering who would be calling there for her. She answered in an evasive manner. "Could you repeat the name, sir?"

"No problem. Aquila Savino," he repeated in a clearer tone. "I'm the assistant principal, Mr. Washington, at her son, Darius's, school. This is the number I was given to reach her."

Aquila composed herself. "Yes, I'm Aquila Savino. Has something happened to my son?" she asked anxiously.

"It seems that Darius has had a slight accident." Mr. Washington heard Aquila gasp.

"Oh my God," Aquila said in an alarmed tone.

"It's not that serious, Mrs. Savino," Mr. Washington assured her. "Darius fell on the playground and skinned his knee. The school's nurse has taken care of him, and he's fine, but I'm required to call the parents and notify them of any accidents."

Aquila took the phone from her mouth for a moment and exhaled a sigh of relief. "Thank you, Mr. Washington," she said in a calmer voice. "I'll try to get there to pick him up in thirty minutes. I have to catch the city bus, but I'll be there as soon as I can."

"Mrs. Savino, that's really not necessary. He's doing fine. He hasn't indicated that he wants to go home. His teacher is taking him back to class now."

Aquila's forehead creased with wrinkles. "Are you sure? I feel like I need to come and get him."

"It's up to you, Ms. Savino. But I assure you, we've taken good care of him."

"I'm sure you have, thank you, but I'll feel better if I see him for myself," Aquila insisted.

"Sure," Mr. Washington relented. "We'll look forward to your visit."

Aquila telephoned Kendra to get permission to leave. She put the telephone on automatic voice mail and went into the daycare to get Abigail. They walked to the bus stop. While waiting for the bus, Aquila noticed the man she'd seen several times walking in her neighborhood. As usual, he stared at her and nodded. She nodded and pulled Abigail close to her. When the bus came, they boarded, and so did the man.

Aquila was tempted to ask him whether or not he was following them, but she decided that if he got off on the same stop as she, that she would dial 911 and report him to the police.

Two bus stops before the school, the man got off the bus and Aquila watched him walk toward McDonald's and sit at the bus stop area in front of it.

Whew. Aquila breathed a sigh of relief. *I must be paranoid*, she mused. *I guess the man lives near here somewhere*. Abigail shifted in Aquila's lap and looked up into her eyes.

"Mommy, I miss Daddy. When are we going home?"

Aquila looked away from Abigail's innocent brown eyes. "I don't know, Abigail. Maybe one day soon," she lied. Aquila felt unstable when she stood up to get off at their stop. "Come on, Abigail. Let's go get your brothers." Aquila looked at her hands. They trembled slightly. Something wasn't right. She could feel it.

Chapter 19

Diana frowned as she tried to open her eyes. She could hear Kendra, Matthew, and Jeffrey as they stood over her bed and prayed for her. It had been a month since her accident. She'd suffered a broken right leg, a broken left ankle, a broken arm, three broken ribs, and a head injury, which resulted in a concussion. Her face was still a little swollen from being knocked into the steering wheel.

The doctors had been concerned that she might have had brain damage from the impact of the accident. After many tests and x-rays, the results proved to be negative.

She listened as Matthew prayed. "Heavenly Father, we come to you with praise and thanksgiving. We honor you and magnify your holy name. Oh, God, you are worthy to be praised."

Kendra had her eyes closed and her hands lifted up toward the ceiling. "Hallelujah, yes, you are worthy to be praised," she witnessed.

"Thank you for forgiving us of every sin, transgression, and iniquity that we have committed against you. Thank you for having mercy on us and giving us grace and favor. Glory to your name, Lord Jesus," Matthew said fervently.

Diana groaned as the pain seemed to shoot through every part of her body. "Lord, have mercy," she moaned.

Jeffrey touched her hand. "That's right; praise Him for your healing, Diana."

Matthew continued to praise God. "Lord, we thank you, Lord you are so good," he declared.

Diana watched her husband as he bowed his head while Matthew prayed.

"Lord, we thank you in advance for Diana's full recovery," Matthew said as he clapped his hands lightly. "Thank you for sparing her life and bringing her through this tragedy. We praise you for keeping her covered under your blood, and for sending angels to encamp around her. God you've been so good to her; thank you, Lord for the blessing that you have bestowed upon her. Lord, we pray that Diana will draw nigh to you, so you can draw nigh to her. Thank you for answering these petitions, in the mighty, precious name of Jesus."

Jeffrey said, "Thank you, Jesus. Amen."

Kendra opened her eyes and said, "Amen and amen."

Tears rolled down Diana's face.

Kendra picked up the Bible and read Psalm 138:8. *"The Lord will perfect that which concerneth me; thy mercy, O Lord, endureth for ever; forsake not the works of thine own hands."* She walked over to Diana's bed and touched her on the shoulder. "God, we give you praise for the work that you are manifesting in your daughter, Diana. We thank you for sparing her life, for saving her soul, and giving her a mind to praise you and honor you." Kendra let tears roll down her face. "Lord, I love you. I give you all the glory. There is none like you, Jesus. From the rising of the sun, to the going down thereof, your name is worthy to be praised. Thank you for healing and saving my friend, in Jesus' name. Amen."

Matthew and Jeffrey said Amen and amen."

Diana mumbled, "Amen."

Jeffrey's beeper went off. He kissed Diana on the forehead. "I need to go, baby. I've been called for an emergency. I'll come back to see you as soon as I can, okay?"

Diana nodded her head and smiled weakly.

Kendra sat beside her bed. Matthew kissed Kendra on the cheek and left.

Kendra smiled at Diana. "It's just the two of us again, girlfriend."

Diana smiled and hoarsely said, "Like old times, huh?" Diana cleared her throat. "Kendra, I want to thank you for putting up with my bad behavior and selfishness." She glanced up at the ceiling for a moment while she talked. "I want to apologize; I'm so sorry—"

Kendra burst into tears before Diana could finish.

Diana couldn't do anything to comfort her. She watched her friend in amazement as she sobbed. She wondered what on earth could have happened to cause Kendra to break down and cry so forcefully.

Chapter 20

Aquila moved around in the small kitchen with the expertise of a chef. She surrounded the roast beef with potatoes and carrots. She chopped a head of cabbage on the cutting board, and then made a corn bread batter to put in the oven.

Pricilla walked into the house at seven forty-two. "Hey, Aquila. What are you cooking? It smells delicious," she yelled.

Aquila smiled. "Just a little something that I stirred up. It's been awhile since we've had a full course meal. I thought I'd show my appreciation by having a nice meal ready for you by the time you got home."

Pricilla scurried to the kitchen. "Girl, I've told you that you don't have to cook dinner for me. I'll eat whatever I can find in the refrigerator."

"I don't mind. I love to cook. When I was with Brandon, cooking was one of the things that made me relax."

"Of course, he benefited from your relaxation," Pricilla said sarcastically.

"I'm sure he did, but now I cook because I *want* to, and it feels good. Hey, maybe I'll open up a restaurant one day," Aquila joked.

"The sky's the limit, Quila. If I've said it once, I've said it twice; you can do all things through Christ who strengthens you."

Aquila pulled a dinette chair out from under the table and sat in it. "I'm really starting to believe that that's true, Pricilla."

Pricilla walked to the refrigerator and placed the vanilla ice cream that she'd bought into the freezer. "It is true. And I know that because I believe that I'm going to find my mother too."

Aquila looked at Pricilla with compassionate eyes. "That's really important to you now, isn't it?"

Pricilla sat at the table with Aquila. "Yes, it is." Pricilla sighed. "I don't know why, but since I've moved to Raleigh, I feel close to her. Sometimes I notice women that I think I resemble her and wonder if they could be my mother."

"Wow. That is amazing." Aquila giggled. "I've done the same thing. At least you're on a mission to find her. Although I've always wanted to meet my mother, I've never been brave enough to try to find her. When First Lady Kendra asked me to stop saying yes ma'am to her because she didn't like being called ma'am, I was a little offended." Aquila looked at Pricilla wistfully. "I guess I started saying ma'am to her, because she has such a nurturing personality that it's easy to get attached to her."

"She does have a strong motherly persona," Pricilla agreed.

Aquila propped her left elbow on the table and rested her face in her hand. "Sometimes I look at her and wish that I had a mother like her. I would give just about anything to be able to say yes ma'am to my mother."

Pricilla gazed at Aquila compassionately. "I feel you, girl."

"She told me that she knew that she was old enough to be my mother, but she preferred that I remained professional."

Pricilla nodded in agreement. "I can relate to what she means. It's best to remain professional in the workplace."

Aquila rested her back in the seat. "I can respect that. I'm just grateful that she gave me the opportunity to work for her. She's an awesome lady."

"Yes, she is." Pricilla was thoughtful for a moment. "I noticed that she wasn't at church last Sunday. I hope she is doing okay."

"I'm sure she's doing fine," Aquila said in a positive tone. "She didn't come into the office this week either. She called and told me that she would be out of commission for a few days because she wasn't feeling well. Maybe she's just tired."

"You're probably right. Being a lawyer, first lady of the church, and overseeing the kitchen has got to be overwhelming at times," Pricilla concluded.

"I'm sure." Aquila stood back up and checked the food in the oven and turned the cabbage off on top of the stove. "Pricilla," she said as she turned around to face her, "the strangest thing has been happening to me."

Pricilla frowned. "What?"

"It seems like everywhere I go, there's this strange man around. He never says anything, he just nods."

"He's following you?" Pricilla asked her in an alarmed tone. "Aquila, you might want to report him to the police."

"Why? I'm not sure that he's following me; he's just there. It's not as though they're going to arrest him. He hasn't committed any crime."

"Stalking is a crime."

Aquila hunched up her shoulders. "I can't prove that he's stalking me. He just happens to *be* in a lot of places that I am."

"I don't feel comfortable about this. Keep your eyes open, and if he approaches you for any reason, be prepared to take him down," Pricilla told her emphatically.

Aquila laughed loudly. "How do you expect me to *take him down*, Pricilla?"

"You need some pepper spray, a knife, or at least keep a whistle in your purse. You can't afford to walk around with no protection."

Aquila shook her head. "I can't afford to let one of my children find pepper spray or a knife in my purse. Carrying something like that will do more harm than good."

Pricilla shook her finger at Aquila. "Just be careful. There are some desperate people walking around downtown, especially this time of year during Thanksgiving and with Christmas right around the corner."

"I understand. He looks like a homeless person though. Whenever I see him, he's either catching a bus, or sitting at the bus stops. He probably rides the bus during the day and sleeps at the shelters at night."

"Maybe." Pricilla meditated for a moment. "Watch and pray, Aquila, and stay alert to your surroundings."

"I will." Aquila's face brightened as she changed the subject. "Speaking of this time of year, do you normally cook for Thanksgiving dinner?"

"Are you kidding me?" Pricilla laughed. "I usually go out and eat Thanksgiving dinner."

Aquila chuckled lightly. "Do you mind if we did that this year? I'm usually chained down to the stove, preparing dinner for Brandon's parents."

Pricilla held her hands out, palms up toward Aquila. "You are free to do what you want to do. It's time for you to break free of Brandon's house rules."

Aquila laughed. "You're right. I'm a free woman," she said excitedly. She danced around in the kitchen.

Pricilla walked into the living room and got the radio and brought it into the kitchen. She turned the radio to a station with some uplifting music. "Now this is the kind of atmosphere that I like, stress free and happy." She laughed.

"I know that's right." Aquila and Pricilla danced around in the kitchen and chatted awhile longer.

"Dinner's ready," Aquila said, taking the food out of the oven. "Dig in." She made the children's plates, and then walked into the living room toward the bedroom, where they were watching TV. She'd opened her mouth to tell the children to wash their hands so they could eat, but there was a loud knock on the door. She jumped. "Lord, have mercy," she yelled.

Pricilla rushed into the living room. "Calm down, Aquila. It's probably just Jeffrey. We have a date tonight."

Aquila held her hand over her thumping chest. "Oh."

"And I thought tonight would be a good time for the two of you to finally meet each other." Pricilla asked who was at the door. It was indeed Jeffrey.

"Do you think he might want to eat dinner with us?" Aquila asked her as Pricilla unlocked the door. "There's more than enough."

"Sure," Pricilla said cheerfully. "He'd probably rather eat with us than go out." Pricilla opened the door and Jeffrey walked in. She introduced Jeffrey to Aquila.

Jeffrey greeted Aquila with a warm smile and a light hug. "Hi, Aquila," he said. "I'm glad to finally meet you."

Aquila hugged him, and then took a step back to get a good look at him. She smiled and said, "It's a pleasure to meet you too. Pricilla talks about you a lot."

Jeffrey looked at Pricilla with raised eyebrows. "I hope she hasn't ruined my good reputation by speaking badly about me," he joked.

Aquila giggled. "No; so far, it's been all good."

Jeffrey smiled and nodded his head.

The children came out of the bedroom and lingered at the door, gazing curiously at Jeffrey. Pricilla told them to come over to her so that she could introduce Jeffrey to each of them. The boys walked over to her. Jeffrey said hello to them and held his hand up to the boys to receive a high five. They obliged him and said hello.

Aquila instructed them to go into the bathroom, wash their hands, and go to the kitchen to eat their dinner. They did as they were told, and then ran into the kitchen to sit down at the table. Abigail ran over to Aquila, grabbed her around her waist, and peered at Jeffrey.

Pricilla laughed softly. "Jeffrey, this is Abigail," she said as she played with the long braid that hung down Abigail's back.

"Hello, Abigail," Jeffrey said, greeting her cheerfully. "How are you?"

Abigail waved at Jeffrey shyly and reached up for Aquila to pick her up. Aquila scooped Abigail up in her arms. "Mommy," Abigail said to Aquila, "I miss my daddy. Is he coming here to see us soon?"

Aquila hesitated a moment before she replied to her. "Maybe, honey. We'll see." She put Abigail back on the floor. "Go eat your dinner, okay?" Abigail ran into the kitchen and sat at the table with the boys. Aquila looked at Pricilla and Jeffrey helplessly. "I don't know what to tell her. This is the second time today that she has asked about Brandon."

Pricilla folded her hands across her stomach. "You might have to sit her and the boys down and tell them the truth, Aquila."

Jeffrey nodded in agreement.

Aquila looked at both of them and shook her head vigorously. "I can't, they are too young to understand. Brandon was never mean to them, so they love him to death. Like most children, they would want me to reconcile with their father." Aquila's facial expression hardened. "I'd rather see him dead before I go back to him." She turned on her heels and walked into the kitchen.

Chapter 21

Kendra was devastated. She'd just had outpatient surgery. The news she had received from her surgeon was heartbreaking. The biopsy she'd had weeks earlier of the ovarian cysts was not a good report. The ovarian cysts had become malignant. Surgery was inevitable. After the outpatient surgery, the doctor had determined the cancer had metastasized to stage II.

Matthew drove them home toward Garner, another city adjacent to Raleigh, in silence. He couldn't think of anything else to say to Kendra. He'd tried to comfort her as best he could with scriptures from the Bible. He assured Kendra how much he loved her, and that he would be with her every step of the way when the time came for her to start her chemotherapy sessions.

"Honey," Matthew said cautiously, "I think that you should quit work. Maybe you should take a leave of absence from work for at least a year. I'll handle your cases. And as far as the soup kitchen is concerned, Ms. Mable has that under control."

Kendra gawked at him. "Are you kidding me, Matthew?" You have more cases than you can handle now. We're partners. I'm well enough to take care of my clients."

Matthew glanced away from the highway for a moment and looked at Kendra. "You are now, but the doctors told you that the more stress you are under, the worse the illness can become."

Kendra sighed heavily. "Matthew, my work is what keeps me going. I wouldn't know what to do with myself, sitting around the house all day."

"You don't have to sit around the house all day. After your six weeks recovery period, you can treat yourself to a spa, or take a vacation, go to Belize, or—"

Kendra shook her head from side to side. "What's the point of going on vacation without you?"

"The point is to relax and recover, not only your body, but your spirit. You know I would love to go with you, but I need to stay abreast of our law firm."

"What about church? I need to be there to help you with the services."

Matthew cleared his throat. "I was thinking about letting Minister Hilliard become the interim pastor until you recover."

Kendra propped her elbow up on the arm rest and put her hand under her chin. "Hmm. That sounds like a good idea. I'm sure his wife, Claudia, would love the idea of becoming First Lady. She's such a bossy little woman."

Matthew chuckled. "She is a bit zealous, but she'll do fine because she truly loves the Lord."

"Yes, I have to admit that she's a prayer warrior." Kendra reached over and touched Matthew's face gently. "I think you should talk to Minister Hilliard, honey. You look stressed out yourself."

Matthew exhaled loudly. "Good, I'm glad that you agree. I'll call him first thing tomorrow morning. If he agrees, I'll make my announcement to the congregation on Sunday."

Kendra sighed softly. "Okay, honey. That sounds reasonable."

Matthew picked up her hand and put it in his. "Once I step down from the position as pastor, I'll be able to devote more time to taking care of you."

Kendra relaxed in the soft tan leather seat of the Mercedes and closed her eyes. "Thank you, honey. I don't know what I would do without you."

Matthew kissed her hand softly. "I'm only doing what God expects me to do as His servant. I love you, and I intend to provide for you and protect you. Just because I'm temporarily stepping down as the pastor, doesn't mean that I'm going to stop serving God. We'll still have our worship services at home until you get better. Right now, my duty is to minister to your needs."

"Momma wants to come over and take care of me while you're at work. I prefer for her to be there with me during the day anyway."

"That's great, but with her arthritis, is she able to take care of you?"

Kendra rested her head on the headrest. "I don't anticipate that she'll have to do anything but sit there with me, or maybe make a light lunch. Other than that, she can sit and watch her soap operas. She'll mainly be there for company."

Matthew released Kendra's hand and pressed the right signal column down to indicate that he was turning onto the off ramp. "It's settled then. While you're at home recovering, you can plan for that much needed vacation."

Kendra smiled. "I think I will plan for a vacation." She reached over and kissed Matthew on the cheek. "I should ask Momma to go with me. In all of her seventy-three years, she's never had a decent vacation. I think it's time she had some enjoyment out of life."

Matthew pulled into their driveway and pressed

the garage door opener that was situated on the sun visor of the car. He drove into the two-car garage. "You amaze me sometimes, Kendra. Even in your illness, you're compassionate and are considerate of other people."

Kendra shrugged her shoulders. "Life is short, Matthew. I guess it takes a serious illness to make you appreciate those that you love."

Matthew opened the door to the house and walked back around to Kendra's side of the car, picked her up, and carried her in the house. He looked at her lovingly. "Hold on tight, baby. You're not as light as you used to be."

Kendra laughed. "Are you trying to tell me that I'm heavy?"

"No, you're just the right size, baby; more for me to love." Matthew carried his wife in the house and put her on the chaise near the bed so he could fold the covers back for her to get in bed.

"Matthew." Kendra called him softly.

Matthew answered her without looking back. "Yeah, baby?"

"I'm so sorry that I wasn't able to give you children."

Matthew stopped what he was doing and turned around and looked at Kendra. "I'm fine without children, Kendra. The important thing is that I have you, baby. We have each other."

"But for how long, Matthew?" Tears streamed down Kendra's face. "How long?"

Chapter 22

Diana sat raised up in the hospital bed and watched a movie on the Lifetime Channel. She periodically glanced at Mable as she read the Bible.

I certainly hope that she doesn't start her preaching again, Diana complained inwardly. Mable looked up at Diana as though she had read her mind.

"I heard that you would be going home soon, honey," Mable said enthusiastically. "God sure has been good to you."

"Yes, ma'am, I suppose He has," Diana said dryly. She turned her head back to the movie. "I will definitely be glad to get out of here."

"I know what you mean. Hospitals aren't my favorite place to be either." Mable put the Bible down and looked at the movie that Diana seemed to be so interested in. She was watching Halle Berry, Jessica Lange, and Samuel L. Jackson in the movie, *Losing Isaiah*.

"This movie reminds me of my own life," Mable said sadly. "I was messed up on drugs for a long time. I still haven't gotten myself together like I want to. I guess I never will." Mable cleared her throat. "Losing a child the way I lost mine, through neglect, tends to mess you up for life."

Diana looked at Mable compassionately. "I'm so sorry for your loss, Ms. Mable. I can relate to your pain because we both have daughters that we yearn for."

Mable clasped her hands together. "I pray that God will make a way for both of us to find our daughters."

Diana had a distant look in her eyes. "I hope so, Ms. Mable."

Mable pulled her posture up straight and smiled. "I didn't mean to come in here and bring you down." She stood up and unwrapped the dish she'd brought in earlier. "Diana, are you ready to try my homemade banana pudding?" she asked her cheerfully. "It's way better than that imitation banana pudding kind that we serve at the soup kitchen."

"Sure, I'll take a sample of it. This bland hospital food is for the birds." Mable scooped two large spoonfuls into a saucer and handed it to Diana. Diana used her good arm to eat with, balancing the bowl with her other arm that was in a cast. "Wow," Diana exclaimed. "This tastes like the banana pudding that my mother used to make."

Mable smiled. "I knew that you would like it." She turned her attention back to the movie that they were watching.

Diana finished the pudding and let the bowl rest on her lap. "Ms. Mable, I was about to find out who my child was before I had the accident." Mable turned her attention back to Diana. "I became so excited that I forgot what I was doing and ran a red light and pulled into the path of an oncoming truck."

Mable clasped her hands together tightly. "I heard that you had driven through a red light, but I had no idea that you had gotten some good news before it happened. Thank God that He brought you through this tragedy. Diana, you should give Him praise because He had mercy on you and let you live, so you *can* find out who the child is."

Diana shook her head in agreement. "I am grateful, Ms. Mable." Diana changed the subject. "Have you talked to Kendra lately?"

"Yes, I suppose she's doing okay. I try not to pry, but she has not been herself lately."

"I know. When she comes to see me, she puts on a good act, but I know that there's something seriously wrong. She sat in here and cried like a baby two weeks ago."

Mable stood up to take the bowl out of Diana's lap. She put her left hand on her hip and frowned. "Are you kidding me?" Mable shook her head. "Poor baby; she must be really going through a tough trial. I will certainly keep her in prayer."

Diana nodded her head. "When I finally got a chance to ask her what was going on, she said she hated to see me in such pain. I know that's not the whole truth, Ms. Mable. I've known Kendra since we were nine years old, and I've never seen her break down and cry like that before. She's always been as tough as nails."

Mable sighed heavily. "I guess she'll let us know what's wrong when the time is right."

Diana shook her head from side to side. "I don't normally discuss my friend's business with anyone, but I'm so worried about her."

"I've been concerned about her myself. I usually try to mind my business, but if Kendra doesn't say something soon, I'm bound to ask her what's going on."

Diana glanced at Mable. "Let's just give her a little time, maybe she'll talk to us soon."

"I suppose you are right. In the meantime, we can pray for her." Diana didn't respond. Mable

walked to the counter in the room and picked her
purse up. "I'll leave the rest of this pudding for
you for later, Diana."

"That'll be great. Thank you for coming by to
see me, Ms. Mable."

"Of course . . . I would have come sooner, but
we were shorthanded in the kitchen, and my
sons keep me on the go. They both play on the
basketball team at Broughton High School."

Diana gently massaged her swollen left knee.
"That's wonderful, Ms. Mable. I wish I were well
enough to go see them play."

Mable nodded her head in agreement. "Yeah,
that would be nice. Maybe you can come to see
them play soccer next year. They're very athletic,
and they're 'A' students too," she said proudly.

"That's great. I know that you are proud of
them." Diana rested her head on the pillow.

"I am." Mable opened her purse, pulled out
her wallet, and slid her sons' pictures out to show
Diana. "I don't think I've ever shown you their
pictures, have I?"

Diana raised her head back up off of the pillow. "No, you haven't," Diana told her.

Mable walked closer to Diana's bed and put the
pictures in her hand. "These are my big sons," she
told Diana with a wide smile on her face. "The one

in the blue shirt is Adrian, the oldest, and Andre, my baby, has on the white shirt."

Diana examined the pictures. Both of her sons were extremely handsome. They both had honey-brown skin, and their wavy hair was cut closely to their heads. They had dark brown, almond shaped eyes and beautiful white teeth. "Wow," Diana exclaimed. "You have some good-looking sons, Ms. Mable. And both of them are dressed so well in their suits, too. They *are* some big guys," she said, laughing. "How tall are they?" Diana handed the pictures back to Mable.

Mable took the pictures and put them back in her wallet. "Adrian is six foot two inches, and Andre is six foot three inches," she said with a smile on her face. She pulled out another picture. "Here is a picture of the three of us." She handed it to Diana.

Diana gazed at the picture. "Ms. Mable, you look so pretty in this picture. You look so much different than you do when you're at work."

"Thanks for the compliment," Mable said, blushing. "I thank God that I look as well as I do, considering the way I treated myself when I was younger."

"You look great, Ms. Mable. And your sons tower over you. I can tell that they are proud of you too."

"I hope so," Mable said softly. She gazed up toward the television that was mounted on the wall. "I pray that God will be with them, and they'll turn out to be a lot more successful in life than I've been." Diana handed her the picture and she put it back in her wallet.

"You are a single mother, Ms. Mable; that in itself is successful," Diana encouraged her.

"I appreciate you saying that, but child, I've lived a rough life. I thank God that's behind me now. Once my sons were old enough, I shared information with them about my drug abuse. I constantly talk to them about the perils of drug use. I encourage them to excel academically and get involved in extracurricular activities at school to avoid having too much leisure time on their hands. I just hope that they listen and take heed."

"I'm sure they are going to grow up to be fine young men," Diana told her.

Jeffrey stuck his head in the doorway. Diana smiled. "Hi, honey. Come in and meet my friend."

Mable walked over to Jeffrey and shook his hand. "Hi, I'm Mable Woodard. It's a pleasure to officially meet you, Dr. Thompson."

Jeffrey smiled warmly at Mable while he shook her hand. "It's a pleasure to meet you too, Ms.

Woodard. My wife has mentioned you quite often. She's very fond of you."

"That's good to know. I think that she is a fine young lady too. When I first met her, she was a mess, though." Mable chuckled.

"I'm sure she was." Jeffrey laughed.

Mable gazed at Jeffrey for a moment before she said, "I believe I've seen you at church a couple of times."

Jeffrey nodded. "Yes, a couple of times; that's about as much as I've attended. I would like to go more, but I can't convince Diana to go with me."

"Diana," Mable said, as she looked Jeffrey up and down. "Girl, you better come to church with this man. As fine as he is some of those hot-to-trot women are gonna try to snatch him up. Everybody don't come to church to hear the Word of God." Mable waved good-bye to them and walked out of the room.

Mable's statement intensified Diana's insecurities about her husband. The passion between them was almost nonexistent, because he had only slept with her on occasion before the accident. She wondered if he had met someone at church, because lately he was determined to spend more time there, with or without her. Now with Mable making the comment that she made,

Diana wondered if she had actually seen him with someone at church.

Diana scanned Jeffrey's face. With a worried look, she said, "Are you having an affair with someone, Jeffrey?"

Chapter 23

The next morning, Aquila watched Darius and Daniel as they boarded the school bus. She waved good-bye to them as she held Abigail's hand. She and Abigail then headed down the opposite direction to walk the four blocks to her job. Two weeks had passed since Aquila had last seen the strange man around, so she began to feel at ease. God had put her former neighbor in her spirit often lately, so she decided to call her to check on her once she got to work.

After answering the messages from the voice mail and ordering office supplies, Aquila telephoned Ms. Carter. The phone rang three times before she answered.

"Hello," Ms. Carter said in a frail voice.

"Hi, Ms. Carter; this is Aquila."

"Lord, thank you, Jesus," Ms. Carter said in a stronger, more excited voice. "Chile, I've been worried sick about you. Are you all right?"

"Yes, ma'am. The children and I are doing fine. We live in Raleigh, North Carolina with a friend of mine."

"Well, it's good to hear from you, baby," Ms. Carter said sweetly.

Aquila smiled when she heard the warmth in her voice.

"You've been on my mind, so I thought I should give you a call to see how you are doing."

Ms. Carter chuckled. "I'm doing fine. I miss you and the kids, though."

Aquila smiled. "We miss you too. But I had to leave Brandon."

"Uh-huh." Ms. Carter nodded her head. "I figured as much."

"He was physically abusing me; I couldn't take it anymore. My friend wired me some money, so I had to leave in a hurry, before he came home from work. I'm sorry I wasn't able to come tell you good-bye in person."

"I thought he might have been beating on you, but you wouldn't say anything. I started to come out and ask you several times, but I didn't want you to think that I was a nosy old lady."

Aquila sighed. "I should have told you, but I felt so ashamed."

"Well, there is nothing for you to be ashamed of. He is the one with the problem, not you." Ms.

Carter said defiantly. "I'm glad that you got away from him."

"Thank God for touching my friend's heart to rescue me. I'm enjoying my life now, Ms. Carter. Darius and Daniel are in school, and I work now. Can you believe it?" Aquila giggled. "Oh, and I've had my driver's license for two weeks now."

"Praise the Lord. God is good, Aquila. Psalm 34:18 tells us that, *The Lord is nigh unto them that are of a broken heart; and saveth such as be of a contrite spirit.*"

"I remember you telling me that. I must have been a pitiful sight some days, wasn't I?"

Ms. Carter nodded her head in agreement. "Yes, you were kinda sad. That's why I always offered you a place to come if you needed to; anytime, day or night."

Aquila stood up and closed the door to her office. "I appreciated your offer too. But I knew if I had come to your house, that's the first place Brandon would have looked for me." She walked back to her desk and sat down. "Besides, I didn't think it was right to involve you in my problems."

"I think it was just a little bit of pride on your part that kept you from saying anything."

Aquila twirled a pencil around between her fingers. "You're right. Pricilla told me the same thing. I guess I wanted you to think that I had a wonderful life."

"Baby, don't ever put on no outside show, trying to convince people that you're *living large,* as the young folks say. 'Cause having material things and no *peace* is a bad way to live."

"I know that to be true now. Since I've been here, I have so much peace and tranquility. I finally know the meaning of Psalm 23."

Ms. Carter smiled broadly. "Glory to God."

A few seconds of silence passed before either of them said anything. Aquila exhaled slowly before she asked Ms. Carter, "Have you talked to Brandon, lately?"

"Not since Thanksgiving Day. He came over and ate dinner with my son and me. I could tell he was fishing for information about you. He mentioned several times that he missed you and the children. I told him that I hadn't heard from you, but I thought to myself, that if I had, I wouldn't tell him. I figured that he must have done something really horrible to you, or you wouldn't have left his butt."

Aquila exhaled a sigh of relief. "I appreciate you saying that. Please don't tell him that I called you today either."

"Honey, that should be the least of your worries. I've seen him coming and going to work every day, so I guess he's accepted the fact that you're gone."

"I hope so. I have no intention of coming back there to stay. As soon as I earn enough money, I'm going to file for a divorce."

"You probably should, Aquila." She paused for a moment. "I see some woman coming over there on weekends, but she always leaves on Sunday afternoon."

Aquila felt a twinge of hurt. "I don't know why I'm surprised to hear that. I don't understand why I feel betrayed. I should be happy that he's moved on with his life. Maybe she'll distract him from thinking about me."

Ms. Carter sighed softly. "I'm so sorry, Aquila. I shouldn't have said anything."

"That's fine, Ms. Carter," Aquila said in a more jovial tone. "At least now I don't have to keep looking over my shoulders, afraid that he's tracked me down. Hopefully, he's found someone who can make him happy. God knows that I could never do anything to please him."

"Maybe so, but men like Brandon don't miss their water 'til the well runs dry. I'm just glad that you got away from him and are making a good life for yourself and those kids."

"Thank you. I'm happy that God made a way for me to get out of that abusive life too." The office phone rang, and a parishioner knocked on the door. Aquila told her to come in. "Ms. Carter,

I need to go now, there's someone in the office, and I need to talk to them."

"Okay, baby. Please stay in touch. I love you. Take care."

"I love you too. Oh, I forgot to wish you a Merry Christmas," Aquila said excitedly.

Ms. Carter chuckled. "Merry Christmas to you too, honey."

"Thanks. Be blessed. I'll talk to you later."

After Aquila helped the person that had stopped by the office, she answered the call that had gone to the voice mail. She hung up the phone and thought about Brandon. A surge of anger temporarily filled her spirit. *He has the audacity to bring some woman in my house after I worked like a fool to keep it up.* Then Ms. Carter's words echoed in her head. *"Having material things with no peace is a bad way to live."*

There was a soft knock on the opened door. It broke Aquila's train of thought; she lifted up her head. A young man from a local flower shop stood in front of her with a bouquet of flowers. Aquila stood up and greeted him cordially, before she asked him, "May I help you, sir?"

He smiled and said, "I have a delivery for a Miss Aquila Savino."

Aquila looked at him strangely, and then she looked at his shirt for a name. "Are you sure you have the correct name, Raymond?"

The young man looked at his order form. "Yes, ma'am; it says Aquila Savino." He pointed toward the kitchen area. "Ms. Woodard directed me to you."

"Who sent them?" Aquila asked him cautiously.

"I have no idea, ma'am. I'm just the delivery guy." He handed the form to Aquila.

Aquila inspected the tulips. "Is there a card attached?" she demanded to know.

With Christmas being only four days away, Aquila figured someone must have sent her the flowers as a gift.

Raymond answered with a curt reply. "Yes, ma'am. If you could sign the form, I'll be on my way." Aquila scribbled her name illegibly on the form. "Have a good day," Raymond told Aquila before he handed the flowers to her and walked out of the office.

Aquila placed the beautifully arranged flowers on her desk. She opened the card, which stated, "Beautiful flowers for a beautiful lady." The card didn't have a signature. She stood in front of her desk and gazed at the tulips for over a minute. She wondered who could have sent her flowers. She was even more confused over who could have known that tulips were her favorite flowers.

She walked out and closed her office door. She stood in front of her office door for a couple of seconds. *Brandon*, she thought. *He's the only one that knows tulips are my favorite flowers.* She dismissed the thought of it being Brandon because Ms. Carter told her that she sees him going and coming from work every day.

It was lunchtime in the soup kitchen. She walked into the dining room of the church and stood in line for a meal, to save money as Kendra had directed her to. She maneuvered her way around the tables of homeless people and found a table at the back of the room. As she sat at the table alone, she watched Mable and the other workers as they catered to the homeless.

Her eyes settled on Mable again. Aquila stared at her for a few seconds with a perplexed look on her face, wondering why she had an uncanny feeling that she knew Mable from somewhere.

Chapter 24

Diana had been in the hospital for six weeks. She was scheduled for three months of rehabilitation, but she was elated to be home. June bustled around in the house making sure that Diana had everything she needed. Jeffrey's son came home shortly after Diana had arrived. He walked over to the hospital bed that they'd rented from the medical supply company and gave Diana a kiss on the forehead.

"Hey, Diana." Michael greeted her warmly. "It's good to see you at home again. How're you feeling?"

Diana tried to position herself better on the bed. Michael helped her by raising the bed. "Hi, son," Diana said cheerfully. "I'm doing much better now that I'm home. How are you doing with your internship?"

Michael exhaled loudly. "It's a trial, but I'm doing okay." Michael chuckled and shook his head from side to side. "I'm the oldest intern in the crowd. If I had gone to school when I was supposed to, I wouldn't be a thirty-two-year-old intern."

Diana smiled warmly at her stepson. "You're still young. It doesn't matter how old you are; the point is that you've almost reached your goal."

Michael placed his hands behind his head and locked his fingers together. "If I can get through this first year, the rest should be a piece of cake."

"You'll do fine, I have confidence in you." Diana lay her head down on the pillow. She glanced around the room. As usual, June had cleaned the place spotless. Her eyes rested back on Michael. "You look more like the pictures of your mother every day. I know she would have been proud of you."

Michael's countenance brightened up. "Dad thinks so too."

"You've progressed to become quite a successful young man over the years."

"Thanks." Michael's eyebrows furrowed. "It's kind of you to say that, Diana."

Diana used her right forefinger to put a lock of hair behind her ear. "I know that your father is proud of you too."

"I hope that I've finally made him proud of me. I have challenged him enough over the years with my rebellious behavior to last him a lifetime."

Michael reflected to earlier years. He had graduated high school only two weeks when his mother passed away from breast cancer. He had a close relationship with his mother, so it was extremely hard for him to cope with her death.

He was so distraught that he began to hang around with teenaged boys from his school that were supposed to graduate with him, but didn't. These teens did nothing more than hang on the street corners drinking and smoking. Michael would be gone for days, and when he did come home, he slept all day, and stayed up all night playing video games.

He avoided Jeffrey because he blamed him for his mother's untimely death. He felt that Jeffrey neglected her because he was focused more on his career than on her. Although Jeffrey was grieving deeply over the death of his wife, he tried to console Michael. He suggested that they work through the grieving process together, but Michael refused any advice or help that Jeffrey offered him.

He lived recklessly throughout the summer months by spending the fifty thousand dollar death benefit insurance money that his mother had left him on frivolous items. He bought a fifteen thousand dollar Rolex watch, expensive clothes, and high end jewelry for a twenty-one-year-old young lady that he'd met through his so-called friends. He blew the rest of the money, twenty-four thousand dollars, on a used BMW that he wrecked and totaled within two months time.

He had a party in the house while Jeffrey was away at a medical convention, resulting in the house being trashed by his friends and strangers that crashed the party. By the end of the summer, Michael's destructive behavior had challenged his father's patience to the breaking point. Jeffrey gave him the ultimatum of enrolling in Virginia Commonwealth University, in Richmond, Virginia, where he'd been accepted, or get out of his house. Michael enrolled in college at Jeffrey's expense, but he failed all of his courses because he rarely attended classes.

He lived in Richmond, Virginia for a year with the young lady he'd met in college. She worked part-time while she attended college. He worked part-time as a Verizon telephone salesperson, but his salary didn't compensate him enough to pay the rent for the apartment that he shared with his girlfriend. Michael called Jeffrey constantly, asking for money. After a year, Jeffrey refused to send him another dime.

Two months later, he asked Jeffrey if he could move back home. Jeffrey agreed on the condition that Michael sought full-time employment and paid the utility and cable bills. Michael moved back in with Jeffrey and gained full-time employment with Alltel as a salesperson for two years.

When he turned twenty-one, he had access to the fifty-five thousand dollar trust fund that his mother had set up for him. He started dating and married his former high school sweetheart, Barbara Webster. They didn't have any type of ceremony; they went downtown and got married at the Justice of the Peace. They moved into an expensive apartment in North Raleigh and furnished it with high end furniture. Five months into their marriage, their relationship began to deteriorate. Barbara refused to seek employment; she became increasingly jealous of any lady that Michael talked to. She visited him so often on his job that he was terminated. Michael was unemployed for a month, but he sought employment diligently. He was offered a job in the marketing department of a major telephone company, which required him to travel to Atlanta, Georgia once a month.

When he came home from a three-day business trip, he opened the door to his apartment, which was empty of every item in the house, except his boxed up clothes. There was a note taped on the refrigerator from Barbara, stating that she didn't want to be married to him any longer. After the shock wore off, he opened his laptop and checked his bank account. She had withdrawn all of his money, except fifty dollars.

He visited his in-laws, who refused to tell him anything, claiming that they didn't know where she was either. Michael knew that they were lying, but there was nothing that he could do. With no money to pay the expensive rent and utilities, he moved back into the house with Jeffrey and traveled back and forth to his job in Atlanta.

After a year, Barbara contacted him with a petition for a divorce on the grounds of a false accusation of mental cruelty and irreconcilable differences. She'd hired a lawyer, using Michael's money, who worked diligently to ensure that she was awarded the right to keep all of the possessions. Michael used the meager funds that he'd earned to pay a less crafty, inexperienced, lawyer to plead his case, but the judge ruled on her behalf. She left town after the divorce decree was finalized and Michael hadn't seen her since. Needless to say, Michael was bitter against women for a long time. When he met Diana, he was positive that she was just another pretty, young, gold-digger out to scam his father the way Barbara had scammed him.

He worked on his job for another six months, and then decided that he wanted to go back to college to earn a degree. So once again, he asked for his father's financial support.

Being the compassionate father that he was, Jeffrey withdrew some of the funds that he'd worked so hard for and paid for Michael's tuition and books at the University of North Carolina. Michael vowed to repay him when he turned thirty and received his final trust fund of one hundred thousand dollars. When he turned thirty, he remained true to his word. Michael repaid Jeffrey all the money he had loaned him from his college days at Virginia Commonwealth University in Richmond and the money it cost him to graduate from the University of North Carolina. The loans totaled sixty-four thousand dollars. His plan was to purchase a house with part of the remaining thirty-six thousand, but Jeffrey advised him to invest the money in mutual funds, CDs, and money market accounts. He suggested that he finish his internship, and wait until he started earning an income before he purchased a house.

Michael gazed off, focusing on nothing in particular and shook his head sorrowfully. He picked up Jeffrey and Diana's wedding picture and smiled.

"But regardless of what I put him through, he's been a good father." He put the picture back on the sofa table and looked at Diana. "I'm proud of him too, although I think he works too much."

"Yes, he is a busy man." *Although, I don't think all of his time is spent working.* Diana had heard two of the nurses talking outside of her hospital room, saying that Dr. Thompson seems to be getting serious about the new nurse. Diana knew that it wasn't appropriate to mention her doubts about her husband to his son, so she didn't voice that thought.

Diana scrutinized Michael's face. She meditated for a moment before she spoke. "Michael, I feel like I owe you an apology. I know I haven't been very cordial to you over the years."

"You don't owe me an apology, Diana. When you moved into the house, I didn't exactly roll out the red carpet for you either."

Diana sighed softly. "I guess it was awkward for both of us, with me moving into your mother's house."

"Yes, it was weird, but I could have done more to make you feel welcome."

Diana remembered the first time that she'd met Michael. She was sitting in Jeffrey's living room, waiting for him to get dressed for their date. They had been dating for nine months.

Michael came home unexpectedly from college. He unlocked and opened the front door. When he entered the family room, Diana stood up and smiled, extending her hand to him to introduce herself. Michael looked at her like she was disgusting, called her a gold-digger, and told her that she needed to get out of his mother's house.

Diana was flabbergasted. She felt disrespected and insulted. Her initial reaction was to retaliate, but she decided to let Jeffrey deal with his incorrigible adult son. She glared at Michael, picked up her purse from off of the coffee table and swiftly walked out of the house and down the steps to her car. She sat in the car fuming for a minute and then drove away.

Once Jeffrey came downstairs and saw that Diana had left, he asked Michael whether she was in the house when he arrived. He was not satisfied with Michael's evasive answer, so he called Diana on her cell phone. After Diana told him what happened, Jeffrey apologized for Michael and asked her to come back. She reluctantly agreed. In the meantime, Jeffrey reprimanded Michael and ordered him to apologize to Diana.

Diana drove back to the house, got out of her car, and stood on the porch, hesitating before she rang the doorbell. Jeffrey met her at the door, and then told her that his son had something that he wanted to say to her. Diana could tell that Michael hated apologizing to her, and she felt like he did so only because Jeffrey had insisted that he apologize.

After that incident, any communication between them was strained at best. Three months later, Jeffrey and Diana had a private wedding ceremony at The Cary Chapel and Gardens in Cary, North Carolina.

Michael stood as his father's best man, but his disposition was not very pleasant toward Diana. He resented her for taking his mother's place, and when he came over to visit Jeffrey, he had little to nothing to say to Diana.

At first, Diana accommodated his rudeness with politeness. Her kindness toward him only made the situation tenser. Michael was so cold toward her that she realized her efforts were in vain. Eventually, Diana's disposition toward Michael changed. She no longer made an effort to try and win him over.

She asserted her position as Jeffrey's wife and began to pack up Denise's pictures, paintings, trinkets, and any accessories that she had decorated the house with. The final straw for Michael was when Diana had Denise's furnishings removed from the house and replaced them with her décor.

"You were young and I understood that you missed your mother. I tried to be understanding, because I'd lost my mother shortly after I graduated high school also." Diana cleared her throat. "I admit that I felt like a second class citizen at times, because I knew Jeffrey still loved your mother very much." Michael dropped his head, but he didn't say anything. "It's okay; I know that your father loves me, but I'll never replace your mother in your and Jeffrey's lives. I wouldn't even try to. I just want you to know that when I had her decorations and furnishings removed, I didn't do it with malicious intent, but I wanted to feel like this was my home too."

"I understand." Michael rubbed his hand through his thick, coarse hair. "Although Mom had been deceased for three years, Dad left everything the way she had it before the day she died." Michael looked at Diana compassionately. "I've never told you this, but I appreciate you redecorating the whole house, because it was difficult to move on without Mom when every item in the house reflected her personal touch."

Diana's eyes filled with tears. "I kept all of her personal items and had them packed up and put in the attic for you. So whenever you move you can take them with you."

"I know, Diana. Dad told me years ago what you'd done with her stuff. I didn't want to accept you, so I did what I could to make you miserable. But now I'm saying thanks. That means a lot to me." Michael noticed the sad expression on Diana's face. "Regardless of the distance between us over the years, I believe that you've been good for Dad, and despite what you may think, I care about you too."

Diana sniffled. "It means a lot to hear you say that, Michael. I know I've not shown it very often, but I love you like you were my own son."

June came into the room and interrupted their conversation. "Excuse me, Mrs. Thompson. There is someone here to see you. Is it all right if I show them in?"

Diana smoothed her hair down and frowned slightly, wondering who had come to see her unannounced. "Sure, June. Show them in."

Michael touched Diana on her hand. "I'll talk to you later, Diana. I'm going upstairs to take a nap. I have an early day tomorrow."

Diana nodded. "Take care, Michael. I enjoyed our talk."

Michael headed for upstairs, using the back staircase.

Diana's eyes roamed back toward the foyer. She was expecting Kendra, Ms. Mable, or someone else she considered a friend to walk through the door. Her mouth dropped open when Sydney stepped across the threshold. "What are *you* doing here?" she asked her in an acidulous tone.

Chapter 25

"I can't come to see my sick little sister?" Sydney retaliated as she flung her arms out dramatically. Diana rolled her eyes. "I'm not sick, Sydney. I've been in a terrible accident; there's a difference." "You've been in the hospital; same difference. Ain't you glad to see me?"

Diana gawked at Sydney. "It depends."

"On what?" Sydney folded her arms across her stomach and glared at Diana.

Diana looked at Sydney from head to toe. "What do you want, Sydney? I was in the hospital for six weeks, and you've just decided to come and see me?"

Sydney's appearance had not changed much over the years. At forty-four, she remained slim and shapely. She had a few streaks of gray hair and her face was more mature; other than that, she looked exactly the way she did as a teenager.

Sydney's eyes pierced Diana's. "What makes you think I want something every time I contact you?" Sydney sat on the recliner at the end of Diana's bed and put her purse on the floor. "Jeffrey called me and told me that you were home from the hospital."

"Humph. How much money did you swindle out of Jeffrey this time?"

Sydney stood up abruptly. "You know what? I am sick of your snooty butt, Diana," she said in a hardened voice. "I've never swindled money from Jeffrey, and you know it."

"You asked him for money behind my back, so that's swindling."

Sydney stared hard at Diana. "I've never asked Jeffrey for money under false pretenses."

Diana looked at Sydney with a smirk. "I know that, Sydney."

Sydney shook her head. "I thought I'd come to see about my only sister, but I see I wasted my precious time and gas driving from Knightdale all the way out here to Cary. I could have saved myself a lot of stress from dealing with that crazy traffic." She stooped over and picked her purse up from the floor. "You don't appreciate *nothing* I do for you," she said harshly." Sydney took a step toward the door. "And for the record, I came by the hospital to see you a couple of times, but you were out like a light," she said in a matter-offact tone.

"You did?" Diana asked her in a soft tone.

Sydney turned back around and faced Diana with a stoic expression on her face.

Diana held her hand out in a peaceful motion. "Sydney, I apologize. I don't remember you coming to see me in the hospital."

"Well, I did come to see you," Sydney stated flatly. She sat back down in the recliner.

Diana smiled and nodded her head. "Thank you. I'm glad you came to see me today too." She looked toward the foyer. "Where are your grandkids?"

"Oh, you mean your great nephews that you banned from your house?"

"I didn't exactly ban them from the house, Sydney. But after they came over here and nearly destroyed everything, yes, I asked you not to bring those rambunctious boys back. At least until they had some home training."

"They didn't destroy *everything*, Diana. You need to stop blowing things out of proportion." Sydney pointed her forefinger toward the foyer. "They only broke two vases and that funny looking statue sitting in the hallway. Boys will be boys; they just have a lot of energy."

Diana raised her head up off of the pillow and looked at Sydney dubiously. "Energy my foot," she exclaimed. Your grandkids are just bad. I purchased those two vases from Venice and that funny looking statue came from Africa. They cost a lot of money," she stated impetuously. Diana took a deep breath, and then eased her head back down on the pillow.

Sydney slid her body toward the edge of the recliner. "I offered to pay you for them, Diana," she said sorrowfully.

Diana smirked. "You couldn't afford to pay for them, Sydney."

"I offered, just the same," Sydney said defensively. "What did you expect me to do; give you half of my blood and the deed to my house?"

Diana laughed. Even in anger, Sydney had a sense of humor. "No, I just don't want those bad grandkids of yours over here anytime soon."

Sydney relaxed her shoulders. She smiled when Diana laughed because she knew Diana had spoken the truth. Her grandkids *were* hyperactive. "You don't have to worry about that. They're gone back to Connecticut to live with their momma." Sydney maneuvered her body back so that she could relax in the recliner.

Sydney's daughter, Teresa, had gotten pregnant during her sophomore year at college. After she had the first baby, she decided to drop out of school and move back home with Sydney and look for work. Sydney wanted a better life for her daughter than she had had, so she told Teresa that she would keep her three-month-old son for six months. By then, Teresa would have finished her sophomore year.

In the meantime, Teresa became pregnant with her second child. Teresa and the baby's father had planned to get married, but that didn't work out. The father of the children quit school and joined the military. He had a monetary allotment taken out for the first child. By the time Teresa had given birth to the second child, he was deployed to Iraq. After his eighteen month tour, he married a woman, also in the military, that he'd met while in Iraq. He financially supported both of his infant sons, but he wasn't available to help Teresa raise them.

Reluctantly, Sydney took both babies in so that Teresa could finish college. She had raised them each since they were three months old. They were now five and six years old.

"It's about time she took those kids off of your hands," Diana stated. "How *is* Teresa?"

"She's doing well now," Sydney said proudly. She graduated from the University of Connecticut last May. She works as a business administrator at the school. She finally saved up enough money to get a decent apartment so she could send for her kids."

Diana nodded her head. "That should be a burden lifted off of you now."

June came back into the room. "Excuse me, Mrs. Thompson; do you need anything else before I leave?"

"No, June; I'll be fine. Jeffrey should be home soon. Thank you for staying later than usual. It'll reflect in your paycheck, okay?"

"Thank you. Have a blessed evening, ma'am." June walked toward the door.

"You too, June," Diana replied. "Drive safely."

Sydney smiled. "Diana, you are spoiled rotten. I wonder what Momma would say about you having a housekeeper?"

"Girl, you know exactly what she'd say. 'Diana, get off of your lazy butt and clean your own house. It's a shame to waste money paying somebody to do what you can do yourself.'" Diana imitated her mother to a tee.

Sydney laughed. "You sound just like her. Momma was something else."

Diana giggled. "She sure was. I still miss her."

Sydney sighed. "Me too." Both were silent for a few moments. Sydney stood and stretched her legs. "What were we talking about before June interrupted us?"

"You were telling me that Teresa had sent for her boys, and I made the statement that it must be a burden lifted off of you."

"Oh yeah. It is a huge burden lifted off of me. It feels good not to have to take care of anybody but myself for a change. By the time I thought I had gotten Teresa off to college so I could relax, she come popping up with a baby, and eleven months after that, another one." Sydney frowned. "Girl, I was so upset with her; I could have spit fire."

"I remember." Diana looked at Sydney with compassionate eyes. "Well, you are a good mother, Sydney, because I don't think I would have taken in two young babies."

Sydney sighed loudly. "I know how it feels to be a young girl having a baby on your own. And I wanted her to finish college. I was only nineteen when I had her. Momma never knew she had a grandbaby on the way before she died. I knew I was pregnant by someone else when I married Gary, the pastor of our church."

Diana gasped. "Are you telling me that Gary isn't Teresa's father?"

Sydney nodded. "Yep. That's what I'm telling you. Teresa's father was Donald Avery."

"What?" Diana exclaimed. "He used to hang around the house all the time; I thought he was a friend of Momma's. How did you get involved with him?"

"He used to hang around the house all the time to help Momma by repairing things for her, but he really liked me. Momma didn't have a clue that we were involved." Sydney crossed her legs and smoothed her hair down.

Diana's eyes widened. "She couldn't have known, or she would have almost killed you and had him prosecuted. So how did you end up with Gary?"

"During Momma's last days, I confessed to Gary that I was pregnant with Donald's baby. I told him that I didn't know what I was going to do, because Donald was a married man."

"Yes, he was, and a so-called deacon in the church. How old was he anyway?"

Sydney's eyes roamed up toward the ceiling as she tried to recall his age. "I think he was about thirty-seven at the time."

Diana's facial features hardened. "You see, that's why I don't go to church now. Some people in church are worse than people in the world. Donald Avery should have been put in jail for child molestation," she said vehemently.

"I was eighteen; there wasn't anything the law could have done about it."

"But he was much older than you, Sydney, and he knew he was married," Diana emphasized again. "He took advantage of your youth."

"I realize that now," Sydney agreed. "But I guess I looked up to him as a father figure because our father passed away when we were little girls."

Diana nodded. She veered the conversation back to Gary White. "Gary used to be a good looking young pastor. All the girls in the church had a crush on him. They had a fit when he married you a month after Momma died and you guys left the church and moved to Connecticut."

"I remember," Sydney smiled. "Gary rescued me from an embarrassing situation with Donald. He let me know that shortly after he saw me in the congregation, he knew I was going to be his wife. But because I was only sixteen at the time, he knew he had to wait until I became an adult. Unfortunately, I had no idea that he was interested in me or I would never have given Donald Avery a second look."

Diana stared at Sydney with her mouth dropped open. "So you and Gary had a good marriage in spite of the fact that Teresa wasn't his child?"

"Yes, we did. Gary was a good man, a great father to Teresa, and he loved the Lord until the day he died. So you see, Diana, everybody in the church isn't a hypocrite. As a matter of fact, there are more people in the church that love God than not." Sydney clasped her hands together. "You

have to love God and have a personal relationship with Him for yourself. Don't look at other
people and decide whether or not you're going to
serve Him, because we are each accountable for
our own souls."

Diana nodded her head, but she didn't reply.
She used the remote control that was on the
table beside her bed, to turn on the television.
Sydney and Diana focused on the evening news
in silence. Ten minutes later, Sydney spoke up.

"Oh, I forgot to tell you, Diana," she said excitedly. Diana turned her attention back to her sister. "Teresa wanted me to let you know that she
is going to start repaying Jeffrey the seven thousand dollars for her tuition that she owes him."

Diana arched her eyebrows. "Jeffrey loaned
Teresa that much money for tuition?"

Sydney scrutinized Diana's face. "Yeah, over
the course of three years."

Diana scrunched up her face. "That's news to
me; he wouldn't tell me how many checks he had
written for her. I had no idea it was that many."

"I know. He told us not to tell you because he
knew you would have a tantrum. I really appreciate him helping my daughter through school."

Diana lowered her head. "I must really be a
hard person to deal with." She looked back up at

Sydney and waited for her to confirm her statement.

Sydney's eyebrows furrowed. "You have your moments. But I know deep down inside, there's a heart in you somewhere."

Diana gazed past Sydney's head. "I'm trying to change, Sydney. Lying in that hospital bed gave me a lot to think about. Until I had the accident, I refused to believe that God really loves us." She looked at Sydney with tears in her eyes. "After Momma died, I was convinced that He was a false hope that people held onto as a coping mechanism."

"He *is* real, honey." Sydney blinked away tears. "Just keep talking to Jesus, Diana. He'll see you through."

Diana nodded her head. "Just keep me in prayer, Sydney."

Jeffrey walked into the house from work. He strolled into the family room where the two of them were and hugged Sydney. "Hi, my beautiful sister-in-law," he said warmly.

"Hey there, my handsome brother-in-law," Sydney responded cheerfully. "How are you?"

"I'm blessed. I see you took my advice and came to visit your sister."

"Yes, but I thought she was gonna throw me out at first."

"Why?" He walked over to the bed and kissed Diana on the forehead. "What did you say to her, Diana?"

"I just asked her what she was doing here. I was angry with her because I didn't think she had come to see me until now. I had to apologize when she told me that she had visited me in the hospital twice."

"That's right, she did. I thought I told you that."

Diana looked confused. "If you did, I don't remember."

"You were in and out of consciousness so much, I'm sure you don't remember. Plus, she called me daily to check on your progress," Jeffrey assured his wife. He collapsed on the sofa.

Diana looked at her sister and nodded in appreciation.

Sydney stood up and peered in the kitchen at the wall clock. "Well, it's getting late, Diana." It was almost nine thirty. She had been at Diana's house since five thirty that afternoon. "I'll come back and visit you again one day next week. I have to drive back to Knightdale, and my car isn't the most reliable."

Diana's eyes twinkled from the excitement of her idea. "Why don't you spend the night, Sydney? We have more than enough space. You have a choice of two guest bedrooms."

Sydney looked surprised. In all the years that Diana had been married, she'd never asked her to spend the night.

"Please, Sydney?" Diana pressed.

Sydney shrugged her shoulders. "Well, I guess I can, but I didn't bring a change of clothing."

Diana scanned Sydney's body. "We are about the same size; you can wear some of my clothes tomorrow. Or I can call June tomorrow morning and ask her to buy you some clothes before she comes to work. She knows I'll repay her."

"Okay, it would be nice to spend some time together." Sydney chuckled softly. "It's been years since we've been able to put our differences aside and act like real sisters."

Diana giggled. "You're right. I really miss having my big sister to talk to."

Jeffrey stood up. "On that note, I'm going to bed. It's been a long day. Do you need anything before I go up, Diana?"

"If she does, I'll take care of her, Jeffrey. You go on upstairs and relax," Sydney told him.

"Thanks, sis." Jeffrey walked over to Diana and kissed her on her lips. "Goodnight, dear. I'll see you in the morning. Call me if you need any help, okay?"

Diana rubbed Jeffrey's right arm gently. "I will, baby. Have a good night."

Sydney and Diana watched Jeffrey as he left the room.

Diana made sure that he was out of earshot before she spoke. "Sydney, I have something to tell you that I should have told you years ago."

Diana felt closer to Sydney since she had shared her secret with her. She realized that Sydney had been as vulnerable as she had been in her youth. She no longer felt jealous of her and, miraculously, the animosity she had carried toward her had dissipated. Diana decided now would be a good time to share her secret with Sydney that she had ached to tell her years ago.

Frowning, Sydney sat back down in the recliner. "What's wrong, Diana? You look so serious."

Diana looked away from Sydney. "I feel so ashamed. You're probably never going to forgive me." Tears rolled down her face. Sydney's face was distorted with confusion, because she couldn't imagine just what it was that her sister could possibly have to say.

Chapter 26

Pricilla shut down her computer. Aquila sauntered into the living room where she sat. "Hey, Quila," Pricilla greeted. "What's going on? How was your day?"

"It was okay," Aquila responded to her somberly. "I miss talking to First Lady Kendra every morning. I hope she's doing okay."

It had been four weeks since Matthew and Kendra stood in front of the congregation and informed them that he needed to temporarily step down as senior pastor.

It was amongst the grumbling and whispering that Kendra tearfully announced to the congregation that she had cancer. She told them that she would be going through the process of chemotherapy, which would leave her sick and lethargic most days. She assured them that she regretted not being able to serve them as first lady of Macedonia Baptist Church. But until God healed her, she needed to use her energy fighting the illness that had attacked her body.

Matthew explained to them that God was his first priority, but that God also requires man to provide for and protect his wife. And that was what he intended to do; take care of his wife until further notice. He told them that he would sincerely miss serving them as the senior pastor, but hoped that they understood.

Their parishioners were deeply saddened, and several parishioners stood up and vowed to keep her lifted up in prayer until God blessed her with a full recovery.

Matthew announced that the interim pastor would be Minister Hilliard, and his wife, Sister Claudia, would serve as first lady. The congregation's reaction was mixed. Some applauded in agreement, while others mumbled their dissatisfaction. Nonetheless, Matthew adjourned the meeting and taught the Word of God with passion, but also with clarity.

Pricilla stood up to stretch her legs. "I hope she's doing okay too. Maybe we should go see her."

Aquila shook her head. "We can't." Pricilla's eyebrows furrowed and Aquila continued. "I called Pastor Woodbridge at his office yesterday to give him a message from one of the members.

I asked him how she was. He said she was recovering well, but that she didn't feel up to having company just yet."

Pricilla sat back down on the recliner. "Oh." She was thoughtful for a moment. "It seems strange with Sister Hilliard sitting in her place at church. Minister Hilliard is a good speaker, but he can't take the place of Pastor Matthew."

Aquila sat on the couch and crossed her legs. "You're right. I began to look forward to hearing Pastor Woodbridge teach the Word. He explains the scriptures in detail. He even applies a sense of humor within his teaching."

Pricilla smiled. "That's true; he's funny. Minister Hilliard does a good job teaching the Word, but his voice is so monotonous that it'll put you to sleep." Aquila laughed. "Pastor looked so weary when he announced that he was gonna step down for a while to take care of First Lady Kendra during her illness."

"He did look tired," Aquila agreed. "I hope they'll both recover and come back to work and church soon." Aquila stared across the room toward the children's bedroom.

"That's what I've been praying for, Aquila." Pricilla's phone rang. She answered it cheerfully. "Hi, Jeffrey. How are you?" She stood and walked to her bedroom.

Aquila checked on the children once more. They were tucked away and sleeping peacefully. She'd become more protective over them and very cautious of her surroundings because she had received flowers at work two days ago with a card that wasn't signed. Her first instinct told her they were from Brandon. She checked the windows to make sure that they were locked. Satisfied, she walked back into the living room and took the seat cushions off of the sofa bed and began to make up her bed.

Pricilla came back into the room. "Why are you going to bed so early, Aquila? It's only eight thirty."

"I'm a little tired," Aquila exhaled loudly. "Since Minister Hilliard's wife became first lady, she took it upon herself to take over the duties of First Lady Kendra. I had my office organized the way that I wanted it, but she seems to think it's her duty to micro manage me." Aquila unpinned her hair out of the French roll she'd worn.

"She does have a reputation for being bossy." Pricilla cocked her head to one side. "Just tell her that you have everything under control, and that First Lady Kendra is satisfied with the way you handle your duties."

Aquila picked her hair brush up from off of the end table and brushed her hair vigorously.

"She's not the easiest woman in the world to talk to, Pricilla."

"Just tell her," Pricilla ordered. "And if she gives you any problems, call First Lady Kendra. She's your boss, not Sister Hilliard."

"I hate to bother her at home, but she did tell me to call her if I needed anything." Aquila put her hair brush down and finished putting the covers on her bed.

Pricilla held her hands out, palms up at Aquila. "It sounds like you have a need, so you should make that phone call, girl. There's no need to be miserable at work when you don't have to be."

Aquila sighed. "You're right. I'll call her when I get to work tomorrow. So how was your day at work?"

"Great," Pricilla said enthusiastically. "I received my first full paycheck today. Being a full-time registered nurse at WakeMed is a lot more lucrative than being an aide at the retirement home. All of that hard work in school is paying off." She showed Aquila her pay stub.

Aquila's eyes stretched open. "Wow," she said emphatically. "That's good, Pricilla. Looking at this makes me want to go into the nursing field."

"Go for it, but only if you know that's what you really want to do, because if your heart's not in it . . ."

Aquila nodded. "No, I'll stick to what I know. Business office technology is what I like, so that's the degree I'll work toward."

"That's right." Pricilla tapped her right hand on her forehead lightly. "Oh. Jeffrey wanted me to say hello to you."

"Tell him that I said hello." Aquila sat in the recliner. "Pricilla?"

Pricilla had started toward the kitchen until Aquila called her name, she thought, with a worried tone in her voice. She turned around to face Aquila. "What's wrong?"

"I don't know if this is something to worry about, but . . ." Aquila hesitated.

Pricilla searched her face. "What's going on?"

"I received some beautiful flowers at my job on Tuesday. The card had a message that said, 'Beautiful flowers for a beautiful lady.' But there wasn't a signature on the card. I don't know what to make of it."

Pricilla came back into the living room and stood. "You probably have a secret admirer. I've seen a couple of guys at church checking you out. But of course, you never seem to notice them."

"I notice them, but I'm not in any position to talk to them. I'm still married, and my children are my priority right now, not another man."

"You won't be married for long, I hope. You and Brandon have been separated for over four months now." Pricilla smiled broadly, hoping to cheer up Aquila. Pricilla hunched up her shoulders. "In the meantime, just enjoy the fact that you have a secret admirer."

"I would like to think that the flowers were from a secret admirer, but it's just odd that the person knows that my favorite flowers are tulips."

"Maybe it's a coincidence." Pricilla sat down on Aquila's neatly made up sofa bed. "Did you tell anyone that tulips are your favorite flowers?"

Aquila laid her head back against the recliner. "I may have mentioned it around someone at church. But I don't remember having that conversation with anyone."

Pricilla shrugged. "I wouldn't worry about it. I'm almost sure that it was one of the guys at church that sent the flowers. It's pure coincidence that they happen to be tulips."

"I just feel uneasy. Brandon used to have tulips delivered to me as a way of making up." Aquila's lips trembled. "I hope that he hasn't found me. The very thought of it makes me shake inside."

Pricilla looked at Aquila suspiciously. "You haven't called him, have you?"

"Of course I haven't called him," Aquila retorted. She put her hand on her hip and glared at Pricilla. "You must think I'm a glutton for punishment, don't you?"

Pricilla was startled by Aquila's quick tempered remark. She folded her arms across her stomach and scrutinized Aquila's face. "No, I just watch you when you buckle under pressure when your kids start asking you about their father.

I told you that you need to go ahead and tell them the truth, so that they won't be under the impression that they are going back home."

Aquila dropped her head and massaged both of her temples. "I guess you're right. I'll talk to them this weekend."

Pricilla's eyes widened a bit. "Aquila, do you think that your neighbor, Ms. Carter, slipped up and mentioned your whereabouts to Brandon?"

Aquila's eyebrows furrowed. "I don't think so. She promised me that she wouldn't say a word to him about our conversation."

Pricilla was thoughtful for a moment. "Well, if I remember correctly, Brandon could be a charmer when he wanted to be. I hope he hasn't sweet talked Ms. Carter into telling him anything."

"Surely she wouldn't," Aquila said in a pleading voice. Aquila hurried over to the door and made sure that it was locked. "I hope that she hasn't betrayed my trust."

Chapter 27

Brandon's plane landed at the Raleigh/Durham International Airport at eight fifteen Friday night. He exited the plane and hurriedly walked down the corridor and took the escalator down to Baggage Claim. Once he'd picked up his luggage, he looked around for Leonard, the private detective he'd hired.

He was about to turn his phone on to call him, but Leonard walked up behind him and tapped him on the shoulder.

"Hey, Brandon," Leonard greeted him in a deep voice. "I tried to head you off upstairs, but you were walking so fast, I couldn't catch up to you."

"I expected you to be here sooner." Brandon replied in an agitated tone.

"I'm here now, so what's the problem?" Leonard retorted in an equally agitated tone. He pointed his head toward the parking deck. "The car's in this direction; let's go."

Brandon walked in a manner that insinuated to others around him that he was a man of great eminence. He didn't bother to reply to the women who smiled and spoke to him. He was a handsome Italian man, with olive skin and green eyes. He was five feet nine inches and had a chiseled body.

Brandon's upbringing had been disciplined. He was an only child, raised by a father in the U.S. Marine Corps and a stay-at-home mother. He'd traveled extensively with his parents as his father was stationed at Marine Corps bases all over the world. His father, Robert Savino, was a strict disciplinary toward Brandon as well as to his mother, Rachael. He belted out orders to Brandon and his mother as though they were one of his subordinates. When Rachael didn't follow his orders precisely, he punished her with physical abuse. After Brandon turned thirteen, depending on the offense, Robert would punch Brandon like he was a man.

Brandon grew up resenting his father and had little respect for his mother. Although he loved her, he considered his mother to be weak because she allowed her husband to verbally and physically abuse her. She was not strong enough emotionally to protect Brandon from his father's excessive beatings.

Robert Savino retired from the Marine Corps after thirty-five years of service. He settled his family in San Diego, California. Brandon graduated high school when he was eighteen. He attended and graduated college from the University of San Diego, in San Diego, California, with a degree in computer science.

He joined the Marines and served for twelve years. After being deployed for a year to Afghanistan and eighteen months in Iraq, he decided not to reenlist when his duties ended. He made his home in Nashville, Tennessee, and was hired at the Nashville International Airport as an air traffic controller. Six months later, he spotted Aquila in a park one day and observed her while she sat alone with an expression of despair on her face. After that, he noticed that she came to the park at least twice a week, alone, and sat on the bench feeding the ducks. He was intrigued by her beauty and innocence. He introduced himself to her, and after talking for hours, they began to meet at the park on a regular basis. Aquila was three weeks away from turning eighteen when she ran away from the orphanage and moved in with Brandon. Brandon was careful not to touch Aquila until she turned eighteen; he didn't want to be charged with child molestation and ruin chances of him being with her forever.

A month after she turned eighteen, he asked her to marry him. Aquila accepted the proposal, and they eloped and married in a chapel in Las Vegas, Nevada. After they were married, he took her to places like Bicentennial Mall State Park, the Grand Ole Opry, and Vanderbilt University Fine Arts Gallery on weekends.

Brandon had sincere intentions of being a good husband, but he soon learned that he was his father's son. He imitated his father's cruelty to his mother with Aquila. To his dismay, he had become as ruthless as his father was. It took Aquila's departure for him to realize that he needed psychiatric counseling. After a few weeks of counseling, his doctor diagnosed him with post-traumatic stress disorder.

Brandon was confident that once he shared this information with Aquila, she would understand. He knew that Aquila was a good wife and that once she heard him out, she'd be willing to forgive him of his trespasses toward her.

"Did you find any more information about my wife since you called me this morning?" Brandon asked Leonard in a gruff tone.

Leonard grunted. "No, I haven't learned any more information. Like I told you before, she and the children live downtown with a friend, in an old shack. She works at Macedonia Baptist Church as the church secretary."

Brandon raised his eyebrows. "My wife *works*? I didn't think she had sense enough to do anything but cook and clean." He smirked.

Leonard snorted. *This guy is a real jerk.* "I followed her to the kids' school a couple of times, but I got off a couple of stops before she did. She'd seen me around a few times before, but that last time, I could tell by her expression that she had become suspicious of me, so I backed off a bit."

They walked across the breezeway from the airport terminal and got on the parking deck's elevator. Leonard pressed the button to go up.

"I hope you haven't spooked her, Leonard," Brandon complained. "It's taken three months to track her down. The last thing I need is for her to jump up and run with the kids before I get a chance to convince her to come back home."

Leonard almost laughed out loud. "You can't be serious. From what I understand, word on the street is you used to beat the mess out of her. If you hadn't paid me so well, I'd never have let you know where she was."

The elevator door opened. The two of them were now standing on the fifth floor of the parking deck. The icy wind whipped around them. It was a dark, frigid December night. In the parking deck's lighting, Brandon's face was so distorted, that he looked like an animal to Leonard.

"Look, I paid you well because word on the street is you'll do anything if the price is right. How I handled my wife is my business," Brandon emphasized coldly. "You did your job, I paid you over and above what you're worth, so shut up," he yelled.

Leonard lost his temper. "You freaking wife beater, don't get nasty with me after I busted my tail for three months for your sorry behind. Don't mess with me, 'cause I ain't the one," he snapped. "You might scare the daylights out of your wife, but I'll work you over and get rid of you." Brandon backed away from Leonard. "The word on the street you heard is true; don't press your luck, buddy. I'll do Aquila a favor so she won't *ever* hear from you again."

"What the heck are you doing referring to my wife by her name, like you know her personally?" Brandon asked him angrily. "The two of you got something going on?"

Leonard stared Brandon down, took a deep breath and walked away from him. "Man, you are one *crazy* son of a gun," he said fervently. "Let's go before I change my mind about what I'm doing."

Brandon followed Leonard to the car. Leonard cranked the car up, blasted his B.B. King blues CD, and the two of them rode silently down the highway, headed for the hotel in downtown Raleigh.

As they neared downtown, Brandon broke the silence. "Leonard, before we go to the hotel, drive me by the place where my wife lives."

Leonard cut his eyes over at Brandon. "It's your dime, man. I'll drive you by there, but I ain't gonna drop you off." Leonard swerved the car around in a service station's parking lot. He turned onto the one-way street going in the opposite direction, away from the hotel. After ten minutes of maneuvering downtown, he parked across the street from Pricilla's house. He pointed his finger toward the house. "This is the house where your wife lives." He stared at Brandon with hard eyes. "Just pay me the rest of my cash, so I can catch a plane back to Nashville tomorrow. 'Cause whatever you do from now on, is on you."

Brandon opened his attaché case and dumped ten thousand dollars onto the seat. He had a sick smile on his face. "Relax, man. All I came to do is take my wife and kids back home where they belong."

Chapter 28

Sydney stared at Diana in disbelief. She sat back in her chair and absorbed her sister's incredible confession. "Diana, I can't believe that you had a baby when you were away at college. Why didn't you try to contact me and let me know?"

Diana slowly shook her head from side to side. "I had no idea where you were. The only thing that you told me after you married Gary was that you were moving to Connecticut. You didn't bother to call me and give me your address, so there was no way to contact you."

"I gave you my phone number, honey; that's all I had at the time."

"When I moved in with Kendra and Ms. Hannah, I misplaced your phone number. When it was time for me to leave for college, I just took off." Diana wiped the tear away that rolled down her face.

Sydney's eyes were full of tears. "I should have insisted that you move in with me," she said passionately. "I was the older sister; Momma would have expected me to take care of you."

Diana looked down at her hands and interlocked her fingers. "You made the offer for me to come and live with you, remember?" She looked back up at Sydney. "I turned you down because I had other plans for my life." Sydney nodded in agreement and Diana continued. "But it's a good thing that Kendra was accepted to the same school, or I would have felt completely abandoned after I got pregnant."

Sydney sighed heavily. "I'm so sorry that I left you so suddenly. I was ashamed of the fact that I'd gotten pregnant by a married man. I couldn't tell you that I was already pregnant with another man's baby when Gary married me. I didn't want to leave a scandal behind on Momma's good reputation in the community."

Diana looked past Sydney's head and up at the 11 x 15 picture of their mother that hung above the mantle over the fireplace. She smiled sadly. "Momma was a sweet lady, wasn't she? I still miss her." She sighed. "Sydney, do you know that I haven't set my foot in a church since she died?"

Sydney's eyes widened. "Are you kidding me? Why?"

"I couldn't see the purpose of going to church. Momma spent her entire life in church. She was there almost every Sunday and rarely missed Bible Study unless she was going through a sickle cell crisis." Sydney nodded. "She dragged us with her every step of the way."

"Yeah," Sydney replied. "It seems like every time we turned around, rain, shine, sleet, or snow, we were sitting in church, front and center." Sydney stood up. "Diana, do you mind if I get something to drink?"

Diana smiled warmly at Sydney. "Honey, help yourself to whatever you want from the kitchen. I'm sorry for being rude by not offering you anything. Do you want something to eat?"

Sydney patted her stomach lightly. "It's been awhile since I've eaten. I would like a sandwich or something light."

"Feel free to make what you want."

"Okay, thanks." Sydney went into the bathroom and washed her hands, and then headed for the kitchen. "Do you want anything?" she asked Diana.

Diana laid her head back on the pillow. "A ham and cheese sandwich would be nice."

Sydney stood at the refrigerator. "Okay," she said loudly enough so Diana could hear her. "I think I'll have the same."

Diana raised her voice loudly enough for Sydney to hear her request. "Could you put some lettuce and tomato on it too, please?"

Sydney had already taken the ingredients out of the refrigerator. "Sure. I'm already making it that way. I remembered how you liked your ham and cheese sandwich when we were growing up."

Diana closed her eyes and smiled. "This feels just like old times, doesn't it, Sydney?"

Sydney stopped what she was doing and walked back toward the family room entrance. "Yes, it does; only the house is much larger and prettier. I feel like the family on *The Jeffersons*. We're moving on up," she sang loudly.

Diana laughed heartily. "You are too funny. Girl, I used to sing that song a lot when we were growing up. That was my dream: to move on up and get my piece of the pie."

Sydney walked back into the kitchen and finished making the sandwiches and poured orange juice into long stemmed, gold rimmed glasses. "Well, God has made your dreams come true, girl." She walked back into the family room with the food on a tray.

Diana looked around at her home. "Yes, He did. I guess I need to be more grateful than I am."

Sydney placed the tray across Diana's lap. "You *guess* you need to be more grateful?" Sydney raised her eyebrows at Diana.

Diana's eyes met Sydney's piercing stare. "I *know* I need to be more grateful," she admitted.

Sydney took her plate and glass off of the tray and sat back down in the recliner. "That's more like it," she said in a soothing tone.

Diana giggled. "You looked just like Momma when you said that." She cocked her head to the side. "I've never noticed until now how much you look and sound like her."

Sydney nodded her head while she bit into her sandwich. After she finished chewing, she said, "Whenever I run into some of Momma's former church members and friends, they always tell me that the older I get, the more I look like her."

Diana swallowed some orange juice and took a bite of her sandwich. She wiped her mouth with the paper napkin that Sydney had placed on the tray. She stared at Sydney for a moment. "Wow, you really do look just like Momma."

Sydney mocked Diana by rolling her eyes up toward the ceiling. Diana laughed. They both ate their food. After they finished, Sydney took the tray back into the kitchen and washed Diana's glass and the plates. She put the tray back in its place and returned to the family room.

Diana thanked Sydney for making her a meal and resumed the conversation. "I used to get so tired of going to church. Momma didn't let us do anything, but go to church." Diana laughed heartily. Sydney smiled and nodded. "Girl, I got so tired of going to church that I started faking illnesses. I would develop a migraine headache, or a severe stomachache at the drop of a hat."

"I remember that." Sydney picked up her glass from the coffee table and sipped her juice. "You weren't fooling Momma though; she was wise to your dramatic acts of sudden illness."

"I knew she was fully aware of what I was doing, but she had an uncanny way of making me think that she believed me." Diana inhaled deeply. "I think she understood me better than I understood myself."

Sydney laughed. "I tried to fool her a few times by faking sick, but she would look at me as though she was baffled, and then her eyes seemed to pierce right through to my soul. So rather than face those eyes, I decided it was best to sit through church and pretend I was into it. You have always been a drama queen, so you got away with a lot during our childhood."

"I had to do something to get Momma's attention. Sometimes she acted as though you were peanut butter and she was jelly. The two of you were close."

Sydney gazed off toward the kitchen. "We were close, but I did not feel close enough to share my secret with her about Donald Avery."

Diana shook her head from side to side. "Momma would have flipped her wig if she had known about that. She probably expected me to get in trouble, but not her angel, Sydney," she teased.

"Diana, stop exaggerating. Momma let you get away with highway robbery." Sydney sighed. "It's a shame that she never got to meet either of her grandchildren. I really hate that I kept my pregnancy a secret from her."

A tear slid down Diana's face. "At least you loved and raised your secret. I have lived with mine for twenty-three years. It's been a nightmare living with the fact that I gave her up."

Sydney looked at Diana curiously. "Did you see the baby after it was born?"

Diana glanced at Sydney and frowned slightly. "Yes, briefly. Why'd you ask that?"

"I was just wondering if you got to hold her in your arms."

Diana looked away from Sydney. "No, I didn't want to because I was afraid if I did, I wouldn't go through with the adoption."

Sydney placed her hands over her face. "I understand," she said sadly.

Diana's countenance brightened up. "I do have some encouraging news though."

Sydney removed her hands from her face and looked at Diana expectedly.

"The private detective that I'd hired was about to tell me her name. She lives right here in Raleigh."

Sydney sat up briskly. "Are you *kidding* me?"

Diana's eyes twinkled. "No, I'm serious. Terry said that the information that he had found traced him to her, and that she's been living here for a while."

Sydney clasped her hands together as though she was about to pray. "That's amazing," she exclaimed. "Well, who is she, Diana?"

Diana shrugged her shoulders. "I have no idea."

Sydney's forehead wrinkled. "Girl, what the heck are you talking about?"

Diana stared at Sydney with glassy eyes. "Before he mentioned her name, I ran the stop light, and that's when the truck ran into me."

Sydney frowned from confusion. "So, you haven't talked to him since then?"

"No, because Jeffrey wanted me to heal before I met her. We discussed it last night, and we both believe that I'm ready to meet her now."

"Does Jeffrey know who she is?"

Diana covered her mouth while she coughed. "No. He asked Terry to keep the information confidential for me. He said he didn't want to know until I knew."

Sydney sat back in the recliner and crossed her legs. "I can understand that he didn't want to meet your daughter before you met her."

"That wasn't his concern. When I was in the hospital and cognizant, I kept insisting that he let me speak with Terry, but he wouldn't."

Sydney frowned. "Why?"

"He was concerned about my physical ability to heal, but more importantly, he was worried about my mental state."

"I see. He wanted you to concentrate on getting well, right?"

Diana exhaled loudly. "Yes, that was one reason. But he knows how stressed out I've been about what might happen after I find her."

"I don't understand, Diana. When you meet her, it's going to be a dream come true, and a heavy load lifted off of you."

"I *hope* that it will be a dream come true. Sydney, so many scenarios could emerge from me revealing myself to my daughter. I don't know if she'll be happy to see me or not. She could have had a terrible life, and she may hate me for giving her away. Suppose she doesn't want to meet me?" Diana put her hand over her heart. "I don't think I'll be able to deal with it if she refuses to see me."

Sydney shook her head vigorously. "No, no, Diana, you need to think positively. She may have been looking for you also."

Diana fanned her face with her hand. She looked at Sydney through bewildered eyes. "I need a drink. Sydney, go look in the pantry and look on the top shelf. Hidden way in the back, you'll find a bottle of vodka—"

Sydney jumped up. "Diana, honey, you need to calm down." She placed her hand over Diana's hand. "I'm not going to get you any alcohol. I'll get you a glass of water or some more juice, but I will *not* help you destroy yourself," Sydney scolded.

Diana glared at Sydney. "What are you talking about, Sydney? I drink occasionally. It's not as though I'm an alcoholic," she said defensively.

"Honey, you can't handle alcohol. Jeffrey told me about your drinking habit while you were in the hospital. He said that he asked June to dispose of any alcoholic beverages she found in the house."

Diana's faced turned crimson. "I can't believe that my husband put my business in the street," she yelled. Diana balled up her fist and hit the side railing on her hospital bed.

Sydney took a step backward. "Honey, Jeffrey only told me about your drinking problem because he was worried sick about you. He was hoping that I could convince you to seek medical attention."

"*Medical* attention? Diana looked at Sydney curiously. "Jeffrey knew why I drank the way I did. Whenever I wanted to ease the pain from the void I felt inside, I'd sip a few glasses of wine or drink a little vodka; I didn't bother anyone. It was therapeutic."

"Well, Jeffrey seems to think that you have a problem. He was just concerned about you, Diana. I think that it's sweet the way he dotes over you."

Diana smirked at Sydney. "Girl, don't let Jeffrey fool you. He's a great provider, but I think he's having an affair with someone."

Sydney shook her head in disgust at Diana. "Why are you so dramatic? You never could accept constructive criticism without turning the spotlight on someone else and away from you," Sydney said angrily. "I don't believe that Jeffrey's having an affair with anyone. Between taking care of you and his duties at the hospital, when does he have time to have an affair?"

Diana looked at Sydney with an expression of disbelief on her face. "Are you *kidding* me? Sydney, doctors and nurses have affairs all the time. Hospital romances are very convenient."

Sydney's eyes pierced Diana's. "I'm sure that there is a lot of that going on, but give your husband the benefit of the doubt. I think that he's faithful to you. You are truly blessed, Diana. Perhaps if you would step foot in church every now and then, you'd know that."

Diana's facial expression turned hard. "You can say whatever you want to, but I've known Jeffrey for over ten years. He's spending his free time with someone, and I'm going to find out who she is."

Sydney exhaled loudly. "Diana, don't let that overactive imagination of yours ruin your marriage." She stooped over the wood and glass coffee table to pick up her empty glass. She stood up and yawned. "Diana, can we finish this conversation tomorrow? I'm exhausted."

"Yes, let's do that." Diana covered her mouth as she yawned. "I'm tired too."

Sydney walked to the kitchen and put her empty glass in the kitchen sink. She sauntered back into the room and stood beside Diana's bed. "I'm gonna go up and get ready for bed. I enjoyed our sister talk tonight. It's amazing how we've lived so close, but yet our relationship over the years has been so distant."

Diana patted Sydney lightly on her arm. "It's pretty amazing. I think we've covered a lot of territory tonight, though. It felt good to confide in you. I've missed being able to talk to you."

"I've missed talking to you too, Diana." Sydney smiled, turned around, and walked toward the recliner to pick up her purse off of the floor.

"Goodnight, Sydney. Sleep well."

Sydney glanced back at Diana. "Goodnight, Diana." She walked toward the foyer.

Sydney and Jeffrey passed each other on the stairs as Jeffrey was on his way down to check on Diana. They said goodnight to each other right before Jeffrey's cell phone rang.

Jeffrey stopped short of entering the den after looking at his caller ID, turned, and walked back into the foyer before he answered his phone.

Sydney paused and glanced back downstairs at Jeffrey. She thought that it was strange that he dodged into the foyer to answer his phone as though he had something to hide.

Maybe my sister's right about Jeffrey, Sydney thought as she proceeded to the guest room. *Maybe he is having an affair.*

Chapter 29

Kendra sat on the side of the bed and stared at the wall. It had been four weeks since she'd had the operation to have the ovarian cysts removed. She was recovering well, physically. She stood up and walked outside of her bedroom and into the hallway and looked over the balcony. Her mother and Matthew were busy trimming the seven-foot Christmas tree that stood in the foyer in front of the double glass door.

She was amazed, yet proud of how much her mother had changed over the years. Hannah gave up her life of sin ten years ago, when she was sixty-three years old. Kendra remembered the Sunday morning that her mother came to their church for the first time. She was dressed really well in her emerald two-piece suit with shoes to match. She walked into church with her head held high and sat beside her daughter.

Kendra didn't know if she should embrace her mother or not, because Hannah did not like public displays of affection. Hannah slid her hand into Kendra's.

Kendra smiled at her mother as they sat on the front row and enjoyed the lesson that Matthew taught that day. He taught about forgiveness. His sermon came from Psalm 86:5:

For thou, Lord, are good, and ready to forgive, and plenteous in mercy unto all them that call upon thee.

Once Matthew prayed, he extended the invitation for those that wanted to be saved, healed, rededicate their life back to Christ, or join the church. Hannah rushed to the altar. Kendra went behind her to encourage and support her. She requested prayer for healing, and she wanted to be saved. Matthew and a few other prayer warriors prayed for her, while Kendra cried, praised God, and hugged her mother. She started attending their services every Sunday and became a member a month later. Since that time, she had been a faithful and avid Christian.

Kendra placed a hand over her abdomen, where her baby had lived for a short six weeks. She had decided to terminate her pregnancy during her first year at law school. At that time, she didn't want to be as horrible a mother to her unborn child as her mother had been to her. Her determination to finish law school was also a deciding factor in having an abortion. She felt that a baby would hinder her career. Tears flowed down Kendra's face as she regretted the decision she'd made so many years ago. She wiped them away on her sleeve.

Matthew looked up and saw her watching them. "Hold on, honey. I'll come up and help you downstairs. We can use an extra hand at trimming this gigantic tree that Mom picked out."

"Okay, baby; let me grab my housecoat." Kendra went back into the bedroom and into the bathroom to wash her face and disguise the fact that she had been crying. By the time Matthew had come up, she had combed her hair and applied some lip gloss.

"You look beautiful, baby." Matthew stood behind her and wrapped his arms around her. Kendra melted in his arms. "What's going on, Kendra? You seem troubled."

"Oh, it's nothing. I'm a little bored. I don't know what to do with myself."

"You'll be healed enough to go on your vacation in two weeks. Mom and I talked about it while we were trimming the tree. She's excited to be going on her first cruise."

"I'm sure she is. She hasn't traveled far outside the perimeter of North Carolina. This will be a good experience for her."

Matthew kissed Kendra's right shoulder. "That's true. The two of you should be able to relax and enjoy each other's company."

Kendra turned around to face Matthew. "I hope so. Momma thinks that I'm a little too uptight. She's always telling me to loosen up and let my hair down."

Matthew laughed. "You are a little intense at times, Kendra. Once you guys get on that ship, I'm sure your mom will find some fun things for the two of you to do."

Kendra smiled. "I know she will. Momma might be seventy-three years old, but she still loves to dance and socialize."

Matthew held Kendra a little tighter. "Yes, she does. Your mother is a feisty lady. I wish I had known her in her younger days."

Kendra frowned and eased out of Matthew's embrace. "No, you don't. Believe me, Matthew, if you had known my mother twenty years ago . . ." Kendra waved her hand in the air. "Let's not dredge up old memories. I just thank God that Momma has changed." Matthew nodded his head in agreement. She tied her robe tighter around her waist. "I'm ready; let's go down and finish trimming that over-sized Christmas tree." Kendra giggled.

Matthew laughed too. "It is humongous, isn't it? I asked your mother to pick one from off of the lot, and I think she chose the biggest one there."

"I hope you two bought enough bulbs. I would have gone to Lowe's and bought a pre-lit tree; it would have been so much simpler."

Matthew walked down the stairs, with Kendra holding on to his hand for support. "Mom likes it, so I indulged her."

Kendra's mother peered at them in a peculiar way. Frowning, she straightened her body and placed her right hand on her lower back. "Mom likes what?"

Matthew replied. "I was telling your daughter that you loved this Christmas tree from the moment you saw it."

Hannah stood back and admired the tree. "I do like it. It reminds me of trees that the family I used to work for, the Patton family, had every year. Remember how we used to wish that we were wealthy black people like them, Kendra?"

"Yes, I remember that, Momma." *Along with the unpleasant memories of those trifling boyfriends you used to bring home every Christmas Eve.* Kendra looked away from her mother and focused on the tree. "Thank God for better days."

As though reading Kendra's mind, Hannah replied. "Amen to that, chile. God has brought me from a mighty long way. He's a merciful and loving God."

"Yes, He is," Matthew witnessed. He looked at his watch. It was two fifty-nine. "I'm going upstairs to take a quick shower. I need to get back to the office. I have a four o'clock appointment. Can you ladies handle this tree while I'm gone?"

"We should be able to," Kendra answered. "If not, it'll be here when you get back," she quipped.

"Okay; I should be back home around six or six thirty." He brushed his lips across Kendra's forehead and sprinted back upstairs.

Kendra walked into the living room and sat on the cream colored loveseat. Hannah followed and sat beside her. She looked back into the foyer and admired the tree. "It is a pretty tree, Momma. You deserve to have something out of life that makes you happy."

Hannah looked at Kendra compassionately. "Actually, I chose it for you, Kendra. I thought you would get some delight out of it. You seem so sad lately."

"I am sad, Momma. I want a baby so badly, and with my health issues, I'll probably never have one." Kendra inhaled deeply and released her breath slowly. She held her head down and cupped her face in her hands.

"You never know, Kendra. Anything is possible with God."

"Yes, that's true." Kendra looked at Hannah sheepishly. "I may have missed my chance at giving birth when I decided to have an abortion in college."

Since her operation, Kendra knew that chances of her conceiving again were slim to none. She hadn't told anyone, other than Diana, about her abortion. The guilt she felt from destroying her baby was tearing her up inside. She'd longed for years to tell Hannah about her mistake. Although her mother had been saved for ten years, she found it difficult, until now, to confide her detrimental mistake to Hannah.

Hannah was shocked at Kendra's confession. "You had an abortion while you were in college?" Kendra nodded. Hannah absorbed the information for a few seconds, and then gazed at Kendra steadfastly. "Why did you do something that drastic?" Hannah asked her sharply without considering her tone of voice.

Tears rolled down Kendra's face. "Momma, please don't judge me. I had just entered law school, and I didn't think that I had any alternative. "

"You did have an alternative. You could have given birth to the child and kept going to school too," Hannah scolded. "I would have kept the child for you, if necessary."

Kendra looked at her mother incredulously. Hannah understood what that expression meant. She wasn't in a grandmotherly state of mind during that time of her life.

"It wasn't as easy to do as it sounded, Momma. Law school is very stressful. At the time, I chose my education and career over my unborn child. I've regretted that decision ever since." More tears spilled out of Kendra's eyes.

Hannah picked up Kendra's left hand and held it in hers. "I'm so sorry, honey. I wish that I had been a better mother to you when you were growing up. I remember you telling me, more than once, that you'll never bring a child into the world if you had to be the kind of mother that I was. If I had been a better mother, maybe you wouldn't have felt pressured to get rid of your unborn child. I've caused you so much pain, baby." Hannah hugged her. "Please forgive me."

"I *have* forgiven you, Momma. I'm sorry that I said those words to you. What I did wasn't your fault. I was selfish and determined at the time that nothing was going to stop me from accomplishing my goals." Kendra wiped her tears away with the back of her hand.

Hannah stood and walked into the dining room and took a napkin from the dining room table. She handed it to Kendra. "It's going to be all right, honey. I believe that God is going to heal you from this disease and that, in time, you'll be able to have a healthy baby too." She lifted Kendra's chin so that Kendra could see the reassuring smile on her face.

Kendra dried her tears away. "Let's hope so, Momma."

Matthew walked swiftly down the stairs and toward the door leading to the garage. "I'm behind schedule, Kendra," he yelled, without looking back at her. "I should be back home no later than six thirty or seven, okay?" Before Kendra could reply, he had opened the door, walked into the garage, and pulled it closed behind him.

Kendra looked at her mother with a panicky expression on her face. "The thing that's eating me alive is that I've never told Matthew what I did." Hannah stretched her eyes open wider and held her hand over her mouth. "He doesn't have a clue that any chance we had at having a baby may have been destroyed when I decided to end my pregnancy years ago. I'm afraid to tell him because I don't think he'll ever forgive me."

Chapter 30

Brandon eased his way in line at the soup kitchen at Macedonia Baptist Church. He was dressed in heavy layers of clothing, with a navy toboggan pulled so far down on his head, that his eyes were almost concealed. Once he was served, he sauntered to the back of the room and sat with two guys. He had been spying on Aquila for three days. He wanted to get her schedule down precisely before he made his move. He watched Aquila as she stood in line to get her food. He held his head down when she strolled by his table.

One of the guys he was sitting with stared after her. He looked at the other man and exclaimed, "Now, that's a beautiful woman. If I had the life I used to have, I sho' would try to talk to her." He and the other man clinked paper cups in a toast.

Brandon immediately became angry. He almost choked on his food. "Man, she wouldn't give you a second thought," he snarled.

The man looked at Brandon and grunted. "Who the heck are you?" he asked loudly. "If I want to dream about being with a pretty woman, you ain't got crap to say 'bout it! Get your butt up from our table anyway," he yelled at Brandon.

Everybody stopped eating and gazed their way. Mable walked over to the table. "Gentlemen, you all know that we don't tolerate this mess. If you can't control yourselves, I'll call the police, and I'm sure they'll be glad to escort you out," she told them sternly.

The men apologized and continued to eat. Brandon bowed his head at Mable, picked up his plate, and moved to a table where he would be sitting alone.

He had rented a car, and after lunch, he drove to the school where his sons attended. He sat on the park bench across from the school and watched as Darius and Daniel enjoyed themselves on the playground. He had planned on going back to the hotel and cleaning himself up.

Today was the last day of school before Christmas vacation. He intended to go to the school's office, show his ID, and sign his boys out of school.

Another man walked up to him and sat beside him on the park bench. "Hey, man." He addressed Brandon cordially as though he knew him. "You got a light?"

Brandon glanced at him. "No, I don't smoke." Brandon answered him curtly, with a superior attitude. He refocused on his children.

"You got kids that go to this school?"

Brandon shook his head. "No. Why?" he asked in a straightforward tone.

"I was just making conversation, man, that's all. Where you from?"

Brandon glared at the man. "Not that it's any of your business, but I'm from New York."

The man was taken aback. "I didn't mean no harm; I thought I recognized a northern accent."

Brandon relaxed a little once he realized the man was harmless. "Are you from this area?"

"Yes, I was born and raised right here in Raleigh." He pulled out a cigarette lighter and kept fumbling with it until he finally got it to light. "There we go!" he exclaimed, and then lit his cigarette. "I used to work in a factory at a major computer company. I've been laid off for two years now. I haven't been able to find work in my field, so I do odd jobs here and there, so I can help keep a roof over my family's head. My wife works as a medical assistant in a doctor's office, but she can't afford to pay the bills by herself. I go to school at night, majoring in accounting. As soon as I finish, we plan to move to Nashville, Tennessee." Brandon looked at the man suspiciously. "What's wrong, man? You look like you've seen a ghost."

Brandon coughed. "Nothing, nothing at all; I just got cold all of a sudden."

"Oh. As I was saying, we decided to move to Nashville and start a new life. My wife has family there."

Brandon stood up and rubbed his gloved hands together. *I guess you can't judge a book by its cover. I thought he was homeless.* "I understand; sometimes it's good to start over. I'm here to find work myself. I'm a teacher," he lied. I have an interview with the Wake County Public School System tomorrow."

He looked at Brandon's frumpy outerwear. "So, you're a teacher?" he asked with doubt in his voice.

Brandon stared into the man's eyes. "Yes, I am. I teach elementary education."

The man held Brandon's stare for a moment, and then glanced toward the children in the school yard. He took another puff on his cigarette and exhaled the smoke before he said, "That's good." He glanced at Brandon's clothing once more. "We need more good male role models in the school system."

Brandon nodded in agreement. He wasn't sure if the man believed him or not, so he decided it was time to end the conversation with him. Brandon looked at Darius and Daniel once more. Faking a laugh, he said, "I guess I need to keep moving so I won't get frost bite."

The man extended his hand out to shake Brandon's. Brandon shook his hand.

"It's a little nippy out here." The man nodded toward the schoolyard. "I'm surprised that they let the children come out to play today. I guess they're keeping warm by running around. Well, it was nice to talk to you, sir. I hope you have a blessed day. And I wish you much success on your interview tomorrow."

Brandon nodded. "Thanks. Good luck on your endeavors too. Sorry for being rude earlier."

"No problem." He chuckled. "I just started talking to you like I knew you. My wife tells me that I act like I don't know any strangers.

"You just never know what people are up to in this day and time."

The man nodded in agreement. "That's true."

Brandon stuffed his hands in his coat. "Have a good day." He proceeded to walk away from the man.

"You too," he replied warmly.

Brandon walked swiftly to his rental car and got in. He looked back to see if the man was watching him. He wasn't. "I guess I'll have to go with plan B," he mumbled aloud.

Chapter 31

Pricilla and Jeffrey walked down the hospital corridor toward the lunchroom. They stood in line and chose their meals. Pricilla ordered a grilled chicken salad with blue cheese dressing and lemon tea. Jeffrey chose broccoli and carrots, rice, baked chicken, and pink lemonade. They walked toward a table in the back of the lunchroom and sat down. Pricilla smiled broadly.

Jeffrey raised his eyebrows at Pricilla. "What's going on with you?" he inquired.

"I have some good news about my mother." Jeffrey listened attentively. "In my research on the Internet I've been doing for the past couple of weeks, I've learned that a woman has been searching for me too. She signed her name Ms. W. I guess she wanted to remain anonymous until she is absolutely sure that I'm her daughter. You'll be surprised at the information that's on the Internet if you have the right search criteria."

"That's true," Jeffrey agreed. "So, what did you find?"

Pricilla's eyes twinkled from the excitement she felt. "It turns out that my mother has been looking for me too. She listed my birth date, the name of the hospital that I was born in, and the fact that the child's name could possibly be Pricilla. How cool is that?"

Jeffrey gazed at Pricilla thoughtfully before he spoke. "How did she know your name if she had given you away for adoption? The birth mother doesn't have the privilege of naming the child that they're giving away. In some instances, they don't even want to know the sex of the child. Wouldn't the adoptive parents have named you?"

"I was under the same impression. Maybe she saw me." Pricilla smiled. "Or maybe she even held me," she said wistfully, "and then named me. Who knows what the circumstances were in her life? She could have decided to give me away shortly after she named me. If my adoptive parents kept my name, that would explain how she knew my name."

Jeffrey looked into Pricilla's eyes compassionately. "Pricilla, honey, I don't want you to get your hopes up. It could all be a coincidence or even a scam. You can never be too sure in dealing with the Internet. For instance, I'd be suspicious of her because she signed her name 'Ms. W.'" Jeffrey opened his hands, palms up, toward Pricilla. "What's that about? It seems to me if she were genuine and had nothing to hide, she would at least sign her first name."

Pricilla's happy countenance changed to frustration. "Jeffrey, it is *not* a coincidence or a scam. What are the chances of two baby girls being born in that hospital on that day, at the same time, whose mother gave them away?"

Jeffrey opened his mouth to speak, but Pricilla held her hand up toward him.

"And what are the chances that both babies were possibly named Pricilla?"

Jeffrey's voice was soothing when he spoke to Pricilla. "You're right. It is a slim coincidence. Whose name is on your birth certificate?"

"My adoptive parents' names are on the birth certificate; George Rufus and Ester Mae Battle. Of course the last name is different from my birth mother's. I don't even remember them that well. I was only six when they died. I've searched the Internet for descendents of the couple, but so far, nothing has surfaced."

"Well, honey, you sound like you are getting close. What are your plans now?"

"I sent an e-mail to the address that the person had on the Web site. It's been four days, but no one has replied to my e-mail. The wait is so frustrating.

"It is frustrating. I've assisted Diana on her search for her daughter too. Sometimes it's hard to decipher the truth from a scam on the Internet." The color drained out of Jeffrey's face.

Pricilla stared at him. "Jeffrey, are you okay?"

Jeffrey rubbed his chin. "I just had a scary thought."

"What?" Pricilla looked at him expectedly.

"What if you are the daughter that Diana is looking for?"

Pricilla shook her head slowly from side to side. "No way," she said with conviction. "Don't even think about that, Jeffrey. There is no way that I could be Diana's daughter."

"I hope not, but there is a slim possibility." Jeffrey stared at Pricilla. "For the sake of everyone involved, I hope not," he said seriously.

Pricilla looked away from Jeffrey's piercing eyes. "I don't think I'm her daughter," she said forcefully. "Besides, the woman signed her name Ms. W.," Pricilla told him confidently. "Diana's last name is Thompson," she reminded Jeffrey as if he didn't know.

Jeffrey chewed and swallowed a piece of baked chicken. He looked into Pricilla's eyes and said, "Diana's maiden name is Wooten."

Pricilla glanced at Jeffrey, and then diverted her attention to the clock on the wall. "I don't want to talk about it anymore. The light-hearted mood that she was in earlier had turned sullen. She picked at her salad to avoid eye contact with Jeffrey.

Jeffrey stayed silent for a couple of minutes. He cleared his throat and asked her cautiously, "Honey, how long have you known this information?"

She glanced at him and looked back down. "I told you; I started surfing the Net just a couple of weeks ago." Pricilla ate a forkful of salad.

Jeffrey ate a forkful of rice, and then he ate some carrots and broccoli, swallowed his food, and wiped his mouth. "You've made a lot of progress in only two weeks."

"I really have," Pricilla said quietly.

Pricilla finished her salad, and Jeffrey ate the last spoonful of vegetables on his plate before either of them spoke again. Pricilla took a sip of her lemon tea before she continued.

"For some reason, I wanted to be employed full time as a registered nurse when I met my mother. I want her to be proud of me."

"You met that goal; you're a full-time registered nurse here at WakeMed. But regardless, I'm sure she would have been proud of you. You have a lot going for you; especially considering the circumstances that you grew up in. Besides, she's not in any position to judge you. *She* gave *you* away."

"Yes, she did. But she might not have been financially secure enough to support me. She had her reasons for giving me up." Pricilla's eyes glazed over with tears. "I need to give her the benefit of being a good person."

Jeffrey touched her hand gently. "I'm sure she had a good reason. Whatever the case may be, I'm glad I met you. I'm going to support you, no matter what the outcome."

Pricilla's face lit up. "Thank you so much, Jeffrey. I don't have a clue as to what kind of family I came from, but I am grateful that you are willing to support me anyway."

Jeffrey shrugged. "We can't help how we came into this world, Pricilla. How we adjust to our situations and what we do to handle life's bumps and bruises is ultimately what counts. You might have been given lemons, but *you* chose to make lemonade instead of feeling sorry for yourself. Your accomplishments at such a young age are to be highly commended."

"Thanks. You sound like an old man, Jeffrey." She laughed.

Jeffrey relaxed in his chair. "I *am* a few years older than you, sweetheart."

Pricilla smirked. "True." Pricilla opened her purse, retrieved her lip gloss, and applied it to her lips.

Jeffrey drank the rest of his pink lemonade. "I have two tickets to North Carolina State's basketball game this Saturday? I know you're a Wolfpack fan, so would you like to go?"

Pricilla put her lip gloss back into her purse. "I'd love to," she said sweetly.

"I know you enjoyed Tyler Perry's play that we saw in October."

"I did. *The Marriage Counselor* was off the hook," she said passionately.

Jeffrey laughed at Pricilla's excitement. It always amazed him at how quickly her moods could change. "I thought it was time to treat you to something else."

Pricilla sat back in her chair. "Great. I'm not scheduled to work Saturday."

"I know. I checked the schedule. I don't have to work Saturday either; unless I'm put on the schedule between today and then."

Pricilla stared into Jeffrey's eyes. "I hope you can go. I really want to see the game."

Jeffrey shrugged. "If something comes up, you can invite Aquila to go with you. I'm sure it's been a long time since she's enjoyed an evening out."

"I'd rather go with you, but I'm sure she would enjoy a night out away from the children. That is, if she can release her paranoia that something might happen to them long enough to find a babysitter."

"Did she ever find out who sent her the flowers?" Jeffrey asked her with concern in his eyes.

Pricilla smoothed her hair down. "No. I still think that one of the men at church sent them to her."

"You're probably right."

Jeffrey's cell phone rang. Pricilla's eyes zoomed in on the phone as he checked the caller ID.

"It's Diana."

Chapter 32

It was Christmas Eve. Kendra walked up the steps to Diana's house and rang the doorbell. Her mother stood behind her. June opened the door and showed them into the house.

"Come in, Mrs. Woodbridge," June greeted her with warmth. "Mrs. Thompson is sitting up today. She's excited about your visit."

Kendra smiled. "Hi, June. Merry Christmas," she said cheerfully. "It's good to see you again. How are you?"

"I'm doing okay. Merry Christmas to you, too, Mrs. Woodbridge. How are you?"

"I'm well, thank God. Thank you for asking." Kendra turned around to her mother. "June, this is my mother, Hannah."

June shook Hannah's hand. "It's nice to meet you, ma'am."

Hannah smiled warmly. "It's a pleasure to meet you too, June."

"Please, let me take your coats," June offered before the two women handed her their coats.

"Thank you, June." Kendra looked through the foyer and saw Diana. Her heart went out to her. Diana had been home from the hospital for two weeks. She sat in a wheelchair with both of her legs propped up in casts. Her left arm was in a cast also.

Hannah admired the Christmas decorations throughout the foyer and the living room. Her eyes followed the winding staircase that was decorated in garland and white lights. She smiled when she saw the huge Christmas tree that sparkled with white lights and red and gold ornaments. It sat in the corner of the family room, near a huge bay window.

Kendra approached Diana carefully and hugged her lightly. "Merry Christmas," she greeted Diana in a melodious tone. "How are you, Diana?"

Diana welcomed Kendra with excitement. "Merry Christmas to you. I'm doing well, how are *you*?"

"I am well, now. The doctor says that I'm healing wonderfully. You seem to be doing okay. I brought Momma to see you. She's been very concerned about you."

Diana smiled at Hannah. "Hi, Ms. Hannah; it has been a long time. You are still as pretty as ever."

Hannah bent over and kissed Diana on her forehead. "I thank you for the compliment." She chuckled. "Even though that's not true, it makes me feel good, so I receive your kind words."

"It's the truth. Please have a seat, Ms. Hannah."

"Thanks." Hannah sat on the burgundy leather loveseat. "You have such a beautiful home. God has really been good to you, Diana."

"Yes, ma'am; He really has been good to me." Diana noticed Hannah's eyes roaming around the room. "Ms. Hannah, would you like to see the rest of the house? It's not all that, but I am grateful to be able to live here."

"I would love to see your house, if you don't mind. I bet people don't ask to walk through a person's house anymore, do they?" she asked Diana coyly.

Diana giggled softly. "I'm sure they do. I don't mind. I know you're from the old school. Let me call June to see if she will take you around."

Hannah smoothed her short gray hair down behind her neck. "Okay. That'll be fine. I know you and Kendra probably have a lot to talk about anyway."

Diana called June, who walked into the room shortly after. "Yes, Mrs. Thompson?"

"June, can you show Ms. Hannah around the house?" Diana asked her.

"Sure, I can. I'll be happy to." She looked at Hannah and smiled. "Come on, Ms. Hannah. We'll start in the kitchen."

Hannah stood up and followed June.

Kendra sat in the burgundy leather recliner. "I love this chair." She reclined it back. "Diana, God has really brought you from a long way."

"He sure has, girl. I am much better than I was the last time you saw me."

"Don't forget to praise Him for His mighty works. God had truly assigned an angel to protect you on the day of your accident."

Diana nodded. "*Somebody* up there was looking out for me," she said sarcastically.

Kendra frowned. "Diana, don't be full of pride. You know that the Lord had you covered under the precious blood of Jesus that day. If you had seen your car, you wouldn't have believed that you survived that accident," Kendra scolded her loudly. "It was nothing more than the grace of God that brought you through."

Diana was surprised at Kendra's tone of voice. "Kendra, I didn't mean to make it sound as though I'm not grateful. I know that God had mercy on me and spared my life."

Kendra's voice softened. "Thank you, Jesus. I'm sorry if I got a little loud with you, Diana, but your tone of voice was so sarcastic. It's good to know that I'm not still dealing with the Diana of times past. You were a piece of work when you got on your soap box about religion, as you called it."

Diana nodded her head in agreement. "I was about to be blasphemous, wasn't I?"

"Yes, you were. I thank God that you're changing. Prayer changes situations and people."

Diana's forehead wrinkled. "I just couldn't understand why the Lord wouldn't heal my mother. She was the most devout person I knew, yet she was in so much pain before she passed away."

Kendra pulled the lever on the recliner so that she could sit upright. "Yes, Ms. Anna was a virtuous woman. She suffered greatly before she passed away, but it's my belief that God's way of healing her was to let her enter into His rest."

Diana didn't say anything for a moment. "I believe that she is in heaven also, Kendra. Momma did her best to serve the Lord with all her might. She really loved God."

"Amen. She was a blessing to me too. There were days when I wished that she was my mother. She took good care of me while Momma went through her episodes with her boyfriends."

"Momma loved Ms. Hannah. She always prayed for her and asked God to save her. She told Sydney and me that your mother had a good heart, but she was confused about where her loyalties belonged. And you know Momma loved you like a daughter."

Kendra smiled as she thought about the warmth and love that Diana's mother had shown her. "There's no doubt in my mind about that. I loved her too. She gave me a lot of good advice over the years. If it hadn't been for her, I probably would have been just like my mother."

Diana gazed at her mother's picture that hung over the fireplace. "Well, at least you still have a living mother."

Kendra glanced at Ms. Anna's picture. "I am grateful for Momma too. I thank God that she is saved. We are so much closer now. I wouldn't trade her for anything."

"I know what you mean." Diana lowered her eyes to the floor. "I didn't fully realize, until after Momma passed, how much I loved her. I was so selfish that I took it for granted that she would always be there when I needed her."

Kendra didn't know what to say to Diana's statement, so she just nodded her head.

Diana picked up the thin iron rod that Jeffrey had given her, from beside her wheelchair, and inserted it into her leg cast and scratched her itching leg. "Excuse me, Kendra, but my leg feels like it's about to itch off. Three more weeks, and these things can come off, thank God."

"That's great, Diana. God is good. You'll be up and about very soon."

Diana carefully pulled the rod out of her cast. "I have a lot of physical therapy to go through, but if it will help me regain strength to walk again, I'm ready for it."

"I'll be happy to see you up and about again." Kendra announced enthusiastically, "Momma and I are going on a cruise in two weeks."

"That's great, Kendra. I'm sure that Ms. Hannah is excited. I can see her on the dance floor now. Who knows, she might meet a man," Diana exclaimed, laughing loudly.

Kendra chuckled. "She probably will because Momma is still feisty. She declares that there's nothing old about her but her clothes."

Diana rested her head on the pillow that was propped in the wheelchair. "I think it would be nice if she met someone."

"Anything's possible." Kendra laid her head on the back of the recliner and admired the Christmas tree. "Wouldn't it be awesome if Momma got married at her age? She never remarried after Daddy and she divorced. I think that would be cool."

"I think that would be cool too." Hannah swished into the room, snapping her fingers in the air. "If God allows my husband to find me, I'll be walking down the aisle like an old school princess," she said emphatically.

Diana and Kendra laughed. "Ms. Hannah, you still got it going on," Diana exclaimed.

"Girl, I ain't dead 'til I die," Hannah joked. She looked at Kendra and laughed. "Isn't that right, baby girl?"

"Yes, ma'am, Miss Feisty." Kendra giggled.

Hannah looked at Diana. "Baby, you have a *beautiful* home," she emphasized. "I love it, love it, love it!"

"Thank you, Ms. Hannah," Diana replied. "I thank God for it. Please make yourself at home."

Hannah clasped her hands together. "I think I will. Would it be okay if I went back upstairs to your sitting room and watched my story? I watch *The Young and the Restless* like clockwork every day."

Diana smiled warmly. "No, I don't mind at all. June likes that soap opera too. Enjoy," Diana told her.

"All right, then. I'm going up."

Kendra and Diana watched her climb the stairs.

Kendra stretched out in the recliner again. "I told Momma about my secret from college."

Diana raised her eyebrows. "Oh yeah? What did she say about it?"

"She didn't say a lot. I think that she was a little disappointed, but I expected that from her. She wanted to know why I didn't consult her before I did something that drastic. But the look I gave her answered that question. We both know that she wasn't ready to be a grandma back then."

Diana glanced up at the ceiling and shook her head from side to side. "That's true. Ms. Hannah would *not* have been the ideal grandma."

"You're right about that," Kendra said solemnly. "But I thank God that she's changed." Kendra's countenance brightened up. "She's praying with me that God will heal my body so that I can conceive when the time is right."

"I'll pray that for you too, Kendra." Diana exhaled loudly. "It must have been confession time for both of us because I told Sydney about my baby last week too. I also told her that I'm in the process of trying to locate her."

"How did she take the news?"

"She was shocked, but she is optimistic that when I find her, the child will be happy that I found her. The thing is, she's an adult now, not a child. Sydney's more confident than I am," Diana said sadly.

Kendra put her hand behind her head while she rested in the recliner. "I agree with Sydney, Diana. I think your child will be thrilled that you found her."

Diana rolled her eyes up toward the ceiling. "We'll see. I'm supposed to find out who she is before the New Year comes in." She inhaled deeply. "I pray that 2009 will be filled with healing and answered prayers."

"It will. I believe God for it," Kendra replied cheerfully.

"Sydney told me something that shocked my socks off too. Being that we grew up like sisters, I know she won't mind me telling you about it." Diana shared the news about the paternity of Sydney's daughter with Kendra.

Kendra sat upright in the recliner. "Are you kidding me?"

"No. I guess we all have some skeletons in our closet, huh? Our lives, at least mine, have been tormented because of the desperate decisions we made in our youth."

Kendra blinked back tears. "Now only God knows if our loved ones will be able to forgive us."

Chapter 33

Aquila finished wrapping the last of the children's Christmas presents. She placed them under the small tree. Pricilla came out of her bedroom and headed for the door.

"I will see you later tonight, Aquila," Pricilla told her. "I regret that I switched places with one of the nurses now. She wanted to spend Christmas Eve with her daughter before she deploys to Iraq. But the good news is, I'll be home on Christmas Day."

Aquila sighed loudly. "Pricilla, are you sure your neighbor will take good care of the kids while I do my last minute shopping?"

"Yes, Aquila," Pricilla said wearily. "Mrs. Turner has great-grandchildren about the age of Daniel, Darius, and Abigail. She takes very good care of them. She's aware that you are very protective of your children. So stop worrying, and take the kids to her house and do what you need to do." She threw her hands up in the air dramatically.

Aquila frowned, and then looked toward the bedroom door where the children sat watching television. "I guess I can leave them with her this once. I'll probably only be gone for a couple of hours."

"If you want to, you can take me to work, and that way you can take them with you," Pricilla stressed in a defeated tone.

"No, that won't work. Taking them will only distract me. I know what I want to purchase at Dillard's for First Lady Kendra. And I saw two pairs of shoes in the Nine West store that I'd like to buy for myself. I can catch the bus to Triangle Towne Center, get my items, and be back in no less than three hours."

"You can do that faster if you drive. You won't have to haul those packages on the bus," Pricilla reasoned.

Aquila gawked at Pricilla. "Pricilla, I haven't been driving that long. There is no way that I'm gonna tackle that crazy traffic on Capital Boulevard, especially on Christmas Eve."

"Well, I offered you the car," Pricilla told her flatly. "Suit yourself, but if you can drive downtown, you can drive anywhere in Raleigh." Pricilla looked at her watch. It was two seventeen. "I need to get going so I can make it to work by three o'clock. I'm pushing it as it is. I'll see you tomorrow."

"Okay. I hope you have a blessed twelve-hour shift."

After Pricilla left, Aquila called Mrs. Turner. She sat down on the couch and crossed her legs.

Mrs. Turner answered the phone on the third ring. "Hello?" she answered cheerfully.

"Hello, Mrs. Turner. This is Aquila." Mrs. Turner greeted Aquila warmly and asked her how she was doing on her job, and then she inquired about the children. Aquila replied that she loved her job and that the children were doing great. She then stated her reason for calling. "Mrs. Turner, I was wondering if you could still keep the children for me for about three hours."

"I'll be happy to keep them. What time are you gonna bring them over?"

"I wanted to go ahead and catch the next bus to the mall. Hopefully I won't be gone for more than three hours."

"That will be perfect; as long as you're back before eight o'clock. My son may come over to pick me up so I can spend the night with his family." Mrs. Turner chuckled. "We decided that would be best, so I'll already be at his house on Christmas Day."

Aquila stood back up and stooped down to pick up the scraps of wrapping paper off of the living room floor. "Oh that's sweet, Mrs. Turner.

Is your husband going to be home in time for Christmas?" Aquila walked into the kitchen with the scraps and threw them into the trash can.

Mrs. Turner's husband was an over-the-road, tractor trailer driver.

"I hope so, Aquila. He had to deliver a load to York, Pennsylvania, yesterday. He's on his way back, but now he's stuck in traffic in Fredericksburg, Virginia. He's supposed to retire in three months. I'll be glad when he does because he's sixty-four years old, and he's too old to be driving up and down the road working as hard as he does."

"Yes, ma'am; you're right," Aquila agreed. "I'm gonna get the kids ready, Mrs. Turner. I'll talk to you when we get over there."

"Well, bring them on over, honey. I'll be waiting for you." She hung up the phone without saying good-bye.

Aquila called the children into the living room and told them her plans. She instructed them to put their coats on, and gave them strict orders to obey Mrs. Turner and be on their best behavior.

Ten minutes later, she was knocking on Mrs. Turner's door. "Hi, Mrs. Turner; they've already eaten, so they shouldn't be hungry. I brought each of them a Lunchables meal and a juice box, in case they get hungry before I get back."

"They'll be fine, honey. If they get hungry, I have snacks in the house. I keep snacks in the house because of my grandchildren. Plus I have three little great-grandkids. So I'm always prepared."

"Okay; thanks, Mrs. Turner. I'll pay you whatever you charge for your time when I get back from the mall."

"Chile, I don't expect you to pay me. It would be different if you asked me to keep them all the time."

Aquila's forehead wrinkled. "Are you sure? I don't want to take advantage of your kindness."

Mrs. Turner put her left hand on her hip. "Girl, I said, no. I'm not gonna let you or anybody else take advantage of me. Sadie Turner ain't nobody's fool. Now go on, before you miss the next bus."

"Yes, ma'am." Aquila took a deep breath and smiled broadly, showing her dimples. "Kids, remember what I said now. Be on your best behavior." She kissed them each on the cheek and looked back up at Mrs. Turner. "Do you have something that I can write my cell phone number on, Mrs. Turner? In case you need to call me."

"I sure do; hold on." Mrs. Turner took a few steps to her small kitchen, grabbed a tablet and pen, and then came back and handed it to Aquila.

Aquila jotted down her name and number, circled them and handed the tablet back to Mrs. Turner. Mrs. Turner looked over the number and put the tablet down on the coffee table.

"I should be back in less than three hours, Mrs. Turner. I'll see you soon." She blew the kids a kiss and walked outside. "Bye, guys," she yelled.

The children said good-bye and Mrs. Turner closed the door. Aquila walked swiftly to the bus stop. She was there for five minutes when the bus pulled up. She stepped on the bus, swiped her bus pass and found a seat in the middle of the bus. She gazed at Mrs. Turner's house as the bus whizzed by.

Aquila's stomach felt like it was in knots. She had a nagging feeling inside. She took a deep breath, and then sat back in the seat and tried to relax.

Chapter 34

Diana listened attentively while Terry rambled off the information that he'd been holding for six weeks. She held Jeffrey's hand tightly.

"And this is her name, Mrs. Thompson," Terry pointed at the name on the document. "She lives in downtown Raleigh. If you like, I can contact her to arrange a meeting."

Diana's hands shook. "No. I—I want to do it myself."

Jeffrey sat in a chair beside Diana's wheelchair and put his arm around her shoulder. "I think you need to wait until after Christmas, Diana."

"I agree with your husband, Mrs. Thompson. I don't think you should surprise her with some heavy news like this on Christmas Eve," Terry stated.

Diana sat back in the wheelchair. "Well, I've waited for years to see my daughter; a few more days of waiting won't kill me."

Jeffrey stood up and faced Terry. "Come into my office, Terry, and we can settle your bill." Terry nodded and followed Jeffrey into his office.

Diana stared at the name. "A few more days, baby, and I can finally lay my eyes on you." Tears rolled down Diana's face. She looked up. "Thank you, Lord," she said softly.

Diana no longer doubted God's unlimited abilities to heal the broken hearted, answer prayer, or demonstrate His unconditional love.

Diana felt an overwhelming desire to share the good news with someone. Ordinarily, she would have called Kendra. Over the years, Kendra had been the one that she relied on to be her sounding board. But now she felt closer to Sydney since they had talked at her house the week before. She wanted to share the news with her big sister first. Diana pressed the button on her wheelchair and rolled into the kitchen. She reached onto the black granite countertop, picked up the cordless phone, and then dialed Sydney's number.

"Hello?" Sydney answered.

"Sydney!" Diana called her name frantically.

"What's wrong, Diana?" Sydney asked her, alarmed by her tone.

"Nothing's wrong. I found out tonight who my daughter is," Diana said, speaking louder than necessary. Sydney held the phone away from her ear. "Sydney, I'm so excited, but at the same time, I'm a nervous wreck."

Sydney giggled. "Well, God answered your prayers. Congratulations," she told Diana joyfully. "You couldn't have asked for a better Christmas present."

"I know. I'm so happy that I don't know what to do," Diana said emphatically. She looked down at her hands. "You should see my hands. They're shaking."

Sydney opened the oven door to check the turkey that she was baking. "I can imagine so. Have you called her yet?"

"No, Jeffrey advised me to wait until after Christmas. Terry agreed with him."

"Who's Terry?" Sydney put the phone on the counter beside the stove because Diana talked loud enough that she heard her clearly.

"Terry is the private detective we hired to find her."

"That's good. I'm so happy for you." Sydney pulled the turkey out, basted it, and put it back in the oven while she talked. "Are you gonna have a big dinner for her to celebrate?"

Diana wheeled her chair back into the family room while she talked to Sydney. "I hadn't thought about giving her a dinner, but that wouldn't be a bad idea. But I want to meet her in private first because I don't know how she's going to relate to me."

"I'm praying that your reunion with her will be a happy occasion."

"That's my prayer too, but I have to be realistic." Diana's tone and facial expression were melancholy. "She could have grown to hate the idea that she had a mother that gave her away."

"Remember, Diana," Sydney wagged her forefinger as though Diana was standing in front of her. "I told you to think positive. On the other hand, she could have grown up yearning for you. If that's the case, I believe that she'll be thrilled that you found her."

Diana expelled a nervous breath. "I hope you're right, Sydney."

"Whatever the outcome is, it is going to take time for you and your daughter to get to know each other."

Diana nodded her head in agreement as though Sydney could see her.

"Diana?" Sydney called her in a soft tone.

Diana cleared her throat. "I'm still here. I just feel so full."

"I understand. Just relax, and let God bless you with His love. If you want to let the tears of joy flow, that's all right too."

Tears streamed down Diana's face. "Sydney?"

"Yes, baby sister?"

Diana sniffled. "Thank you for putting up with me all these years. I apologize for mistreating you, and I want to ask you to please forgive me."

Sydney's eyes filled up with tears and they trickled down her face. "There's nothing to forgive. You're my sister, girl."

"Thanks. I appreciate you more than you'll ever know."

Sydney heard her grandsons coming down the hallway toward the kitchen. She grabbed a napkin and wiped the tears off of her face. "What are you doing for dinner tomorrow?"

"Not much. Jeffrey said that he would make some steaks and baked potatoes for Christmas dinner. That's his specialty." Diana laughed. "I can't make anything for Christmas dinner; not with one good arm."

"You didn't ask June to cook you guys a small dinner?"

"No. I released June for vacation. She won't be back until the day after New Year's Day. I told her that she needs to spend time with her family."

Sydney motioned for her grandsons to sit at the table. "That is nice of you, Diana."

Diana rolled her wheelchair back into the kitch-
en. She rolled to the refrigerator, opened it, and
retrieved a bottle of water. "It's the least that I
could do. June is so faithful. Jeffrey gave her a huge
bonus this year, so I think she's satisfied."

"If you treat people right, they won't mind
sticking by you when you need them," Sydney
assured her.

Diana sighed lightly. "I've finally come to that
conclusion too."

"Would you mind if the kids and I come over?
Teresa and the boys came home for Christmas,
and I'm baking a turkey. We're also having ham,
collard greens, yams, green bean casserole, corn
on the cob, corn bread stuffing, a chocolate cake,
and two sweet potato pies." Sydney sat down at
the table with her grandsons. She reached across
the table and pinched their jaws lightly.

"Yummy!" Diana said excitedly. "I haven't had
a meal like that in years. What time is dinner?"
Diana held the bottle in her lap, twisted off the
top, and drank some of the water.

Sydney held her head back and let out a heart-
warming laugh. "Does three o'clock sound good?
Teresa and I can pack up the whole dinner and
bring it over to your house."

"Three o'clock is perfect," Diana told her cheerfully. "I'll let Jeffrey know when he finishes tak-

ing care of business with Terry. I know he'll be thrilled to get a home cooked meal."

"And Diana, don't worry about the kids. Teresa has them under control. That girl is strict."

"I'm sure. She's young, so she still has patience with children." Diana giggled. "You were too old to be worried with them; that's why they ran over you."

Sydney laughed. "You're right. I didn't feel like dealing with those boys half the time because I was tired."

"Okay. They'll be fine. And Jeffrey will be here to help discipline them, so I'm not worried about it. All right, I'll see you guys tomorrow. Bye."

"I'll look forward to coming over. Bye."

Diana dialed Kendra's number after hanging up with her sister.

"Hey, girl," Kendra replied when she heard Diana's voice. "You couldn't get enough of me and Momma today, huh?"

"I enjoyed you all's company. But I have some good news to share with you."

Diana updated Kendra on the latest news about her daughter. After she revealed her name, Kendra screamed.

Diana frowned and looked at the phone as though she could see Kendra. "What's wrong with you, Kendra?"

"Diana, I *know* her."

Diana's countenance was distorted. "How? Where do you know her from?"

As Kendra began to explain to her just how she knew the girl, Diana dropped the phone in shock.

Chapter 35

Brandon walked up to Mrs. Turner's house and knocked on the door. It was four fifteen in the afternoon. He had watched Aquila walk the children to her neighbor's house, and then get on the bus. He decided now would be the perfect opportunity to make his move. He knocked on the door once more.

Mrs. Turner shouted through the door. "Hold on! I'll be there in a second."

Brandon saw her peep through the mini blind at him. She cracked the door open slightly.

"Yes?" she asked him crudely, with a stoic expression on her face.

Brandon flashed a smile at her, revealing perfect white teeth. "How are you, ma'am? My name is Brandon Savino—"

"And?" Mrs. Turner raised her eyebrows at him. "What do you want?"

Daniel started toward the door after hearing his father's voice. He pushed his body against Mrs. Turner's and tried to look outside.

Mrs. Turner looked down at him. "Go back inside, Daniel," she said softly.

Mrs. Turner's rudeness irritated Brandon, but considering the fact that he knew he was a stranger to her, he held his peace. "Ma'am, I'm Aquila Savino's husband. I just flew in from Nashville, Tennessee. I wanted to surprise her . . ." Brandon stopped talking mid-sentence because Mrs. Turner's face was distorted with a scowl.

"I've known Aquila ever since she moved here with Pricilla, and she hadn't mentioned anything to me about a husband."

Brandon tried to sound pleasant. "Yes, ma'am. Maybe not, but she has one."

Mrs. Turner stared into Brandon's eyes. "It's mighty funny that she's here and you're there. What's that all about?" She stepped out on the porch and folded her arms.

Brandon stepped back, stunned at her boldness to inquire into his business. He had a full view of her now. He decided that she wasn't the type of woman to play around with. At five feet ten inches, Mrs. Turner stood taller than Brandon. Her pecan brown skin was flawless and smooth for a sixty-four-year-old woman. She had on glasses, but her big, piercing, dark brown eyes shone brightly through them. He surmised that she weighed over two hundred fifty pounds.

Brandon took a step back. "We're separated, Ms.?"

"It's *Mrs.* Turner. Uh-huh. How did you know to come to my doorstep? Aquila doesn't live here."

"I know that she lives next door, Mrs. Turner. I knocked on the door to her house several times, but no one answered."

"Was she expecting you? Don't you have her phone number?"

"Actually, no, she isn't expecting me. I guess she got a new number when she came here. Her cell number that she had in Nashville is no longer in service. I missed her and my children, so I decided to fly to Raleigh to spend Christmas with them."

Mrs. Turner examined his expression. "Oh yeah?" she asked him doubtfully.

Brandon stood up straighter so that it didn't feel like Mrs. Turner was lording over him. "Yes, ma'am. We've been separated too long, and I wanted to try to reconcile with Aquila."

"Well, that would be nice if that's what *she* wants." Mrs. Turner sighed loudly. "Look, Brandon, I don't try to get in married folks' business, but Aquila hasn't so much as mentioned your name since I've met her. So it seems to me that some rotten eggs are in the chicken coop."

Brandon frowned. "I don't understand?"

"That simply means that what you're saying doesn't make sense, and it's not adding up. You show up on my doorstep looking for your wife, yet she doesn't have the slightest idea that you're in town. So again, how did you know to come to my house looking for your wife?"

Brandon was about to lose his temper with Mrs. Turner, but he counted to ten under his breath and exhaled slowly. "I figured that since you were her closest neighbor, you could shed some insight as to her whereabouts."

Mrs. Turner's eyes flashed from Brandon's head to his feet with one blink. "And what makes you think that I'm gonna give you any information about Aquila? I don't know you. For all I know, you could be some pervert."

Brandon's patience was growing thin with Mrs. Turner, but if his plans were to work, he'd have to suck it up and let her insults roll off of his back. "Mrs. Turner," he said in a gentle tone, "I understand your concern." He pulled out his wallet. "Here is my identification, and these are pictures of my wife and children."

Mrs. Turner took the driver's license out of his hand and checked the ID closely. Satisfied, she looked at the pictures of Aquila and the children. "Well, I guess you are who you say you are." She gave him his driver's license and the pictures back. "I'm not gonna tell you where she is, but I *will* tell her that you came by looking for her and the kids."

Brandon felt defeated. His plans were to get inside, have a short conversation with her, and then take the children with him back to the hotel. He knew that if he had the children, Aquila would be desperate to get them back. He wouldn't have to threaten her to come back to him because by him having the children, reconciliation was guaranteed. His plan was foolproof. He couldn't let Mrs. Turner know that he was aware that she had the children, or it would blow his cover.

"Okay, Mrs. Turner," he said in a melancholy tone. Mrs. Turner turned around to go back into the house. Brandon raised his voice and spoke loud enough so the children could hear him, hoping that at least, Darius would come back to the door. "I'll come back later. Hopefully, she'll be back soon." It worked. Darius came running to the door.

"Daddy! Daddy!" Darius pushed past Mrs. Turner and hugged Brandon around his legs. "I missed you," he told Brandon passionately. "Are you gonna take us home now?"

Brandon pretended to look surprised. "Hey, sport!" he exclaimed in a jovial tone. He picked up Darius and hugged him. "I didn't know you were here."

Daniel ran to the door. "You were right," he said to Darius, "it is Daddy." He ran to Brandon and grabbed his hand.

Brandon picked him up and hugged him too. "Hey, buddy. I am glad to see my boys," he said sounding relieved. "Look at how big you guys are." He put Darius and Daniel down. He had a wide smile pasted on his face. "I understand your line of questioning now, Mrs. Turner. You were protecting the children."

Mrs. Turner's posture relaxed. "I sure was." She observed Darius and Daniel as one clung to Brandon's arm and the other one held onto his leg. She shivered from the cold burst of wind. Daniel and Darius had on short-sleeved shirts and no shoes. She didn't want them to get sick so she told them to go back inside.

Darius looked up at her and whined, "Is Daddy coming inside with us?"

Mrs. Turner could tell by the way they held onto their father that they would be heartbroken if she sent Brandon away. She hesitated for a moment before she looked at Brandon and asked him, "Would you like to come in? It's cold out here."

"Yes, ma'am, I'd like that." Brandon followed Mrs. Turner into the small living room. He looked around for Abigail. "Did Aquila take Abby with her?" He knew that she hadn't because he saw them all walk in the house with Aquila.

"No, Abigail is in my room taking a nap. Let me take your coat, Brandon."

Brandon unbuttoned his coat and gave it to Mrs. Turner. "Thank you. I appreciate you letting me come in out of the cold."

Mrs. Turner took his coat and put it on the wooden coat hanger that was in the corner of the room. She turned back around to face him. "You're welcome." She gestured toward the couch. "Have a seat."

Brandon sat on the couch. Darius and Daniel sat beside him.

Mrs. Turner continued, "It's a good thing for you that Darius ran out to greet you because I was getting very impatient with you. I was about to go back in the house and close the door in your face."

Brandon smiled. "I could tell that you were suspicious of me. And I don't blame you. You never know who you're dealing with in this day and time."

Mrs. Turner laughed. "Yes, and especially when someone of your complexion comes strutting up here claiming to be my neighbor's husband."

Mrs. Turner was surprised that Aquila's husband was Italian. The children's complexions were light brown; they were at least two shades darker than both their parents. It never occurred to her that they were bi-racial.

Brandon nodded. "Yes, ma'am. I do understand."

There was a silence in the room. Brandon played with the boys. Abigail woke up and sauntered into the room. She looked at Brandon and, without saying a word, ran up to him and jumped in his lap. Brandon hugged and kissed her.

Mrs. Turner observed how Brandon and the children related to each other. "These children must really miss you. Maybe you and Aquila can work out your problems. I hate to see children grow up without a father."

Brandon looked at Mrs. Turner and smiled. "I agree with you totally. That's why I came to Raleigh to try to work things out with my wife, so I can get my family back."

Mrs. Turner leaned her head to one side. "Well, God is able," she assured him. "There's nothing too hard for Him to do."

Brandon shifted in his seat. He had spotted Aquila's phone number on the coffee table. He needed to divert Mrs. Turner's attention so he could decipher it better. "Mrs. Turner, will it be a bother if I asked for a drink of water?"

"No, it's not a bother. I'll be back in a minute." She walked into the kitchen.

While she was in the kitchen, he looked at the number closely, and committed it to memory.

When Mrs. Turner returned with the bottled water, Brandon drank it and stood up. "Mrs. Turner, I thank you for your hospitality. I'm gonna go back to my hotel room and clean up. Please tell Aquila that I will be back later tonight." Brandon held the empty bottle in his hand.

Mrs. Turner held her hand out, indicating that he should give her the bottle. He put it in her hand.

"She should be back soon. Are you sure that you don't want to wait for her?" she coaxed, unaware of Brandon's devious plan.

Brandon gave Mrs. Turner a clandestine smile. "I'm sure. I'll give her a call before I come back over."

The children started crying, especially Abigail. "Daddy, no, please don't leave!" she cried.

Brandon dropped down on his knees and hugged them. "I'll be back soon, guys."

"Maybe you should take them with you, Brandon. I'll call Aquila and let her know that you took them to the hotel. But you need to give me your cell phone number and the number at the hotel."

Brandon stood up. "Sure, I'll be glad to." He wrote his number on the tablet beside Aquila's number. Mrs. Turner instructed the children to get their coats and hats.

Brandon gave her a handshake and a light hug. "Thank you so much, Mrs. Turner. We'll see you later. And by the way, Merry Christmas to you."

"You have a Merry Christmas too, Brandon," Mrs. Turner replied warmly.

Brandon gathered the children, and they followed him to the car. Mrs. Turner watched them drive off.

Sometime later, Aquila knocked on the door. Mrs. Turner opened it for her. "Hi, Mrs. Turner," Aquila greeted her cheerfully. "I'm sorry, it took a little longer than I expected. It is a mad house in the mall." Mrs. Turner had the heat turned up to eighty degrees. Aquila immediately took off her coat and hung it on the coat hanger.

"I know it was. You were a brave soul to go to the mall on Christmas Eve."

"I hope the kids didn't give you any trouble." Aquila looked around. She expected them to come running out of the kitchen or one of the bedrooms. She looked at Mrs. Turner again. "Where are they?" she asked her anxiously.

"I called you and left a message on your phone. You must have it turned off. Their father picked them up; they just left not too long ago."

Aquila looked at Mrs. Turner with fearful eyes. "Brandon?" Mrs. Turner nodded. She fell to the floor on her knees. "No, no, no," she sobbed.

Mrs. Turner walked behind her and tried to pull her up. "My God, baby, what's wrong?" Mrs. Turner did her best to explain, over Aquila's sobbing, where the children were. "The children were so glad to see him that I let them go with him to the hotel—"

Aquila grabbed Mrs. Turner around her waist. "You don't understand!" she cried. "Brandon used to beat me senseless," she said between sobs. "That's why I left him. And now he's got my children," she moaned pitifully.

Mrs. Turner put her arms around Aquila. "Oh, Lord, baby, I'm so sorry. I didn't know."

Aquila stood up with the assistance of Mrs. Turner. Her knees wobbled as she staggered to the couch to sit down. She laid her head back and stared up in the ceiling, wondering if she would ever see her children again.

Chapter 36

Pricilla sat in the lunchroom with her laptop open, checking her e-mail. Her eyes opened wider when she saw one e-mail in particular. It was sent at seven thirty-one that evening.

She clicked on the e-mail and read it. The e-mail read: *Hi, Pricilla. I may be the person that you've been trying to find. I've hesitated replying to your e-mail because I didn't want to give you false hope. I believe that I am your mother, but I'm not absolutely sure. I have been searching for my daughter for a while also. I would love to meet you so we can talk. Please reply so that we can arrange to meet the day after Christmas. Be blessed.*

Pricilla let out a quiet, "Yes!" Two of her colleagues sitting at a table near her turned around to look at her.

Pricilla flipped her cell phone open and dialed Aquila's number. The phone went to voice mail.

She called Jeffrey. His phone went to voice mail also.

"Where is everybody?" she mumbled out of frustration. Gloria, one of the nurses sitting at the table beside her, asked her if she were okay. Pricilla smiled at her sheepishly. "Oh I'm fine. I didn't realize I had spoken aloud. I've just received some good news, and I can't reach anyone to share it with."

"Well, I'm here if you want to talk to me," she looked at her name tag, "Pricilla. Anytime someone gets a positive report on anything, I'm happy for them."

Pricilla glanced at the nurse's name tag. "Thanks, Gloria. I appreciate your kind words. I'll be glad to share with you later, but it has to be confirmed first."

"I understand." Gloria stood up and extended her hand to Pricilla. Pricilla smiled and shook her hand. "Allow me to formally introduce myself. My name is Gloria Driver; I've been an emergency room nurse at WakeMed for five years. And . . ." Gloria reached into her purse and handed Pricilla a business card. Pricilla glanced at the card and frowned slightly. Gloria continued. "I'm a part-time real estate agent, so if you are ever in the market for a house, please give me a call."

Pricilla examined the card, and then looked back up at Gloria. "Thanks. I'm not in the market right now, but I'll be glad to refer you to someone I know that *is* in the market for a home."

"Okay, thanks." Gloria looked at her watch. "Break time goes by so fast. I hope to see you again soon. It was nice to have met you. Take care."

"You too. It was nice to have met you also." Pricilla looked at the clock on the lunchroom wall. She had ten minutes left on her break. She clicked on the reply button and began writing.

Hi, thank you for replying to my e-mail. I'm not sure if I am your daughter either, but I'd love to meet with you to find out. I will have to work the day after Christmas; I'm a nurse. But I do have Christmas Day off. However, I'm sure that you will be spending Christmas Day with your family. If the 27th is convenient for you, please let me know. We can arrange to meet at whatever time is convenient for you. We can decide where you want to meet. Be blessed.

She was about to press the SEND button, when her phone rang. She answered it without looking at the caller ID.

"Hello, sweetheart," Jeffrey said in a sexy tone.

Pricilla smiled broadly and ran her hand through her neatly cut short hair. "Hey, you," she teased him. "I tried to call you a few minutes ago."

"I was in the shower. I saw where your number appeared on my missed calls. Why didn't you leave a message?"

"I decided to try you again later." Pricilla sighed lightly.

"How's your night going?" Jeffrey asked her with concern in his voice.

"It's going well. I'm on my lunch break now, or what's left of it." She looked at the clock; she had seven more minutes until her break was over. "How's your night going on this beautiful Christmas Eve?"

Jeffrey laughed. "It *was* going well. I've been called back to the hospital to assist with a surgery. It seems that most of the surgeons are gone on vacation. I suppose they're gone skiing, or basking in the sun on one of the islands."

Pricilla giggled. "I'm sure. I've got some exciting news!" she said in a bubbly voice.

"Oh yeah? What's going on?" Jeffrey raised his eyebrows in anticipation.

"Ms. W e-mailed me earlier this evening. She told me that she thinks that I'm her daughter, and she would like to meet with me after Christmas."

Jeffrey frowned. "She wanted to meet with you after Christmas?"

"Yes," Pricilla replied defensively. "What's wrong with that?"

"That's a short notice, isn't it?"

"I told her that I had to work the day after Christmas, but that we could arrange to meet on the 27th, if that was convenient for her."

Jeffrey cleared his throat. "Honey, do you even know where she lives? Does she still live in Nashville, where you were born?"

Pricilla covered her mouth. "Oh my God," she whispered. "I didn't even think to ask her where she lived. And she must have assumed that I still lived in Tennessee too."

"You two can't meet if you don't know where each other lives. I don't want to burst your bubble, but communicating about something this serious on the Internet is so impersonal."

Pricilla became frustrated with what she considered to be Jeffrey's pessimistic remark. "It's the sensible thing to do, considering we don't know each other," she huffed.

"I think at this point the two of you should exchange phone numbers."

"Well, that is a good idea," Pricilla said in a calmer voice, "but what if she doesn't want to exchange numbers over the Internet?"

"Then I would be suspicious of her motives. If she doesn't want to talk to you in person, over the phone, then she has something to hide."

Pricilla meditated for a moment. "You're probably right. I think I will ask her to call me before we meet." She looked at her watch. "Oh no!"

"What's wrong," Jeffrey inquired.

"My break was over two minutes ago. I need to get back to the nurses' station."

Pricilla closed her laptop without sending the message.

"Oh yeah, you'd better get going. I'm about to drive into the hospital's parking deck now, so I may lose my signal on this phone. I called to see if you wanted to spend the night together at a hotel. I'll make the reservations after the surgery is completed."

"Sure," Pricilla said hastily. "Call me later and give me the details. I'll meet you there after my shift ends tonight at three A.M." She heard Jeffrey say, "Okay," before his phone went out. Pricilla bustled toward the elevator doors with her laptop computer and phone in her hand. The elevators weren't coming as fast as Pricilla wanted them to, so she took the stairs to the second floor. In the process of walking upstairs, she dropped her phone on the stairs and it broke into pieces.

Pricilla sat at the nurses' station and called Aquila to let her know that Jeffrey and she had plans for the night. She made her rounds attending to her patients and worked three more hours before she took another break. She walked down the hallway to the small break room and bought some coffee out of the vending machine. She sat at a table and opened her laptop and composed a similar e-mail as before to her alleged mother. She asked her what city she resided in. She decided not to take Jeffrey's advice and ask for a phone number. She didn't understand why, but she didn't want to hear the woman's voice until she saw her in person.

Five minutes later, she had an instant message from Ms. W. She wrote: *Pricilla, I live in Raleigh, North Carolina. I'm aware that you may still live in Nashville, where you were born, but I'm prepared to fly there to meet you on the first plane smoking. I hope to hear from you soon. Be blessed.*

Pricilla couldn't believe her eyes. She stared at the words. *Oh, God,* she thought. *She lives in Raleigh? My mother has been right here under my nose?* "Thank you, Jesus!" she said aloud. She glanced at her watch. It was time for her to go back to her duties. *God, you're awesome,* she prayed silently. She wrote: *Believe it or not, I live in Raleigh too!*

Pricilla closed her laptop and prayed silently. *Lord, please let this woman be my mother.* Pricilla's eyes were moist with tears. *If she's not, my heart is going to shatter into a million little pieces.*

Chapter 37

Kendra and Matthew sat on a pallet on the floor in front of the fireplace. Kendra's mother had gone to a Christmas Eve service at her friend's church. They drank sparkling grape juice and ate pizza.

"This fire feels so warm and toasty," Kendra stated. She snuggled against Matthew. "We should do this more often."

Matthew put his arms around her. "It is nice." He lay on his back on the pallet and put his hands behind his head.

Kendra gazed into Matthew's eyes. "Honey, can we talk?"

Matthew's body tensed. "Sure, if that's what you really want to do." Matthew studied Kendra's face, then pulled her on top of him and kissed her passionately. "I thought you wanted to spend Christmas Eve relaxing."

Kendra laid her head on Matthew's chest. "I do, but I really need to talk to you about this before I lose my nerve."

Matthew ran his fingers through Kendra's thick, beautiful hair and moaned. "Kendra, it can't be that serious." He gently moved his finger up and down her back.

Kendra buried her face into Matthew's chest and kissed him softly. "Honey, it is *that* serious." She glanced up at him coyly. "I don't know where to start. But I'm asking you to *please* be patient and listen to me before you say anything."

Matthew sensed the despair in Kendra's voice, so he lifted her off of his chest and sat up. He gazed into her eyes. "Okay. I'll do my best."

Kendra shifted her eyes away from Matthew's piercing stare and focused on the fire in the fireplace. "Honey, do you remember when we were in law school, and we had that terrible disagreement about my salvation?"

Matthew frowned. "Yes, that was a long time ago, baby. How does that argument pertain to what you're about to tell me?"

Kendra cleared her throat and blinked back tears. "I tried to tell you several times about my condition, but the time never seemed appropriate. Either you were too engrossed with your studies, or at your part-time job, or I was busy."

Matthew scratched his head. "Yes, we were both swamped with our classes, and our part-time employment. But I don't understand; what *condition* are you referring to?"

Tears streamed down Kendra's face. "My condition of being pregnant."

Matthew stared at Kendra incredulously. "You were pregnant during law school?" Kendra nodded and dropped her eyes to the floor. "What happened to the baby? Did you miscarry? Why didn't you tell me, Kendra?"

"I tried to tell you several times. When you told me that you didn't think that we were right for each other, I didn't know what to do at that point. When you broke up with me, I had no one to turn to. Momma certainly wasn't in a position to help me, and Diana was going through something because she regretted giving her child away."

"What happened to my baby, Kendra?" Matthew asked her sternly.

Kendra stood up and paced the floor. "I wanted to finish school; I had no other alternative . . ." Kendra's knees were about to buckle, so she sat on the couch and forced herself to look at Matthew.

Matthew stood up abruptly; his eyes blazed as he scrutinized Kendra's face. "Are you telling me that you terminated the pregnancy? My son or daughter?"

Kendra dropped her head in her hands. "Yes, Matthew, that's what I'm saying. Please, please forgive me."

Matthew swiftly walked to where Kendra was sitting and stood in front of her. "Kendra, you had no right," he said angrily. "How dare you expect me to forgive you for that? You know I've wanted a son, heck, a daughter would have been fine with me. But because of your selfishness, you made a rash decision to destroy something that would have meant the world to me."

Kendra's voice was tremulous. "That's not fair, Matthew. We talked about children several times and you made it crystal clear that you didn't want children until after you were practicing law and married." She sobbed quietly.

Matthew glared at Kendra. "I would have made an exception, if I had known you were pregnant." He gestured his hands at Kendra wildly. "You should have known that."

Kendra scurried to the dining room to get a napkin. She came back and stood a few feet away from him. "How was I supposed to know that, Matthew? I could only believe what you told me." Kendra wiped away the tears with the napkin. "All I know is that I was pregnant and alone. You had broken up with me, and I had nowhere to turn. The best solution for me at the time was to do what I did."

"The best solution would have been to consult with me, the father," Matthew said indignantly.

"You knew that I was a man who tried to serve the Lord, and *that* was against my belief."

"I know that you broke up with me because you said that I wasn't right for you because I wasn't a Christian woman." Kendra took a deep breath and composed herself. "But you failed to take the mote out of your own eye. Had you been such a Christian man, you wouldn't have taken our relationship there by pressuring me for sex from the beginning."

Matthew opened his mouth to speak, but clamped his lips together. He knew that Kendra was right. His pride, however, wouldn't allow him to admit it. "Kendra, we've tried to have a baby for years. And now, given your condition, we probably won't ever have kids. I hate, with every fiber in my being, that you aborted my baby." His countenance was distorted with pain. "And *why* in heaven's name did you wait fifteen years to tell me?"

Kendra walked over to where he was standing and put his hand in hers. "Matthew, I can't explain to you why I waited so long to tell you about it, but I know within my spirit, I couldn't keep it from you any longer."

Matthew slid his hand out of Kendra's. "Tell me something, Kendra, what else are you keeping from me?"

Kendra looked at him with sorrow in her eyes. "I have no other secrets. It's been a tremendous burden on me, keeping that from you. Since I've been diagnosed with cancer, I didn't know how much time I had left, so—"

Matthew grabbed Kendra and hugged her tightly. "Don't speak anything negative into your life, Kendra."

Tears slid down Kendra's face. "I'm so sorry, Matthew."

They heard the garage door open. Kendra wiped her tears away with the soiled napkin. A few seconds later, Hannah opened the door and walked into the house. She could feel the tension in the air and noticed that Kendra had been crying.

"Kendra, are you okay?" Hannah asked her daughter.

"Yes, Momma. I'm okay. We were just having a difficult discussion, but I'll be all right. Sooner or later, I'll be just fine."

Matthew loosened his embrace. He took a step backward. Hannah lingered in the doorway, but she didn't say anything else. Matthew turned and bustled toward the door past Hannah. "I need some air." He went to the garage, got in his car, backed out of the garage, and sped away.

Hannah hurried into the den toward Kendra. Her face was distorted with frown lines as she observed the despair in Kendra's eyes.

Kendra collapsed on the couch and gazed at the door as though she was in a trance, wondering when Matthew would return home. Tears slid down her face.

Hannah sat on the couch beside her and touched her arm gently. "Kendra, what's wrong?" she asked her in a soothing voice.

Kendra looked at Hannah and burst into tears. "I told him about the baby, Momma," she said, sobbing. Hannah rubbed Kendra's back to console her. Kendra put her head on Hannah's shoulder. "He was so angry and hurt by my confession that he probably won't come back home." She looked up into Hannah's face. "Considering how deceitful I've been with him, I can't blame him if he never comes home."

Chapter 38

Aquila frantically searched for her cell phone in her purse. It was buried underneath her wallet and other items that she had stuffed into the small purse. She opened it to check for messages. "Oh Lord, my phone *has* been off," she told Mrs. Turner. "I had it on the charger before I left home because the battery had died. In my rush to get the kids over here, I unplugged it and threw it in my purse, and I forgot to turn it back on."

She pressed the END button to turn it back on, and then listened to her messages. Sure enough, Mrs. Turner had left her a message telling her about Brandon taking the children. There was a message from Pricilla, asking Aquila to call her as soon as possible. Another message from Pricilla stated that she wasn't coming home after she got off work at three A.M. because she and Jeffrey were going to spend the rest of the night at a hotel. She told her that she'd see her around three or four o'clock on Christmas Day. Pricilla sounded excited as she told Aquila that she had some wonderful news to share with her. Aquila wondered momentarily, what it could be, but she had a more pressing issue to contend with: her children.

While Aquila listened to her messages, Mrs. Turner remembered that Brandon had jotted his phone numbers on the pad. Her countenance brightened. She stood up, walked over to the coffee table, and reached down to pick up the pad. "Aquila, I just remembered that Brandon wrote his phone numbers down on the pad besides yours." She handed the pad to Aquila. "Before he left, he said that he would call you to let you know he had the children." Mrs. Turner frowned slightly. Aquila gave her a curious look. "Now that I think about it, when I talked to him on the porch, he claimed he didn't have your phone number. It didn't even occur to me, until now, that he must have seen your number on this pad." Mrs. Turner shook her head. "I bet that's why he asked me for a drink of water, so that he could copy your number. He's a sly ole fox, isn't he?"

"He's always considered himself to be a clever man," Aquila told her. Her eyes had a twinkle of hope in them as she reached out for the pad. She pressed the END button when she heard the automated voice messenger say, "End of calls." She was about to dial the number when her phone rang.

"Hello?" she answered anxiously.

"Hello, Aquila." Brandon responded with an obvious smile in his voice.

"Bring my children back home, Brandon." Aquila blurted out in a voice of sheer desperation.

"That's what I intend to do, sweetheart," Brandon crooned. "I called to let you know that we'll be there soon."

"Why'd you steal my children!" she yelled through the phone. "You had no right, Brandon," Aquila said in a weaker, trembling voice.

"I didn't steal *your* children," Brandon said in a gruff voice. "They're our children, and you had no right to take them away from me."

Aquila didn't want to exacerbate Brandon's anger for fear that she'd never see her children again. She tried to reason with him. "It wasn't my intention to take the children away from you, but I couldn't take anymore abuse from you. I just had to get away from you for just a little while," she lied.

Brandon took a deep breath so that he could calm down. He cleared his throat. "I sincerely apologize. I've just been under a lot of pressure lately. I promise you that I won't hit you again. I just want my family to come back home."

Aquila couldn't believe that Brandon was so nonchalant about what he'd done to her. His hollow promise not to hit her again echoed through her head as though he'd said it from a snow capped mountain. Nonetheless, she had to pretend to accept his apology in order to coax him to bring her children home.

"I understand that you've been under a lot of pressure," she said weakly. "I accept your apology, but Brandon, please bring my children back to me."

"I will bring them back on the condition that you agree to come back home with me," Brandon stated flatly.

"I'll do whatever you want me to," Aquila agreed solemnly. "Just come here right away so we can talk about it, okay?" she pleaded.

Brandon had a triumphant smile on his face. "Okay, sweetheart. I'll see you in about an hour. The children and I are having dinner right now, and as soon as we finish, we'll be on our way."

Aquila breathed a sigh of relief. "Thank you, Brandon. I can't wait to see you guys."

Aquila couldn't care less if she ever saw Brandon again, but she said what she had to say to convince him to bring her children back to her.

Once she got them back in her possession, she'd have to find the courage to deal with him.

"Okay, honey." Brandon replied. We'll see you soon." He hung up the phone.

Aquila closed her cell phone with trembling fingers. She laid her head back against the sofa, and then looked back up at Mrs. Turner. "He said that he would bring them back in an hour."

Mrs. Turner sincerely apologized to Aquila about letting Brandon take the children. She described the encounter she had with Brandon and told Aquila how well he and the children related to each other.

Aquila's eyes were red and puffy from crying so much. "Brandon loves his children, Mrs. Turner. He wouldn't do anything to hurt them. He just has a problem controlling himself where I'm concerned."

Mrs. Turner used her left forefinger to push her glasses up on her nose. "What is his problem with you, Aquila? The way he talked about you today, I thought he loved you to death."

Aquila's laughter was filled with sadness. "That's the problem; he does actually love me to death. He's literarily tried to love me to death, by beating me to death."

Mrs. Turner's face was distorted from confusion. "What's wrong with him? He sure had me fooled. You should have heard him saying, yes ma'am and no ma'am. He was so polite."

"Brandon has the ability to come on like Prince Charming when it serves his purpose. His problem with me is he's a jealous maniac. When I met him, and for a short while after we were married, he treated me with such respect and love. And one day, like Dr. Jekyll turned to Mr. Hyde, he was a changed man."

Mrs. Turner shook her head slowly from side to side. "Does he have a mental problem or something?"

Aquila hunched up her shoulders. "Sometimes I think that he does. I wonder if he was affected when he was deployed to Afghanistan or maybe when he was in Iraq. His moods change so suddenly at times."

"Are you sure that he won't harm the children?"

"I'm certain about that. Like I said, he is charming with everybody except me. His co-workers really like him. He has quite a few friends who think he's a good man, and some of our neighbors think the world of him."

Mrs. Turner propped her elbow on the chair's arm rest. She rested her face in her right hand. "He could have a mental problem, but he's wise enough to conceal it from everybody."

Aquila interlocked her fingers as she rocked her upper body back and forth on the couch. "He doesn't try to conceal it from me. I seem to be the target that triggers his anger."

"Well, he looks like he's a lot older than you," Mrs. Turner speculated.

Aquila gazed at the floor with a pensive expression on her face. "He is older than I am; he's thirty-six and I just turned twenty-four."

Mrs. Turner scrunched up her face. "Well, how old were you when y'all got married?"

Aquila glanced back up at Mrs. Turner. "I was eighteen and he was thirty."

"He robbed the cradle," Mrs. Turner said indignantly. "He should have been put in jail."

Aquila smiled sadly and said, "He was wise enough to wait until I turned eighteen, and he married me before he touched me. So there was no chance that the law could intercede."

"Uh-huh," Mrs. Turner surmised. "He's probably insecure and jealous because he thinks someone younger will take you away."

Aquila sat up abruptly. "I don't know how he could be insecure. I didn't go anywhere but to the grocery store and back home," she said defensively. "He took me anywhere else I went. And you saw how I dressed when I came to Raleigh." Mrs. Turner nodded her head. "I dressed like an old lady. Not only did I dress like one, I acted old too. I never wore makeup or got my hair done."

"No matter how old fashioned you dressed, or whether you wore makeup, you are a pretty girl, Aquila. And not only that, you have a gentle, kind spirit. When he sees you now, he's gonna be surprised. You look really glamorous now. He was probably controlling because he didn't want to lose you."

Aquila rolled her eyes up toward the ceiling. She was offended by Mrs. Turner's remarks because she felt like Mrs. Turner was trying to vindicate Brandon's behavior. "Well, he should have found a better technique than physical abuse to control me. 'Cause all he did was cause me to hate him."

Mrs. Turner held up her hand toward Aquila. "Oh, I'm not excusing him for that, baby," she said apologetically. "He needs to be put in jail. If I had known he had abused you, he would have never left here with your children; that's for sure."

Mrs. Turner's husband, John, unlocked the door and came in. He greeted Aquila and gave his wife a questioning look.

Aquila stood up. "I'm gonna go home and put up these packages, Mrs. Turner. Brandon should be there in less than an hour." She glanced toward John, but wouldn't look directly at him because she was ashamed of her unkempt appearance. "It's nice to see you again, Mr. Turner." He replied likewise to Aquila. She walked to the corner of the room, grabbed her coat, and put it on. She hastened toward the door with the packages in hand.

Mrs. Turner followed Aquila to the door and touched her on the shoulder. "I'm gonna call you every fifteen minutes to make sure you're okay. Or if he gives you any trouble, blink your lights twice, and I'll call 911," she suggested.

Aquila nodded. "Aren't you expecting your son to pick you up?"

"I can call him and tell him that John is home now, so John can drive us to his house tomorrow if need be."

Aquila unlocked and opened her front door. She mechanically placed the beautifully wrapped packages around the Christmas tree. She pulled off her coat, hung it in the closet, and sat on the couch for a few minutes. She tried to call Pricilla to let her know what had transpired with Brandon. Pricilla's phone service stated that her number was unavailable and she could not be reached at the moment.

She dropped her head into her hands and said a prayer. "Lord, please give me the strength to be able to deal with Brandon. Please help him to understand that I don't want to be married to him any longer. Since I've been living here, I know that you have a better life for me than what I endured with him. As long as you give me breath, strength, and courage, I don't intend to let him abuse me anymore." She exhaled loudly. "Lord, I know that I'm wrong for saying this, but I'd rather see him dead than let him touch me again."

Aquila's prayer was interrupted by her ringing cell phone. She answered promptly. Brandon told her that he was on his way, and he should be there in a few minutes. Aquila told him okay and hung up the phone. She went to the bathroom to brush her teeth and saw the unkempt image of herself in the mirror; her mascara had run down her face, and her hair was displaced as though she hadn't combed it all day. She didn't want the children to see her in such disarray. She decided to take a quick shower and change clothes.

She put on a red crew neck sweater, a pair of black jeans, and a low heeled pair of black boots. Her eyes were still puffy from crying, but she reapplied makeup to disguise it the best that she could. There was a knock on the door. She hurried out of the bedroom and asked who it was.

Abigail tapped on the door once more. "Open the door, Mommy," she said sweetly.

Aquila flung the door opened and scooped Abigail up in her arms. Daniel and Darius hugged her gently around the waist. She shifted Abigail to her left hip and used her right arm to hug Darius and Daniel. Brandon strolled in confidently behind the children and closed the door.

"Oh my God," Aquila said nervously, "I'm so glad you guys are back. She kissed Abigail on her cheek and put her down. "I missed you guys," she exclaimed. They told her that they missed her too, but they'd had fun with Brandon. They ran to the Christmas tree and rummaged through the presents. Aquila glared at Brandon. To her surprise, she didn't fear him. Instead, she felt a wave of hatred wash over her entire being. "You must be out of your mind," she scolded.

Brandon looked at her with uncertainty. She had never approached him with such aggression. "Hey, baby," he said softly. His eyes scanned her body. "You look beautiful; you've changed your entire appearance.

Aquila gawked at him, ignoring his compliment. "Don't you dare stand there and act like you haven't done anything wrong," she said vehemently. "What makes you think that you can slither to my neighbor's house and take my children from me like a thief in the night?" she shouted.

She remembered the scripture that she'd read recently in Proverbs 17:12. *Let a bear robbed of her whelps, or cubs meet a man, rather than a fool in his folly.* When Brandon took her children, the crippling fear she'd felt toward him was replaced with a mother's spontaneous courage to protect her young ones.

The children stopped rummaging through the packages and focused on Aquila with wide open eyes. "Mommy, are you mad at Daddy?" Abigail asked innocently.

Aquila cleared her throat. She blinked back angry tears. "Sweetheart, yes, I am a little upset with your father."

"But why, Mommy?" Darius asked her. Aquila glanced at Darius, but she was too angry to respond to him properly. She just shook her head and said nothing.

Brandon stooped down to the children's level. "I think I upset Mommy because I went away with you guys and she didn't know where you were."

Daniel walked over and put his hand into Aquila's. "Mommy, please don't be mad with Daddy. We had fun with him. He took us to McDonald's, and we played, and then we went to his hotel room," he said excitedly. Darius and Abigail's eyes sparkled with excitement too, as they giggled and nodded their heads in agreement.

Aquila forced herself to smile at Daniel before she patted him on the arm and walked to the couch. "That's great, honey," she told him softly. She plopped down on the couch and gazed steadfastly at Brandon. Brandon stood in the middle of the room, rubbing his hands together. "How did you find us?" she asked him forcefully.

Brandon glanced at the children and put his hands in his pockets. "Can we talk in private? I don't want to have this discussion in front of the children."

Aquila looked at the children, who were chasing each other around the room; playing the game of 'Tag.' She cut her eyes back at Brandon. "Kids, go to Aunt Pricilla's room and look at TV while Daddy and I talk, okay?"

Daniel looked at Brandon. "Daddy, please don't leave without us. Okay?" Darius and Abigail stood in the doorway to Pricilla's bedroom, looking at Brandon with pleading eyes.

"I won't," Brandon said confidently. "But I need to talk to your mommy first, okay?" Satisfied that Brandon wouldn't go anywhere, they nodded their heads and went into the bedroom and turned the TV on to the *Disney Channel*.

Aquila stood up and walked into the kitchen. Brandon followed her. She stood near the sink with her arms folded across her stomach. "I asked you how you found us," Aquila demanded to know.

Brandon noticed Aquila's eyes shift toward the set of knives that were placed on the backside of the countertop. He stood a few feet away from her, heedful not to make her feel threatened. "I hired a private detective."

Aquila shook her head in disgust. "Brandon, why can't you just leave me alone?" she huffed.

Brandon eased closer to her. "I can't leave you alone because you're my wife."

Aquila shook her head from side to side. "All I was to you was a punching bag."

Brandon's forehead wrinkled, and his eyes were sorrowful. "I'm so sorry. I'll never hit you again." Aquila looked at him with blatant disbelief. "I promise you that I've changed," he said passionately. "Since you've been gone, I realized how badly I've treated you, and I promise you, I'll never, ever lay another hand on you."

Aquila scoffed. "How many times have I heard that lie, Brandon? Fifty, sixty, a hundred?" she said sarcastically.

Tears stood in Brandon's eyes. Aquila was not impressed; she'd seen him shed crocodile tears several times. "Please forgive me." He let a tear roll down his face, and then he moved closer to Aquila. She moved closer to the knives. "If you'll take me back, we can go to a marriage counselor. I just need you back in my life, Aquila," he beseeched.

Aquila's composure was obstinate. Brandon wiped the tear away with the back of his hand. He sat down at the kitchen table and tried to look pitiful. "On the phone earlier, you said that if I brought the children to you, you would do whatever I wanted."

Aquila looked away from Brandon's stare. "I'm sorry, I—"

"At least let's talk about it, for the children's sakes." He relaxed his back in the chair and looked at Aquila with pleading eyes.

Aquila's quick angry reaction startled Brandon. He sat up straight. She walked up to his face and stared down at him. She was amazed at her new-found courage. Her fear was replaced with the confidence of a woman who had embraced inner empowerment.

"The only thing we need to talk about is getting a divorce," she told him solemnly. "I will never allow you or any other man to abuse me again. So don't try to use my children to sweet-talk me back into your life because I'm too through with you.

You almost killed me the last time, but God made a way for me to escape." Aquila talked with such strong emotion, that she was almost breathless. She stopped for a moment to catch her breath, and then continued. "I would be a fool to even entertain the idea of living with you again."

Brandon dropped his head into his hands. Aquila moved back over to the counter in front of the sink, within reaching distance of the knives. Brandon looked back up at her and cracked his knuckles loudly. He probed Aquila's face, and then expelled a deep breath. Once Brandon cracked his knuckles and snorted like a bull, Aquila knew what was coming next. His next move would be to strike her. Aquila looked at him unflinchingly and planted her feet firmly on the floor. She positioned herself to where she could easily grab a knife if she had to.

Brandon saw the scenario of what Aquila had prepared to do. He realized that Aquila was not afraid of him anymore, and that she was prepared to defend herself. He quickly withdrew his intentions. It was time to use a more dexterous approach to convince her to submit to his authority. He sat perfectly still in the chair and spoke to her softly.

"I'm truly sorry, Aquila. I will never hurt you again. I love you, and I'm willing to do whatever it takes to make it right with you. If you want to get your high school diploma, go to college, or get a job, I'm willing to support you. I know that I was wrong by trying to control you, but if you'll give me one more chance, I'll make it up to you," he pleaded.

Aquila looked at Brandon in amazement. "I already have my high school diploma *and* I work. I've accomplished the two simple things that I wanted to do when I lived with you."

Aquila's announcement about her job was no secret to Brandon. Nonetheless, he acted like he didn't have a clue. "Congratulations," he said, trying to sound surprised, but excited. "I'm proud of you."

Aquila shook her head from side to side. "Don't pretend to be proud of me when that's the very thing that you pounded on me about before I left you." Aquila's face became distorted with pain. "How could you do that to me, Brandon? All I wanted to do was go to school and better myself, and you denied me that right."

Brandon looked at Aquila compassionately. "I . . . really don't have an explanation." He diverted his eyes toward the back door of the kitchen.

"So why should I go back to Tennessee with you and live the miserable life you supplied me with?"

Brandon was thoughtful as he rubbed his hands together. He glanced at Aquila and looked down at the floor. "All things considered, you shouldn't. But I have seen the error of my ways." He looked back up at Aquila with pleading eyes. "If you allow me to, I'll show you how much I've changed. We can work out our marriage together."

Aquila put her left hand on her hip. "Brandon, I did everything humanly possible to please you, but you didn't appreciate me. It seemed like the kinder I was to you, the meaner you became to me. The last time you beat me, I knew I had to flee for my life because I could see in your eyes that you wanted to kill me."

Brandon dropped his head. "Aquila, I don't know what came over me, but I do not have a desire to kill you."

Aquila sighed. "The same thing came over you as always. You looked at me and decided today would be a good day to beat up on Aquila."

Brandon shook his head. "I never meant to hurt you. I just hate it when you defy my orders."

"Your orders?" Aquila scoffed. "Brandon, you're not in the military anymore." Aquila pointed to herself. "And in case you haven't noticed, I'm not one of your subordinates in the Marines. I'm a grown woman."

"I know you are a grown woman, and I sincerely apologize for treating you like a child."

"No child deserves to be abused the way you abused me." Aquila gazed at Brandon. "You need to seek help for your mental issues."

Brandon sighed. "I probably do, Aquila. I promise you that I will seek help if you come back home and support me." He looked up at the ceiling; his eyes were watery. "I won't be able to do it without you."

For the first time since he'd abused her, Aquila felt sorry for Brandon. She dropped her eyes toward the floor. She looked back up at him with compassion. "I'm sorry, but I can't allow myself to be vulnerable to your needs anymore." She composed herself. "And I will not be manipulated into living a life of turmoil and fear. You may be willing to change, but as far as I'm concerned, our marriage is over."

Brandon blinked back tears and stood up carefully as not to spook Aquila because she still hovered near the knives. "Well, if that's how you really feel, there's nothing more that I can say." He stared into Aquila's eyes. "If it means anything to you, I do love you, and I sincerely apologize for hurting you."

Aquila looked away from his pleading eyes. "I'll have to learn how to forgive you, Brandon, for the kids' sake. But I don't want to be married to you any longer."

Brandon cleared his throat. "I understand." He realized that his strategy to manipulate Aquila into coming home with him had failed. Since the begging and self-pity strategy failed, he planned to use what mattered most to her; the children. He let his eyes roam around the room. "So you had rather let your children live here, in this ragged house, than in the nice home that I provided for you?"

Aquila looked at Brandon with determination in her eyes. "This place may be ragged, but since I've been living here, I have peace of mind. For a while, I missed living in our—or rather, your beautiful home. But I'd rather live in peace in this house, than live a life of torture with you." Brandon shook his head in disgust. "And as far as the children are concerned, they're going to live wherever I live."

Brandon saw the determination in Aquila's eyes. He realized that there was nothing else he could say to convince her to come home. He scrutinized her face for a moment, and then said, "Okay, I guess you've made up your mind."

Brandon felt like the only alternative left was to play on the children's emotions. He turned his back to Aquila and walked to the living room and toward the bedroom where the children sat. "I have to leave guys," he said in a melancholy tone. "I'll see you later, okay?"

Aquila followed Brandon into the living room.

The children ran out of the bedroom. "Daddy, wait!" they screamed. "We want to go with you," Daniel shouted. Darius didn't say anything, he just held onto Brandon's arm.

Abigail started crying. "Don't leave me, Daddy," she pleaded.

Brandon hugged them. "I have to go guys. I'll be back to see you tomorrow so we can spend Christmas Day together, okay?"

"Mommy, make Daddy stay," Abigail cried pitifully. Daniel and Darius cried too.

Aquila picked Abigail up and held her tightly. She rubbed Daniel and Darius on their backs. "He'll be back to spend Christmas with you guys tomorrow." She lifted Darius's chin with the palm of her hand so that he looked into her eyes. "Okay?" Darius yanked his head out her hand and buried his face into Brandon's body and cried.

Brandon felt triumphant; his scheme had worked. He spoke loud enough for the children to hear him over their crying. "They can spend the night with me tonight if you don't mind," he told Aquila.

Darius stopped crying long enough to ask Aquila, "Can we, Mommy, please?"

Aquila shook her head. "I'm not letting you guys go anywhere else without me." Abigail burst into tears again.

Brandon smiled victoriously. "Why don't you come too?" he asked Aquila.

Daniel stopped crying long enough to exclaim, "Yes, Mommy, that would be fun." Darius agreed.

Aquila sighed heavily. She looked at Brandon and shook her head in defeat.

"I guess that will be okay," she said reluctantly. She put Abigail down. "Well, I need to pack us some clothes for tonight and tomorrow." She headed for the children's bedroom, and then turned around and looked at Brandon. "Do you mind taking the kids in the bathroom and cleaning their faces?"

"Not at all," Brandon stated eagerly. He motioned for the children. "Come on, guys." They followed him into the bathroom.

Aquila walked into the children's bedroom and closed the door. She dialed Pricilla's cell phone number again. Her phone went straight to voice mail. *What in the world is going on with Pricilla's phone?* she thought. She dialed Pricilla's work number at the hospital. The nurse told her that Pricilla was with a patient and stated that she could take a message. Aquila left the message for Pricilla to contact her as soon as possible. She told the nurse that the matter was urgent. The nurse told her that she would relay the message.

Aquila called Mrs. Turner. Her husband answered the phone, and after Aquila asked to speak to Mrs. Turner, he called her to the phone.

"Hello? Are you okay, Aquila?" Mrs. Turner asked her anxiously.

"Yes, ma'am, I'm fine." Aquila hesitated for a moment before she spoke again. "Mrs. Turner, Brandon and the children are begging me to go back to the hotel with them. I wanted to let you know where I am, so you won't be worried." Aquila sat on the bed.

Mrs. Turner frowned. "Are you sure that's a good idea?"

"I'm sure. The kids wanted to spend Christmas Eve with their father, and then come back here on Christmas morning."

Mrs. Turner exhaled loudly into the phone. "Well then, let them spend the night with him, and he can bring them back in the morning."

Aquila got off of the bed and began to take some of the children's clothes out of the drawers. "I can't take that chance," she stated emphatically.

"What chance? What are you saying, Aquila?"

"I can't take the chance on him skipping town with them."

Mrs. Turner rubbed her left arm. "Has he threatened to do that?"

Aquila pulled the small suitcase from under the bed. "No, ma'am; I just don't intend to let them out of my sight as long as he's in town."

"Where is he now?"

Aquila double checked to make sure that she had packed their underwear. "They're sitting in the living room, waiting for me." She tried to zip up the bulging suitcase. It was too small to hold the clothes that she'd packed. Aquila dumped the clothes out of the small suitcase and reached under the bed for her large suitcase. Frustrated from having to repack the clothes, she exhaled loudly as she stood up. "Mrs. Turner, I need to pack the rest of our things. Don't worry; I'll be okay, as long as I'm with my children. You have my cell number; call me if you feel the need to. And I can give you Brandon's cell phone number and ask him for the number to the hotel."

Mrs. Turner picked up the pad that Brandon and Aquila had written their numbers on. "I already have those numbers, remember?" She examined the numbers and tossed the pad back on the table. "But I still feel uneasy about you going with him."

Aquila tried to sound cheerful to ease Mrs. Turner's concerns. "I'll be fine; I'll call you tomorrow to wish you a Merry Christmas, okay?"

Mrs. Turner sighed loudly. "Okay, but please be careful. And if he starts acting crazy, don't hesitate to call the police."

"Don't worry, I will. Thanks for everything, Mrs. Turner." Aquila said good-bye and finished packing their clothes.

Mrs. Turner went to the window, opened her blinds, and looked out into Pricilla's driveway. She checked to see what kind of car Brandon was driving. "John, come here," she called to her husband. John looked at her strangely, but he went to see what she wanted.

"What type of car is that?"

"It's a Toyota Corolla. Why?"

"I need to know what type of car Aquila's husband is driving. I have a strong feeling that I'm gonna need to report him to the police."

Chapter 39

Pricilla unlocked the door to her house. "Merry Christmas, everybody," she said in a melodious tone. She walked through every room in the house. *Where in the world is everybody.* She walked back into the living room. The presents were still wrapped neatly around the tree. *Something's wrong. It's three forty on Christmas Day and . . .* She ran out of the house and next door to Mrs. Turner's house. She knocked hard on her door several times, but no one answered.

Frustrated, Pricilla walked down the porch steps. She couldn't call anyone because she had dropped her cell phone on the stairs in the hospital and it had shattered to pieces on her way back from lunch last night.

She ran to her neighbors, the Redmonds', house. The Redmond family's home was located on the other side of Mrs. Turner's. She asked them if she could please use their phone to make an emergency call, and they allowed her to. She called Aquila, but her phone went instantly to voice mail. Then she dialed Mrs. Turner's cell phone number. Mrs. Turner answered, and after Pricilla explained why she had called, Mrs. Turner updated her on what had transpired.

"You mean to tell me that she hasn't come back home yet? Oh my God, I started to insist that she stay home. I hope she is all right," Mrs. Turner said into the phone.

Pricilla nervously patted her left leg. "I do too. He must have threatened her, because I don't think she would have gone with him otherwise. Brandon is crazy." Pricilla's voice trembled slightly. "Oh my Lord, I hope nothing has happened to Aquila."

"I asked her did he threaten her to make her go with him, and she said no."

Pricilla paced back and forth in the Redmonds' small living room. "Mrs. Turner, Aquila was probably afraid to say anything."

"I have his phone number and the hotel's number. Hold on and let me call the numbers from my son's home phone." Pricilla waited impatiently. When Mrs. Turner came back to the phone, she said. "Pricilla, I'm so sorry, but both of those numbers were bogus. I'm really sorry."

"Did she tell you what hotel they were staying in?" Pricilla asked her frantically.

"No, she didn't," Mrs. Turner said wearily. "I don't know *why* I didn't ask her. But I did notice the kind of car he was driving; it was a white Toyota Corolla."

Pricilla patted her temple lightly, trying to will herself to think clearly. "Okay, okay; I'm going to walk to the police station and see what they can do."

The police station was only two blocks away from Pricilla's house. It took her less than five minutes to get there. Pricilla went into the police station and came out even more upset than when she had gone in. They informed her that they couldn't do anything until Aquila had been missing for twenty-four hours or more. The last time they had been seen was at nine thirty-five the night before according to Mrs. Turner.

Pricilla went back to her neighbor's house and called Mrs. Turner. She told Mrs. Turner that she hated to keep interrupting the Redmonds because they were having Christmas dinner.

"I hate for you to have to keep interrupting their dinner too. I'm coming home, Pricilla. That way, you can use my phone and call the local hotels and hospitals and such."

"Okay, that will be better. I'll have more privacy," she whispered to Mrs. Turner. "I'll wait for you inside my house.

Pricilla thanked her neighbors for letting her use the phone. She walked back outside into the frigid air, and then went to her house to warm up and wait for Mrs. Turner to come home.

When he drove into their driveway, Mrs. Turner's husband blew the horn to let Pricilla know that they had arrived home. Pricilla rushed outside and followed them into their house. Pricilla hugged Mrs. Turner and greeted her husband. Mrs. Turner told her to go ahead and start making the calls. Pricilla called the hotels and hospitals. None had any information to give her. She left Mrs. Turner's phone number for the hospitals to call in the event that Aquila turned up for emergency care.

Pricilla looked at her watch. It was six o'clock Christmas evening. She would have to wait at least three hours and thirty minutes before she could file a missing person's report with the police. *I wonder if they'll do anything then,* she mused.

Mrs. Turner urged Pricilla to eat something. Pricilla tried to force down the food. Ten minutes later, Mrs. Turner's phone rang. She answered it and listened intently, saying, "Yes," occasionally. Pricilla watched her anxiously. Finally, Mrs. Turner hung up the phone. "Pricilla," Mrs. Turner called her name as evenly as she could. "That was the hospital where you work. They called to say that an ambulance had brought Aquila—"

Pricilla jumped up from the kitchen table. "Oh my God," Pricilla's voice trembled. "How is she?"

"They just said that we need to get to the hospital as soon as possible."

Chapter 40

Pricilla and Mrs. Turner rushed through the emergency room doors. Mrs. Turner inquired about Aquila at the Intake window. The lady directed them to the nurses' station. One of Pricilla's co-workers was sitting at the nurses' station.

"Hey, Pricilla," Jackie, her co-worker said. "You're back at work already? You can't get enough of this place, huh?"

Pricilla didn't bother to greet her. "Jackie, which triage room is Aquila Savino in?"

Jackie frowned at Pricilla. "Who?"

Pricilla breathed heavily. "Aquila Savino," she said slowly to make sure that Jackie understood her.

Jackie entered the name into the computer. She looked up at Pricilla with sorrowful eyes. "She was the young lady that was brought into E.R. by ambulance a short while ago."

"So what triage room is she in, Jackie?" Pricilla asked her impatiently.

"Oh, that was your friend, the one that lives with you? Poor baby, she looked so pitiful."

Pricilla glared at Jackie. "Which room, Jackie?" she demanded to know.

"She's in room three, but they're still—" Jackie didn't get a chance to finish her sentence because Pricilla and Mrs. Turner walked away while she was talking and bustled down the hall toward room three.

Pricilla opened the door. Aquila lay on the gurney as the doctors worked on her. Pricilla couldn't tell if she were unconscious or had been given medicine to put her to sleep. "Aquila," she said softly.

The nurse stopped her at the door. Pricilla still had on her nurse's uniform. The nurse looked at her nametag. "Pricilla, you can't come in here while the doctor is working on this patient. You know hospital regulations. Are you related to this patient?" Pricilla nodded and tears rolled down her face. The nurse's face softened. "Please, come outside, and as soon as we get her stabilized, we'll let you know something; okay?" She ushered Pricilla back into the hallway.

Pricilla sat in the waiting area with her eyes pasted toward the door. Mrs. Turner sat beside her.

"She's going to be all right, baby," Mrs. Turner assured Pricilla.

"Mrs. Turner, I don't know; she looked terrible. Her skin was so pale, she looked dead," Pricilla cried. Mrs. Turner reached onto the table and pulled a Kleenex out of the box and handed it to her.

"God forbid. Let's pray." Mrs. Turner held out her hand toward Pricilla. Pricilla joined hands with her. "Lord, our Father," Mrs. Turner began, "first of all, we give you praise and thanksgiving. Hallelujah. We come to you tonight and ask for your mercy on Aquila. God, we ask that you will please instruct the doctors on what to look for and to give them the wisdom to know what to do to heal her.

"God, it's only by your healing power that she will withstand this tragic injury. We plead with you in the precious, powerful name of Jesus to spare Aquila's life. Send your ministering angels in the room with her, to protect her from the enemy that tried to destroy her.

"God, if you will, please speak to her and comfort her." Mrs. Turner squeezed Pricilla's hand. "And give her the strength to call on you, Jesus. Hallelujah. We thank you in advance for healing your precious child, in Jesus' name. Amen."

"Amen," Pricilla whispered.

The doctor came out of the room. He had a grave look on his face.

Pricilla looked up and saw him. She turned to Mrs. Turner. "Oh my God; she's dead, Mrs. Turner," she cried. Mrs. Turner patted her on her hand.

Pricilla stood up to meet the doctor. Her legs shook. "Is she . . ."

The doctor stared into Pricilla's eyes with a stoic expression on his face. "Are you related to Mrs. Savino?" he asked Pricilla in a melancholy tone.

Pricilla nodded her head. She exhaled the breath that she held and said, "Yes, she's my sister." She had looked after Aquila ever since the day she arrived at the orphanage. So even though Aquila wasn't her biological sister, in Pricilla's heart, Aquila *was* her sister.

"Well," he looked at her nametag. "Pricilla, she has been injured pretty badly. She has a broken leg and her right shoulder has been dislocated. CMT reported on their way here from the ambulance that she was initially lucid, but shortly began to deteriorate neurologically. Therefore, we knew she had suffered a contusion. Test results confirmed it.

"She's in shock from an intracranial injury." Pricilla gasped and the doctor continued. "We've been monitoring her vital signs carefully and frequently for evidence of any altered cerebral functions. She's been given an anti-inflammatory drug to prevent swelling of the brain.

"We have to surgically remove the hematoma and repair the ruptured blood vessels, and it has to be performed right away." He handed Pricilla a form. "Since you are the next of kin, you need to sign this consent form, giving us permission to operate."

Pricilla grabbed the clipboard out of his hand and scribbled her signature on the form. "Doctor, please do the best that you can to save her."

"You know I will, Nurse." He bustled down the hall and got on the elevator.

Mrs. Turner pulled Pricilla by the arm. "I understood some of what he was saying, but you tell me, in plain words, what he's talking about," she said.

Pricilla rubbed her right temple as she explained to Mrs. Turner what the doctor meant. "Basically, he said that she has a blood clot around the brain and blood is accumulating in the skull. They have to operate to remove the clot and repair the ruptured blood vessels."

Mrs. Turner put her hand over her mouth. "Oh, God, that sounds so serious."

"It is." Pricilla collapsed on the couch. "Please keep praying for her, Mrs. Turner." She lay back on the couch and took some deep breaths to calm down.

An hour had passed, and there was still no word from the doctor. Pricilla stood up abruptly. "I'm going to the nurses' station and call Pastor Woodbridge and First Lady Kendra to let them know that Aquila has been injured. First Lady will want to know because Aquila's the secretary at church. "

"I think that's a good idea, Pricilla." I need to call my husband and let him know what's going on. And then I'm gonna sit here and pray silently that God pulls her through."

Pricilla had a bewildered expression on her face. "Yes, Mrs. Turner," Pricilla said not sounding too hopeful. "Please pray."

Chapter 41

Pricilla looked up and saw Brandon running down the hallway toward them. She stood up and charged at him insolently. "You have a nerve coming here," she yelled at him. "Why aren't you in jail anyway?"

Brandon stopped a few feet away from Pricilla. "I'm here to see how my wife is doing. How is she?" he asked anxiously.

Pricilla got up in his face. "You sick—"

Mrs. Turner yanked her back. "Now is not the time, Pricilla."

Pricilla pointed her finger at Brandon's face. "How do you *think* she is after you tried to kill her?" she asked him fervently.

Brandon held his hands up in the air in a peaceful gesture. "I promise you, I didn't push her over the balcony. She ran and tripped, and somehow she lost her balance and fell over the balcony."

Pricilla looked at him doubtfully. "Is that what *really* happened to her, Brandon? Because given your track record of abuse, I don't believe a word that comes out of your lying mouth."

Brandon sat down on the couch with a defeated, worried expression on his face. "Pricilla, I'm not lying; she fell over the balcony from the third floor of the hotel. The tree standing in the middle of the lobby broke her fall, but she hit the floor really hard."

Pricilla stood a few inches in front of him with her fist balled up. "Why was she running in the first place?" she asked him harshly.

"We were about to leave to come to your house. We'd had a heated discussion—"

Mrs. Turner tightened her grip on Pricilla's arm and urged her, with a stern push, to sit down. Pricilla sat on the chair opposite of Brandon. "Why couldn't you just leave the girl alone, Brandon? Hadn't you done enough damage to her?"

"I love her, Pricilla. I flew to Raleigh to try and reconcile with her."

Pricilla cocked her head to one side as she glared at Brandon. "Are you insane? Why would she want to reconcile with you after you almost beat her half to death?"

Brandon held his head down shamefully. "I regret *ever* touching her. I've sought counseling for my anger. The doctors have diagnosed me with post-traumatic stress disorder."

"I don't give a flip about your diagnosis, Brandon. You had sense enough to control it on your job, and with other people, so I don't believe that that's what you have. You just wanted to control Aquila," Pricilla said furiously.

Mrs. Turner patted her hand. "Pricilla, you need to lower your voice."

Pricilla inhaled and expelled a slow, deep breath. "Brandon, you need to be locked up. How did you talk her into going with you anyway?"

Brandon glared back at Pricilla. "I didn't threaten her, if that's what you think. I asked her to come with us after the children started crying because she refused to let them out of her sight again. She agreed to come to satisfy the children."

"I guess she did agree to join you," Pricilla huffed. "You used the children as a pawn to get her to come with you. As afraid of you as she was, she would have never gotten in the car with you, unless you threatened her with leaving town with her children."

Brandon looked at Mrs. Turner for support. "Was that the impression that you got, Mrs.

Turner? You are my witness that the kids begged me not to leave them."

Mrs. Turner stared at Brandon unflinchingly. "Yes, they were glad to see you, but they're children. Obviously, you didn't allow them to see you whupping up on their momma." She paused for a moment before she said, "You sure enough had me fooled. I thought you were a man that really missed his family. If I had known that you were a sorry wife-beater, you would have never put your foot across my threshold, and God knows you wouldn't have left with those children."

Pricilla jumped in where Mrs. Turner left off. "You said that the two of you were having a heated discussion. Did she take off and start running because you threatened to do something to her?"

Brandon put his hands together in a prayer mold and bumped them against his forehead lightly. "I slapped her before I realized what I was doing."

Pricilla glared at Brandon; she had an expression of disgust on her face. "So much for PTSD," she said sarcastically. "Your butt needs to be in prison, where you can meet your match."

"I apologized to her profusely, but she ran out into the hallway. When I ran after her and called her name, that's when she looked back and tripped and went over the balcony. By the time

I reached the balcony, people were looking up, and accusing me of pushing her over."

Pricilla nodded her head. "You probably did push her," she stated harshly.

"No, I didn't, Pricilla," Brandon said as calmly as he could. "The police questioned me, handcuffed me, and took me to the police station. But a witness explained to the investigating officer exactly what he saw. So they let me go."

Pricilla studied his face, trying to decide if he were telling the truth. "They still should have arrested you for assault. You caused her to have the accident."

Brandon stuffed his hands into his pockets. "They probably will charge me, Pricilla. It depends on the outcome of her injury. They have my personal information, and they warned me not to leave town."

"Good," Pricilla clasped her hands together. "I hope they put you away for life."

Brandon exhaled loudly. "Pricilla, regardless of what you think, I do love Aquila."

Pricilla smirked. "I'm sure you do. You love her to *death*."

Mrs. Turner interrupted them. "Brandon, where are the children?"

Pricilla flung her hands up in the air. "That's right, where *are* they, Brandon?"

"A policewoman took care of them while I was being interrogated. Once I got to the hospital, I asked the volunteer at the information desk to watch over them, because they said children under the age of twelve couldn't come up." Brandon walked to the nurses' station. "Is my wife still in surgery?" he asked them frantically. "Nobody's telling me anything," he complained.

"Sir, you'll know when we know," the nurse said solemnly. "The doctor will be up to talk with you when he's finished."

Brandon sauntered back over to where Pricilla and Mrs. Turner sat. "I need to go downstairs and check on my children."

"I'll do that," Mrs. Turner volunteered. She stood up, picked up her purse from off of the table, and walked toward the elevator.

"Brandon," Pricilla looked intently at him while she questioned him, "did the children witness their mother falling over the balcony?"

"No. They were in the bedroom part of the suite looking at a movie. Aquila and I were in the living room. She ran out of the room and outside, after I—"

Pricilla finished his sentence for him. "After you *slapped* the fire out of her."

Brandon turned the left side of his face toward Pricilla. "Actually, she attacked me first."

"If she did, I'm sure it's because you provoked her," Pricilla huffed.

Brandon had tried most of the night until about one o'clock in the morning to get Aquila to come back home with him. He shared the information about his diagnosis of post-traumatic stress disorder. He told her that he had been in therapy and was now taking medication to help him cope with his illness.

To his dismay, Aquila didn't respond the way that he had expected her to. She told him that she understood his behavior better now and that she would pray that God would heal him. She looked at him earnestly and told him that she was sorry, but she couldn't go back home with him and risk getting beat up again. She left him standing in the living room of the suite as she turned and walked into the bedroom and got in bed with her children.

Brandon slept on the pull-out couch. Late the next morning, Aquila awoke to the children playing with their toys on the floor with Brandon in the living area. Brandon had ordered breakfast for them from room service. Once they had eaten and Aquila supervised their baths, the children watched the DVD, *Madagascar II*, with Brandon.

While they watched the movie, Aquila took her shower and dressed. Aquila came out dressed in a black sweater with a pair of dressy jeans and high heeled black boots. She had made up her face and had pinned her dark hair up into a French roll. She wore long dangling black and silver earrings and a silver necklace that complemented the black sweater.

Brandon was awed by her appearance when she came into the room. He was so impressed that he jumped up and hugged her tightly. He kissed Aquila on her lips and complimented her with excitement. Aquila was uncomfortable with Brandon touching her, so she pulled away from his embrace.

Brandon interpreted her reaction as rejection. He immediately accused her of having cheated on him since moving to North Carolina. Aquila observed Brandon become more irritated as the moments passed by. She looked at the children and didn't want them to see their father in this agitated state. She calmly told them to take their toys into the bedroom and play while Brandon and she talked.

After the children went into the room and settled on the bed with their toys, Aquila followed them and inserted another DVD, *Kung Fu Panda,* into the DVD player. She turned it up louder than she normally would have to drown out Brandon's and her conversation. She reluctantly joined Brandon in the living area.

She remembered that he said he was on medication, so she asked him softly, if he had taken his meds for the day. He told her no, that he hadn't taken any since he'd left Nashville because he'd forgotten to pack them. He asked her again sternly who she was seeing. Aquila assured him that she hadn't been with anyone. Brandon paced around in the room. He told her that he didn't believe her because she would not have changed her appearance so drastically unless she was involved with someone.

Brandon watched Aquila intently as she frantically fumbled through her purse. He cursed at her and asked her what she was looking for. Aquila nervously told him that she was looking for her cell phone to call Pricilla to pick her up. He accused her of trying to call her man to pick her up.

Aquila had become frustrated with his irrational behavior. She defended herself by reminding him that he had no right to accuse her of being with someone, when he had practically moved a woman into her house. Brandon tried to act surprised and asked her what she was talking about. Aquila told him not to deny it because Ms. Carter had told her about the woman who visited his place on weekends.

At that point, Brandon grabbed Aquila's left arm tightly. He had a wild look in his eyes when he told her that it was her fault that he brought another woman home. His rational excuse was that if she hadn't left him, he wouldn't have needed another woman.

Aquila was in pain, but she didn't scream, because she didn't want the children to hear her. So she used her free arm to reach up into his face and scratch him as hard as she could. Brandon immediately let her go and slapped her hard across the face with the back of his hand. Aquila whimpered and ran outside of the room and into the hallway with the intention of asking someone to call the police. When Brandon ran out behind her and called her, she looked back and twisted her ankle running in the high heels. She lost her balance and fell over the balcony.

Pricilla examined his face closer. There were three long red fingernail marks running along the side of his face. "Good for her," she said sarcastically. Brandon looked away from Pricilla and cleared his throat loudly.

Kendra and Matthew exited the elevator and walked up to Pricilla. "How's Aquila doing, Pricilla?" Kendra asked her softly.

Pricilla hugged Kendra and then Matthew. "We haven't heard anything since they took her to the operating room."

Matthew looked at Brandon. "You must be Brandon."

Brandon extended his hand to Matthew. "Yes, I am."

Matthew reluctantly shook his hand, giving him a stern look. Kendra looked at Brandon and shook her head and turned her back to him.

The doctor walked swiftly toward them. Brandon walked up to him. "How's my wife, Doctor?"

"Oh," he looked at Pricilla, "I wasn't aware that her husband was here before I operated."

"He wasn't," Pricilla scoffed. "Anyway, how is she doctor?"

"It was touch and go, but she's going to make it. She has a strong will to live. We took care of the most serious problem first, which was the brain hemorrhage, and then we worked on her shoulder and the broken leg. She's got a tough road ahead of her, but she's going to make it through. Hopefully, she won't have any complications. We're monitoring her around the clock to prevent that. She's still in critical condition, but if she keeps improving, we'll transfer her out of the intensive care unit, and into a lower level of critical care."

"Thank you, Doctor," Brandon said. He shook his hand. "Can I see her now?"

"Brandon, I think you are the last one she wants to see," Pricilla said harshly.

Kendra touched Pricilla on the shoulder. "Pricilla, no; not here."

"She's still unconscious and heavily medicated. Mr. Savino, you can go in and see her for five minutes." The doctor turned to Pricilla. "And since you're her sister, you can visit with her for five minutes also. I have to attend to another patient, but if you have any questions, I'll be available later." He bowed his head at everyone else, and walked away.

Matthew and Kendra sat in chairs across from each other. Mrs. Turner came back up from checking on the children and joined them. Pricilla introduced them to each other, and then she followed Brandon down to the ICU.

Kendra looked at Matthew. "This has been an unforgettable Christmas Day."

Matthew nodded and eyeballed Kendra harshly. "It's definitely been a Christmas full of surprises; that's for sure."

Chapter 42

Mrs. Turner looked from Kendra to Matthew. "Yes, it sure is a tension filled day."

For the next ten minutes, neither of them spoke. Matthew picked up a *Black Enterprise* magazine and read the "Moneywise" article.

Kendra stood up when she saw Pricilla coming toward them. "How is she?"

Pricilla hunched her shoulders. "Unconscious, but she looks a lot better than she did when I saw her earlier."

"Praise God." Kendra clasped her hands together. "Aquila feels more like a daughter to me than a secretary. I've become rather attached to her."

Matthew grunted. He stood up and walked toward the window. Kendra blinked back tears. Mrs. Turner observed both of them closely.

Brandon walked back into the waiting room. "Pricilla, I want to spend the night here so I can be around in case Aquila wakes up. Can you take the children home with you?"

"Yes, I'll take them home, but I'm taking care of them for Aquila's sake, not because I'm doing any favors for you," Pricilla stated as she glared at Brandon. "I expect you to call me the minute that she wakes up. And don't say anything stupid to upset her either," she ordered.

Brandon was about to retaliate, but Matthew walked swiftly back to where everyone stood.

"We're going to keep Aquila lifted up in prayer," he said in a calm manner. "Let's try to set aside our differences and pray for her." He gave Pricilla a hug. "We'll be back tomorrow to see how she's doing." He turned to Kendra. "Are you ready?" he asked her coolly.

"Yes, I am," she answered curtly. Kendra turned around and hugged Pricilla. "We'll see you tomorrow, okay? Try to get some rest."

"I will. Thank you for coming, First Lady."

Pricilla hugged Matthew, and he patted her on the back. Matthew cut his eyes away from the painful look in Kendra's eyes when she looked at him. Kendra forced a sad smile at Mrs. Turner and followed Matthew to the door. She wondered if Matthew would ever forgive her.

After Matthew had returned back home on Christmas Eve, he had slept in the guest bedroom. He had avoided having a serious conversation with Kendra on Christmas morning.

When Kendra approached him to talk, he told her that he didn't want to discuss the issue. She asked him when could they talk, and he told her no time in the near future. He stayed to himself and would not eat dinner with Hannah and her. Matthew was a stubborn man.

It wasn't until after the phone call from Pricilla informing them about Aquila that he agreed to do his pastoral duty. They rode to the hospital in silence. Kendra dreaded the ride back home; she knew it would be very uncomfortable. And even worse, she hated going home, knowing the only response that she would get from Matthew would be the silent treatment.

Mrs. Turner waited until they were out of sight. "Girl, what in the world is going on with your pastor and his wife?"

Pricilla frowned. "What do you mean, Mrs. Turner? I didn't notice anything going on with them."

"You're probably too upset about Aquila, 'cause anybody can see that something is not right with those two."

"I hope they're okay. But, they're only human. Pastors and their spouses have marital problems sometimes too, just like everybody else."

"I suppose so," Mrs. Turner said doubtfully. "Are you ready? I know Darius, Daniel, and Abigail must be exhausted by now."

"Yes, ma'am, I'm ready. I'm sure they're scared not knowing what's going on with their mother."

Pricilla and Mrs. Turner took the elevator down to the lobby, picked up the children, and drove home.

After they arrived home, Pricilla gave Abigail her bath, and then she supervised the boys as they took a bath.

"Auntie Cilla," Daniel asked. "Is Mommy coming home tomorrow?"

"No, she won't be home tomorrow, sweetie. She's really sick and she needs to stay in the hospital a little while longer," Pricilla answered.

"Can we go to stay with Daddy at the hotel until she gets better, then?" Darius asked.

"Don't you want to stay here with me? I'll take very good care of you guys."

"I guess so." Darius looked at Daniel. "I miss Mommy so much."

"I do too. But we'll all have to be brave and pray that God will make her better, okay?"

"Okay," Daniel said. Darius nodded his head in agreement.

"You know what?" Pricilla said to them. They looked at her expectantly. "When you guys finish with your baths, I think that it will be a good idea if you made get well cards for your mother." They smiled brightly. "I'm gonna go and check on Abigail. No playing around in the tub, now. I don't want you to get hurt."

Pricilla went and peeped in the bedroom. Abigail had fallen asleep. She tucked her in bed and turned off the light. She went back into the bathroom and instructed the boys to get out of the tub. She helped them dry off, and they put on their pajamas. Pricilla led them to the kitchen table where she placed crayons and paper for them.

"You guys make your cards while I check my e-mail, okay?"

"Okay. Auntie Cilla?" Darius called her name timidly. "We didn't open our Christmas presents here yet. Daddy bought us some, but we left those at the hotel."

"Wow. So much has gone on today; I almost forgot it was Christmas." Pricilla looked at the clock. It was after ten o'clock. "After you make your mother's cards, you both can open one gift. Tomorrow, you can open them all, okay?" They both nodded eagerly and started working on their cards. Pricilla smiled at them and opened her laptop.

She clicked on the e-mail from Jeffrey and read it.

Hi, Pricilla. Since I can't call you, I wanted to let you know that I enjoyed our time together last night and today. I have to work tomorrow, and I know that you're off, but I hope that I'll hear from you soon. Take care. Love you.

She replied to his e-mail, telling him that she enjoyed their time together also. She informed him about Aquila's horrible accident and asked that he would pray for Aquila's recovery. She then replied to an e-mail she'd received from her alleged mother.

Hi, Ms. W, I'm sorry that it took so long to reply to your e-mail. A close friend of mine was in an accident today, and I've been at the hospital most of the evening. I would love to get a chance to meet with you tomorrow, but ten o'clock is definitely too early. I will be at WakeMed most of the day checking on my friend. Perhaps we could meet later at around five o'clock? If this is convenient for you, let me know where you'd like to meet. Be blessed.

By the time she'd read and replied to Jeffrey and her alleged mother's e-mail, the boys had finished their get-well cards. Pricilla praised them for the wonderful work that they had done. They placed the cards on the coffee table and opened their presents. Pricilla let them play with their trucks for thirty minutes and walked them to their bed and tucked them in for the night.

Whew, I am so tired. She was about to close her laptop when she noticed that Ms. W. had e-mailed her back. *"Pricilla, I'll be happy to meet you at WakeMed around five o'clock if that's convenient for you. I have a four o'clock appointment. Is the lunchroom, okay? Perhaps I can buy you a meal for an early dinner. Be blessed."*

Pricilla responded with, *"Yes, that sounds good. I'll see you tomorrow at five o'clock. Oh, how will I know you?"*

A few seconds later, she replied. *"I'll have on a North Carolina State cap."*

Pricilla smiled. *"Great. I'm a Wolfpack fan also. I'll wear my cap too."*

Pricilla rose early the next morning and cooked breakfast for the children. She called the hospital to check on Aquila. They said that her condition had improved. While she washed the dishes, the children opened their presents and played with their toys.

She had asked Mrs. Turner the night before if she could babysit because the children weren't allowed to visit Aquila in ICU. She agreed. An hour later, she was escorting the children over to Mrs. Turner's house. She made sure that she had their get-well cards before heading off to the hospital. While sitting in her car, waiting for it to warm up, she suddenly began to feel nauseous.

Oh my God, after all these years, I'm finally going to meet my mother. She put the car in reverse and backed out into the street when the coast was clear.

Thirty minutes later, she was at the hospital. She went up to the Intensive Care Unit to check on Aquila. The nurse told her that she could only stay for fifteen minutes.

Pricilla walked into the room using stealthy movements. Brandon sat on a chair that was pulled up to Aquila's bed. His elbows were propped on his legs and his face was cupped between his hands. Pricilla watched him for a moment before she spoke. "How is she, Brandon?" she whispered.

Brandon was startled by Pricilla's appearance. He jerked his head up and looked at her with bloodshot eyes. He cleared his throat before he spoke. "Her eyes fluttered open a few times, but otherwise, she's stable, thank God."

Pricilla glanced at Brandon. "You know, I have a tendency to want to believe that you love Aquila. But it's a sick kind of love."

Brandon gave Pricilla an acrid look. "Who are you to judge me, Pricilla? I have made some really bad mistakes with her, but I do love her. I'm seeking counseling for my illness."

"You don't have an illness, Brandon," Pricilla told him critically. "You have a wicked temper, which you reserve especially for Aquila."

Brandon's voice deepened. "Say what you will, but I know how I feel about my wife."

Aquila's heart-rate machine started beeping faster. The nurse came running into the room. "I don't know what's going on with the two of you, but it needs to stop right now. This patient is in enough distress. As a matter of fact, I'm going to ask both of you to leave *now*."

Brandon kissed Aquila on the forehead. "I love you," he told her.

Pricilla whispered in her ear. "Be strong, Aquila. I'm here for you. Your kids are doing fine." She and Brandon glared at each other and left the room.

Pricilla left the hospital to run some errands. She stopped by Mrs. Turner's house to check on the children. By the time she got back to the hospital, it was four thirty. She went into a bathroom and freshened up and reapplied her makeup.

Pricilla walked into the lunchroom and sat at the very back, so that she could see her mother when she walked in. She looked at her hands; they trembled. She looked back up. A few feet away, near the cafeteria entrance, was a woman wearing a North Carolina Wolfpack cap. The woman's cap was pulled down close over her eyes. Pricilla waved at her.

Kendra had walked into the cafeteria entrance at the very moment that Pricilla waved at the woman. Kendra assumed that Pricilla was waving at her. She smiled and waved back at her and proceeded to walk toward her. Diana wheeled her wheelchair alongside Kendra.

Pricilla stood up to greet and hug Kendra. "Hey, First Lady Kendra," she said cheerfully."

Kendra smiled warmly as she hugged Pricilla. "Hi, Pricilla." She looked down at Diana in the wheelchair. "I'd like you to meet Diana. Diana, this is Pricilla; she's a faithful member of our church." Diana rolled her wheel chair toward Pricilla with her arms stretched out to hug her.

Before they hugged, Kendra saw Jeffrey approaching them. "Hey, Diana. What are you doing here?" he asked.

Diana looked up at him and frowned slightly. "I had an appointment today, remember? They removed the cast on my arm," she explained to him. "Kendra was kind enough to bring me to my four o'clock appointment."

Pricilla looked at Jeffrey quizzically.

Jeffrey introduced them. "Diana, this is Pricilla. I've been meaning to tell you about her, but the time never seemed right."

Diana's eyes widened. "How long have you two known each other?"

"I've been seeing Pricilla for about eighteen months now," Jeffrey replied casually.

Kendra looked at him incredulously. "Wow," she exclaimed. "You sure know how to keep a secret."

Jeffrey looked at Kendra with pride in his eyes. "Yes, I hadn't planned on keeping Pricilla a secret, but I hadn't had a chance to tell Diana about her." He looked back down at Diana. "I wanted to tell you about her in a different atmosphere . . ." his voice trailed off. He put Pricilla's hand in his. "Well, now you know."

Diana glanced from him to Pricilla. "Why am I not surprised?" she asked sarcastically. She looked at Pricilla from head to toe.

Just then, Diana looked up and spotted her husband walking toward them. "Hi, honey. Did your cast removal go all right?" he asked his wife.

"Yes, it went well, honey." Diana looked at her step son. "Michael," she called Jeffrey Jr. by his middle name, "does your father know about Pricilla?"

When the two Jeffrey's were together, Jeffrey Jr. went by his middle name, Michael.

"Yes, he does, Diana," he chuckled. "I'm sorry to keep her a secret from you, but you weren't too fond of the other girlfriends I had," Michael told her.

Diana had managed to run all of his former girlfriends off and he didn't want to take that chance with Pricilla.

"That's because they were only after the money that they *thought* you had. They were definitely up to no good, baby. A mother knows these things," Diana quipped.

Jeffrey Sr. patted his son, Jeffrey Michael, on the back. "I agree with your step-mother, Michael. They *were* gold-diggers," he laughed. Jeffrey Sr. glanced from Michael to Pricilla and smiled. "Well, I'm pleased that God has sent you a virtuous woman."

"Thank you for the compliment, Dr. Thompson," Pricilla responded to him. She cleared her throat nervously as she watched the woman wearing the Wolfpack cap proceeding toward them. "Everybody, please excuse me for a moment," she said with a quiver in her voice. "I was just about to meet someone who I think is my . . ." Pricilla choked up. "My mother."

"Hi, Pricilla. I'm so glad to see you again. It's been too long," Mable said with a tremble in her voice. She took off the North Carolina Wolfpack cap and blinked back tears.

Kendra looked at Mable and frowned. "Mable? *Pricilla* is your daughter?" Mable nodded. "My Lord, this is a small world," Kendra exclaimed.

Diana looked perplexed. "Mable, this is the baby you told me about?"

Mable smiled. "Yes, this is my baby." Mable touched Kendra on her arm. "Pricilla's the daughter that I've talked to you about for the last five years. I finally got the nerve up to try and find her. And the Lord answered my prayers. I hadn't seen her since Social Services took her away from me when I lived in Nashville." Mable looked up. "Thank you, Jesus. Lord, you truly are a merciful God." She pulled Pricilla close to her. I've been waiting for this moment for over twenty-three years." She traced her trembling hand around Pricilla's face. "My sweet, beautiful daughter; you look exactly like you did when you were three years old."

Pricilla buried her head into Mable shoulders, and cried.

Jeffrey Michael hugged Pricilla and told her that he was proud of her for finding her mother. They were both relieved to know that Diana wasn't her mother. Ms. *W.* turned out to be Mable *Woodard.*

Pricilla hugged him back and giggled. "Thanks, *Michael,*" she quipped. "I'll see you later hopefully."

Jeffrey Sr. bent down and kissed Diana on the cheek. Tears streamed down Diana's face as she imagined the joy she'd feel when she met her daughter.

Mable hugged Diana and told her that she believed that when the time came, her reunion with her daughter would be a blessed event also. Kendra and everyone else said good-bye to Pricilla and Mable as they walked outside to get better acquainted.

Dr. Jeffrey Thompson, Sr., and Dr. Jeffrey Michael Thompson, Jr. went back to work.

Kendra looked at Diana. "This has been an interesting afternoon. I would have never guessed in a million years that Mable's daughter was Pricilla."

Diana shook her head. "It's a small world." She glanced up at Kendra with a confused look on her face. "How did they not know each other though? Mable worked in the soup kitchen and attended church services. And you just said that Pricilla was a faithful member of your church."

"That is strange." Kendra was thoughtful for a moment. "Mable and her daughter frequented the same place, yet they never met. I've known Mable for five years and Pricilla moved here a little over two years ago." Kendra sat at the nearest table.

"I don't understand how they could have basically walked in the same circles, but never got to know each other," Diana repeated.

Kendra twisted her wedding band around her finger. "All I can say is that maybe God didn't allow their paths to cross until He knew that the timing was right."

Diana's eyebrows furrowed. She sighed loudly. "That's possible because I worked in the soup kitchen for months, and I didn't meet Pricilla until today."

"Well, you only worked on weekdays, and Pricilla didn't come to church every Sunday because she worked on some Sundays. Maybe that's how she and Mable missed each other." Kendra rubbed her temples. "I don't know how they missed each other for two years, but I do know that God performed a miracle when He let their paths cross."

"I have to agree with you, Kendra. Their reunion was nothing less than a miracle."

Kendra stood up slowly. "Come on, Diana. I'm going to go upstairs to see if they'll let me see Aquila.

Diana pressed her wheelchair button and followed Kendra to the elevator. Once inside, Kendra pressed the elevator button for the fifth floor. Diana and Kendra were silent while they rode on the elevator. Once the elevator door opened, they exited and followed the signs that led to the Intensive Care Unit. Kendra talked to the ICU nurse. She directed them to Aquila's room. Diana rolled into the room behind Kendra.

Kendra expected to see Brandon sitting in the room with Aquila since he'd spent the night watching over her. He wasn't there because he'd left an hour before they arrived to go to his hotel room to shower and shave. Kendra was relieved that he wasn't in the room. Having to introduce Diana to Aquila's husband, the man that abused her, would have been awkward. The introduction could possibly have had some serious repercussions for Brandon.

Ever since Diana told Kendra the name of her child, Kendra couldn't wait to introduce them.

"This is Aquila, Diana," Kendra stated while she straightened the blanket to cover Aquila's feet.

Diana looked at Aquila with compassion. "She looks so peaceful. She's beautiful." Diana rolled up to the bed. "Aquila, I don't know if you can hear me, but . . ." Diana's eyes filled with tears. "Aquila, I'm your mother, honey. Please, please, be strong and pull through this terrible tragedy so that I can beg you to forgive me for giving you away." Diana picked up Aquila's hand and held it to her face. Teardrops fell onto Aquila's hand.

Kendra stood at the foot of the bed and watched Aquila force her eyes open. "Thank you, Jesus," she whispered. Kendra shed tears of joy for Diana. Her heart hurt for the child that she'd aborted. She wondered if Matthew would be able to forgive her for the desperate decision that she'd made so many years ago.

She smiled through the tears as she watched Diana plead with her daughter to wake up. She pulled a Kleenex from out of the box on the table and wiped her tears away. She thanked God that He had given Diana a second chance to amend her mistake.

Aquila stared at Diana's head. *Maybe I'm dreaming or dead*, she thought. Aquila couldn't believe her eyes or her ears. She'd prayed for her mother all of her life. Her mind was fuzzy. If it were a dream, she didn't want to wake up. If she were dead, she thought she must have gone to heaven. Her eyes, though unfocused, roamed around the room. She was really groggy, but she thought she saw someone standing at the foot of the bed. *Maybe it's an angel*, she thought before she felt the warm tears run down her hand. She forced her head, which felt like it was weighed down with lead, around so she could see the top of the head again. "Momma?" she said weakly.

Diana jerked her head up. "Yes, sweetheart," she said softly. Diana looked at Kendra and emphatically said, "God has truly been merciful to me." She held Aquila's hand tightly and looked at her with tears in her eyes. "Yes, sweetheart; I'm your mother."

Tears spilled from Aquila's eyes. "I've prayed for this day forever," she said hoarsely.

"So have I, baby; I've carried you in my heart since the day you were born."

"How," Aquila's mouth felt like cotton was stuffed inside, "did you find me?"

Diana kissed Aquila's hand. "It was only by the grace of God that I found you, baby. It never even occurred to me the day that I talked to you in the soup kitchen that you were my daughter."

Aquila blinked her eyes several times to clear her vision. She stared at Diana for a moment before she said, "Miss Diana, *you're* my mother?" Aquila asked her in a whisper.

Diana nodded her head. "Please forgive me for giving you away. As long as there is breath left in my body, I'm going to do whatever it takes to make it up to you." She dropped her head on Aquila's bed and sobbed pitiful, heart-wrenching tears.

Aquila smiled slightly, rubbed Diana's hand softly with her thumb, and drifted back off to sleep.

Epilogue

After Aquila was strong enough to sit up in the hospital, Diana explained to her why she gave her up for adoption. Initially, Aquila was confused about her mother's decision, but over the weeks, she tried to understand Diana's reasoning.

Diana shared her life's story with Aquila to help her get a better understanding. Aquila told Diana that although their plight in life was different, she could identify with her being a young impoverished girl, with little to no choices in life. Being the meek, kindhearted person that she was, Aquila forgave Diana, and in her heart, she carried no malice toward her.

Diana told her that for years her heart had been broken over her decision. Aquila let her know that God had heard both of their prayers because Psalm 34:18 states: *The Lord is nigh unto them that are of a broken heart; and saveth such as be of a contrite spirit.*

Within three months of their reunion, Diana and Aquila's mother/daughter bond was as natural as breathing air.

A month after Aquila was released from the hospital, Diana, with the help of Sydney and June, hosted a dinner party for Aquila to meet her family members. Sydney's daughter, Teresa, was thrilled to meet her first cousin. Teresa's children and Aquila's children were about the same age, so they bonded right away. Pricilla, Mable, Matthew, and Kendra attended the dinner also. Since Mrs. Turner had become an integral part of Aquila's life, Diana invited her to come too. But Mrs. Turner declined because she and her husband, John, had already made plans to go on a Mediterranean cruise to celebrate his retirement.

It was the first week in June. Diana and Jeffrey's house was full. Aquila and the children moved in with them shortly after Aquila was released from the hospital. Diana felt blessed to share the five thousand square foot house with her new found family. Originally, she had felt unwelcomed in Jeffrey's huge home when she moved into it. She believed now that God had ordained her to marry Jeffrey, a great provider who was more than willing to provide a place for her daughter and grandchildren.

Diana had a permanent limp from the injury of the crushed leg, but she didn't mind, she was grateful that she could walk. Daniel bustled into the kitchen after Diana had called the children into the kitchen.

"Yes, Grandma?" Daniel answered enthusiastically. Darius raced into the room behind Daniel.

"Are you guys ready? It's the last day of school," Diana exclaimed. "You should be excited."

"We are excited, Grandma," Darius replied. He hopped up on the barstool smiling with his two front teeth missing.

When they moved into the house with Diana and Jeffrey, the children were withdrawn; they felt displaced. They clung to Aquila and wouldn't sleep in the bedrooms that had been assigned to them. They claimed that the house was too big and scary. Every night they ended up in Aquila's queen-sized bed with her. It was not an ideal place for them to be because Aquila was still healing from her injuries.

They wanted to go back to Pricilla's house to live. Aquila explained to them that Pricilla's house was being renovated, so no one could live in it until it was fixed. Pricilla visited them as often as she could when she wasn't working. She suggested that Jeffrey and Diana put them in

the same bedroom, like they were at her house.
It worked. They stopped going to Aquila's room
and slept soundly.

Once Jeffrey adjusted to having small children
in the house, he planned activities for the boys at
least once a week. He took them to little league
practice, fishing, or rode his bicycle in the neighborhood with them.

Abigail was satisfied as long as she was with
Aquila or Diana.

Diana held her hands over her ears. "Look,
you guys are going to have to stop calling me
Grandma."

"But you *are* our grandma," Abigail said as she
put her arms around Diana.

Diana picked her up. "Yes, I am, baby, but I
can't *stand* that name. It makes me feel like an
old woman. I know what I want you guys to call
me."

"What?" Darius and Daniel asked her simul-
taneously.

Call me, 'Mama D.' I like the sound of that.
From now on, I'm Mama D. Is that clear?"

"Yes, ma'am, Grandma." Diana cut her eyes at
Daniel. "I mean, Mama D." He laughed.

Aquila walked down the stairs that led to the
kitchen while she talked to Pricilla on the phone.
"Girl, I'm amazed that I didn't see the strong re-
semblance between you and Ms. Mable before."

"I can't believe that she was right under my nose for two years, and we didn't meet until six months ago," Pricilla exclaimed.

"Now I understand why Ms. Mable looked so familiar to me. Your mother must have been the spitting image of you when she was young."

"She was," Pricilla agreed. "When you get a chance, I'll show you the pictures she has of herself in a photo album. If I didn't know any better, I'd swear she was me."

Aquila giggled. "That's awesome. Well, I'll talk to you later."

Pricilla laughed. "Okay. Bye."

Aquila hung up her cell phone and hobbled into the kitchen. "Momma, are you sure that you don't mind taking them to school? I can postpone my physical therapy appointment."

"I don't mind, honey. You need to get your physical therapy so that your shoulder can heal properly. If you're going to enter college in the fall, you need to be physically fit, so you can concentrate solely on your education."

Aquila smiled broadly and kissed Diana on her right cheek. "Okay, Momma." She hesitated before she spoke again. "Brandon just called."

Diana scanned Aquila's face and put her left hand on her hip. "What did *he* want?"

"He wanted to let me know that he had put the child support money in the mail. He wants to keep the children during the summer months. I told him that I would have to pray about it." Aquila leaned against the kitchen's center island and sniffed the tulips that Gregory had sent to her.

It turns out that the tulips that she had received at work several months ago were sent by Gregory Penn. Gregory was the owner of the cleaning service that the church utilized. He had overheard Kendra and Aquila talking about the beautiful red roses that Matthew had sent Kendra. He heard Aquila say that the roses were exquisite, but that she preferred tulips. He thought that Aquila was beautiful, but despite the happy façade she wore, she seemed really sad. The next week, Gregory had tulips delivered to her office.

He had more tulips sent to her office with a card attached, wishing her a speedy recovery because he didn't have her home address. This time he signed his name. Kendra had made a special trip to Diana's house to deliver them to Aquila.

"That's the thing to do; pray about it," Diana assured her. "Do you trust him to keep the children? I hope that he's not trying to talk you into reconciling with him."

"Absolutely not," Aquila said with a frown on her face. "He's finally accepted the fact that we are over."

"Well, he must really have humbled himself and tried to get his life right with God the way that he promised you before he left Raleigh." Diana sat down at the kitchen table. "I'm just glad that he agreed to give you a divorce in exchange for you not pressing charges against him."

"I am too, Momma. After I showed him those pictures that Pricilla took of the bruises I had after he had beat me up, he readily agreed to give me a divorce. He knew he would do some jail time." Aquila walked to the refrigerator and got the orange juice. She reached up in the cabinet to get a juice glass. "Plus, he knew that with having a record, he would lose his job as an air traffic controller." She smiled as she said, "It feels so good not to have to look over my shoulders anymore. I wish him God speed, but I'm glad to be free of him." She poured the juice in her glass.

"God is a healer, baby. And a miracle worker; believe me, I know. God changed me, so I know he can change anybody. Brandon is no exception where God's power is concerned."

"Amen." Aquila sipped her juice and admired her flowers.

"It looks like you have a secret admirer already," Diana joked.

Aquila blushed. "Oh. Gregory is a nice man, but I'm not attracted to him." She frowned slightly. "Besides, I have to get a divorce from Brandon before I can even think about another man."

Diana laughed heartily. "I know what you mean." She raised her eyebrows at Aquila. "But only God knows what the future holds."

Aquila waved off Diana. "Momma, you're going to be late for work. Look at the time."

Diana looked at the clock on the wall. It was seven thirty-four. "Wow. Come on, kids, let's go," she yelled to Darius and Daniel, who had gone into the family room to look at cartoons. "I don't want to hear Jeffrey's mouth because I'm a few minutes late. I'm glad that Jeffrey finally opened his medical practice, but it's hard having your husband as your boss," she laughed.

When Mable introduced Pricilla to her younger brothers, Adrian, eighteen, and Andre, seventeen, they received Pricilla well. Over the years, they had witnessed the depressed state that their mother suffered while yearning for the daughter she'd lost.

They encouraged her to search for her daughter on the Internet. Mable was basically computer illiterate until they taught her how to use a computer and the Internet. So during her leisure time, she searched for Pricilla until she found her.

Mable's first order of business was to ask Pricilla to forgive her for letting Social Services take her away. Mable explained to her about the kind of life that she'd lived in Nashville. She admitted to Pricilla that she was on drugs, which resulted in her losing Pricilla because she was too strung out and high to take care of her.

Mable answered any questions that Pricilla asked. During the first few weeks after Mable told her about the sordid life that she'd live in Nashville, Pricilla distanced herself from Mable emotionally. She found it hard to accept Mable's irrational dependency on drugs to the point that she would leave her with neighbors for days. Mable told her that one day, when she had come home from off of a high, her neighbor had reported her behavior to Social Services and that's how she'd lost her. Mable explained to Pricilla that she couldn't stay clean long enough to prove to Social Services that she could take care of her. She told her that years had passed before she found sobriety, and by then, Pricilla had been adopted.

Pricilla felt bitterness toward her mother until Matthew and Kendra counseled and prayed for her. Matthew asked her to meditate on Ephesians 4:31 and 32: *Let all bitterness, and wrath, and anger, and clamour, and evil speaking, be put away from you with all malice. And be ye kind one to another, tenderhearted, forgiving one another, even as God for Christ's sake hath forgiven you.*

Pricilla forgave her mother and thanked God that He allowed them to reunite. She testified to Ephesians 3:20: *Now unto him that is able to do exceeding abundantly above all that we can ask or think, according to the power that worketh in us.* She attributed that scripture to the fact that she had read in a magazine years ago that Raleigh was chosen to be the second best city to live in. She thought that she was moving to Raleigh to make a better life for herself. But now she realized that God was so awesome that *He* directed her steps in order that her desire to find her mother could be fulfilled.

Over the course of six months, Pricilla and Mable's relationship grew stronger. But it took time for them to bond like mother and daughter.

Pricilla had her house renovated with the addition of an upstairs master bedroom and bath. She signed the deed over to Mable so that she and her brothers would have a decent home to live in.

Pricilla and Jeffrey had set a date to get married. Jeffrey moved out of his parents' house so Aquila and the children could move in. He purchased a three-bedroom, two-bath house through Gloria, Pricilla's co-worker, for them to start their marriage in. He was proud to furnish it with his mother, Denise's, furniture and paintings.

Kendra and Diana sat at the table having lunch in their favorite restaurant. "Diana," Kendra said, beaming, "Matthew and I have gone to counseling, and we've come to the conclusion that we're gonna stay together. I reminded him of the scriptures that he quoted to Pricilla when she was going through with bitterness toward Mable." Diana nodded. "He realized that not only must he preach forgiveness, but he must practice it too."

Diana smiled and nodded. "I prayed fervently that the Lord would work it out for the two of you. I also apologized to Jeffrey for accusing him of cheating on me. I investigated those secret phone calls he made; and the time he spent away from home was to get his business started."

Kendra giggled. "I'm happy that he wasn't cheating too. I know Jeffrey seems to be a man of integrity. But you can't be too naïve when it comes to protecting your marriage." Diana nodded her head in agreement.

"I have more good news," Kendra said excitedly. "The cancer is in remission."

Diana clapped her hands lightly. "Kendra, that is so wonderful. God is a good God," she exclaimed. They agreed in a quiet prayer that God would continue to have mercy on her and heal her completely. They prayed Isaiah 53:5: "*But he was wounded for our transgressions, he was bruised for our iniquities; the chastisement of our peace was upon him; and with his stripes we are healed.*"

"I decree that it *is* so and it *is* done, in Jesus' name," Diana stated.

Kendra nodded. "Amen and amen."

Moments passed before either of them spoke. "Diana, we are so blessed. God allowed you to find your daughter, Sydney, and you reconciled. And Mable found her daughter."

Kendra inhaled deeply before she continued. "And the miraculous thing is that Aquila and Pricilla have been together practically their whole lives. It's just amazing to me," Kendra exclaimed. "God is awesome."

Diana's face beamed with happiness. "Yes, He is. It's as though God directed all of our lives to interweave at His appointed time."

"And I found forgiveness in God for what I did," Kendra added. "Matthew and I have considered asking someone to be a surrogate mother for us."

Diana gazed at Kendra. "Are you guys sure about that?" That can get to be kind of messy sometimes if the woman changes her mind and wants to keep the baby."

Kendra's eyebrows furrowed. "Yes, we've considered that too. I just want Matthew to have his own child."

Diana looked at Kendra with compassion. "I understand."

"We're still praying about what to do. But if the Lord directs us not to do it, then we're going to adopt two children." She clasped her hands together in a prayer mold. "Either way, I'm finally going to be a mother," Kendra said excitedly. "Can you believe it?"

"That's great, Kendra," Diana said, exhilarated. "*Now* I'm a firm believer that God is a forgiving God and will always be near us, even in the midst of making desperate decisions."

"I agree with you, Diana," Kendra stated. "God is a merciful God."

Diana opened her wallet to retrieve a debit card to pay for their meal. She looked at the picture of Aquila and the children and smiled. "Amen and amen."

Discussion Questions

1   Diana believed that giving her baby away for adoption was the right decision at the time. Her reasoning was that she wanted to continue pursuing her goals. Do you think that she was totally selfish? Do you believe she made the right decision, based on her economic status?

2   After graduating from college and obtaining her master's degree, Diana's life changed dramatically for the better. Yet, despite her many blessings, she still seemed to be ungrateful. Why do you suppose her heart was calloused against unfortunate people such as the homeless?

3   Diana harbored unforgiveness in her heart toward God because she believed that He allowed her devout mother to die. Do you believe that God *allows* situations to hap-

pen to us (such as Diana's accident) so that we will draw nigh to Him? Do you believe that bad things happen to good people so that God's glory can be manifested?

4   What are your feelings about Diana and Sydney's relationship over the years? My sister and I have a close relationship. Are the majority of sisters close? Or do you think most have a relationship like Diana and Sydney's?

5   Jeffrey put forth a great effort to understand and comfort Diana. Although he hated the smell of alcohol, he tolerated Diana's excessive drinking. He admitted to his son that he was at his wit's end. Should Michael have encouraged him to leave her? I believe he loved his wife through sickness (depression and alcoholism) and health (during her good days). What are your thoughts?

6   Jeffrey Michael lived in the house with Jeffrey and Diana during most of his twenties and until he was thirty-two. In the early years of their marriage, he was very disrespectful to Diana. Do you think Jeffrey Sr. should have put him out? What was your opinion of

Michael, being a grown man, still living with his father and stepmother?

7   Kendra also made a desperate decision in her youth for the same reasons as Diana; she wanted to accomplish her goals. Considering the fact that she had a bachelor's degree at the time, don't you agree that she could afford to take care of her child?

8   The manner in which Kendra was raised had a huge influence on her decision. Do you think she felt justified (at that time) in having an abortion? Do you think her mother's immoral standards were the deciding factor to her having the abortion? What are the odds that she would have made the same mistakes with her child, as Hannah made with her?

9   Matthew was a highly respected pastor. When Kendra confessed her secret to him, after fifteen years of marriage, he was livid. Kendra hoped that he would understand and forgive her because he preached forgiveness to his congregation. To her dismay, he didn't forgive her right away. Do you believe most men, especially pastors, would have reacted the way Matthew did?

10 Matthew was devastated that Kendra had aborted his baby. He was indignant when he told her she had no right, and how could she expect him to forgive her. He reiterated that she knew he was a Christian and that abortion was against his beliefs. Kendra reminded him that had he been such a Christian man, he wouldn't have pressured her for sex before marriage. These days, it seems as though some saved people, especially men, try to justify fornication. What are your thoughts?

11 Aquila ran away from a hard life in the orphanage, only to find herself in a more distressing situation. Because of her lack of money, education, and with three small children, she stayed with an abusive husband for years. Despite the fact that he may be an excellent provider, what other reasons might a woman stay with an abusive man?

12 What are your thoughts about Brandon? Did you surmise that he abused Aquila because his father abused his mother and him? Was his PTSD diagnosis the cause of his behavior? Or do you think it was a combination of what he'd suffered as a child as well as what he'd experienced in the war?

13 Should Brandon have expected Aquila to reconcile with him after seeking counseling? What would you have done?

14 Pricilla seemed to have had her life together. Her heart's desire was to find her biological mother. When she learned the truth about Mable's past, do you agree that she was righteous by being bitter against her mother?

15 Do you believe the majority of adoptive children have a favorable reunion with their biological parents?

UC HIS GLORY BOOK CLUB!

www.uchisglorybookclub.net

UC His Glory Book Club is the spirit-inspired brainchild of Joylynn Jossel, Author and Acquisitions Editor of Urban Christian, and Kendra Norman-Bellamy, Author for Urban Christian. This is an online book club that hosts authors of Urban Christian. We welcome as members all men and women who have a passion for reading Christian-based fiction.

UC His Glory Book Club pledges our commitment to provide support, positive feedback, encouragement, and a forum whereby members can openly discuss and review the literary works of Urban Christian authors.

There is no membership fee associated with UC His Glory Book Club; however, we do ask that you support the authors through purchasing, encouraging, providing book reviews, and of course, your prayers. We also ask that you respect our beliefs and follow the guidelines of the book club. We hope to receive your valuable input, opinions, and reviews that build up, rather than tear down our authors.

What We Believe:

—We believe that Jesus is the Christ, Son of the Living God.

—We believe the Bible is the true, living Word of God.

—We believe all Urban Christian authors should use their God-given writing abilities to honor God and share the message of the written word God has given to each of them uniquely.

—We believe in supporting Urban Christian authors in their literary endeavors by reading, purchasing and sharing their titles with our online community.

—We believe that in everything we do in our literary arena should be done in a manner that will lead to God being glorified and honored.

—We look forward to the online fellowship with you.

Please visit us often at:
www.uchisglorybookclub.net.

Many Blessing to You!
Shelia E. Lipsey,
President, UC His Glory Book Club